WOLF DIVIDED
THE GREY WOLVES SERIES, BOOK 19

QUINN LOFTIS

PROLOGUE

"We rarely think about the long-term effect of our actions. A single choice can impact our—or someone else's—lives, a month, year, decade, or even longer. So we should think carefully before we act. Even our words have lasting effects. We must remember we are not alone in this flowing river we call life. And we have to be conscious of what's downstream." ~Dillon

"All I want to do is burn some vampires. Is that too much to ask? No, no, it's not. Instead, I get to stare at your smiling faces and *not* eat cotton candy. Ugh." Myanin groaned after she and the rest of their hunting group flashed, thanks to Aphid, into the living room of the Colorado pack mansion. The male fae didn't hang around nor explain why he was leaving. He was just there long enough for everyone to let go of him, and then he was gone. Apparently, he had somewhere he needed to be.

"Fane said there'd been some developments that must

be explored before we continued killing off vamps." Dillon said, and then clenched his jaw

"Did you guys get to kill even one vampire?" Kara asked. She, Nick, Dalton, and Jewel were exactly where they'd left them a little over an hour before.

Tanya sighed. "Not a single one."

Dillon glanced at her. "There will be another hunt soon enough, mate."

"I wish you were wrong," she told him softly. "But since you're not, I feel like we should be out there doing something about it."

"We will," Gerrick offered. "As soon as Fane gives the go ahead."

Dalton tucked Jewel closer to him, as if he needed to protect her from Dillon's words. "And what were these new developments?"

Dillon recounted everything Fane had told him, from Tenia's phone conversation to the news Lilly had shared, Thadrick's information, and Claude's message. It was safe to say things were an absolute disaster.

"Alice is in a coma?" Jewel's words were heavy with empathy.

"Unfortunately." Dillon pinched the bridge of his nose and briefly shut his eyes before opening them again.

Kara curled into a ball on the couch. "Why can't we try to get in her head?"

It was late, and Dillon was feeling every minute of his one hundred sixty years. He was tired, his wolf wanted to hunt, and he could feel the restlessness in his pack, most likely being fed by his own anxiety. "Because Fane wants to wait until Rachel and Sally can do some research on how to protect you two, or whoever tries to contact her," Dillon explained. "Alice is a healer, but she isn't pack. Not yet. Our priority is the safety of those who are pack. We can't help anyone if we don't take care of ourselves and those we love." He sighed and ran a hand down his face. "Fane said that when Tenia spoke to Alice, the healer sounded defensive of Cain and didn't seem inclined to trust Tenia. This was before she was attacked by Claude and then fed Cain's blood, of course. So we have no idea what the situation is now."

Dalton's gaze met Dillon's long enough that the alpha growled. His beta dropped his eyes. "Did Tenia get the impression that Alice has ... *feelings* for the vampire king?"

"I don't know why she would defend the bloodsucker if she didn't have feelings for him," Tanya said, her eyes briefly meeting Dillon's.

Dillon didn't want to think about the consequences that could come to pass if Alice—a gypsy healer who should have a *Canis lupus* mate, because they *always* had a werewolf mate—chose a vampire as her lover. He wouldn't be her true mate. So what would he be?

"If she does care for him, what does that mean for her?" Jewel questioned. "You mentioned Sally said the only way Alice would get better was by taking the blood of her mate."

Dillon nodded.

Kara blew out a breath. "If—and it's a big if, considering she's in a vampire-virus induced coma—she does meet her mate, would she accept him? I mean, if Alice falls in love with Cain, *could* she leave him for her true mate?"

Dillon's stomach churned at the question. Memories that he preferred would stay buried came bubbling up to the surface. He knew exactly how Alice would respond to meeting her mate, no matter what her feelings were toward the vampire king. Tanya's hand ran down Dillon's back, and he felt her love pouring through their bond. He didn't deserve her, but he thanked the Great Luna every day for her.

"The true mate bond would eclipse any feelings she has for Cain," Tanya answered.

Dillon looked at her, the one member of their pack that could hold his gaze, and he saw no judgment there. Although she had every right to judge him, to hate him, she loved him unconditionally. But then his mate was remarkably forgiving.

"You sound very sure of that." Jewel's words were slow, and Dillon could feel her gaze boring a hole in him.

"I am," Tanya raised her chin in that regal way of hers. "Because we've experienced it firsthand."

Kara breathed out. "Oh, snap."

Dillon chuckled darkly. "Oh, snap, indeed."

Jewel's brow furrowed. "Would you elaborate?" Dillon had become used to the curiosity often shown by Dalton's mate. It was no wonder she was a genius. Her tenacity for learning eclipsed anyone he'd ever met.

"Jewel, I don't—" Dalton started, but Tanya cut him off.

"We have time to kill. There is no shame in our past. At least none that hasn't been dealt with and overcome. Fane told us to hold tight until he's decided our next course of action, so we could be here a while."

Myanin plopped herself on a love seat. "A good story always helps pass the time." Gerrick sat beside her and laid his arm across the back, his hand resting on his mate's shoulder. "And this one sounds like a doozy."

"You don't have to, really." Kara held out a hand to stop Tanya.

"Yes, she does." Myanin said. "She's the one who said they had firsthand experience. She can't say something like that and leave us hanging."

Dillon pinched the bridge of his nose. *"You really want to share this?"* he asked his female through their bond.

"It might be good for the healers to know. If they are able to contact the new healer, they will need to warn her. Alice's feelings for Cain could have dire consequences for her and her future mate."

"I don't deserve you," he told her. It was something he'd said many times over the past two decades they'd been mated.

"No, you don't," she teased. *"But I love you anyway, and I wouldn't change the past because it gave us Jacque and Slate."*

She never ceased to amaze him. Letting out a deep breath, Dillon looked at Dalton, his beta and close friend. He'd never even shared this story with Dalton because it wasn't something that was easy for Dillon to talk about. But, as usual, his mate was right. They could learn something from the past, and the knowledge might end up being vital for Alice ... and for others. "As you all know, Jacque is my daughter, but Tanya, my true mate, is not her mother."

Myanin purred. "I love a good scandal."

Kara rolled her eyes. "You should, considering the big-ass scandal you caused."

"Touché, little healer." The djinn tipped her head.

"I can already see the title of the made-for-TV special," said Kara, using her hands as if to emphasize the title. "*Sex, Lies, and Cotton Candy.*"

"Not bad, but it's not my story we're discussing." Myanin looked at Dillon. "Carry on. We will all keep our mouths closed." She looked pointedly at Kara. "And judge you silently instead."

Dillon gave her a dry look. "Thank you for that."

His mate took his hand and entwined their fingers. "We can tell them together. It is, after all, not just your story."

Dillon nodded and then opened the door to their past. A past part of him wished he could change, but one he would never consider changing. Because, as Tanya said, it resulted in the birth of his daughter and grandson. "Once upon a time, my parents were killed by hunters who mistook them for natural wolves. After that, I lived as a lone wolf..."

CHAPTER
ONE

"Just because you've moved out and grown up doesn't mean you stop needing your parents. In moments of folly, their words are your guiding light. When life kicks you to the curb, they are there to hold you up. When you've been too long wandering in the wilderness, they help you find the path back home. But, as with many things in life, you don't understand the importance of their presence until they're no longer there." ~Dillon

1980

Dillon didn't exactly throw his stuff in his duffel bag, but he didn't bother folding his clothes neatly, either. Colin, his pack mate and the closest thing he had to a brother, watched. "You can't just leave," Colin told him.

Dillon didn't pause. "I have to, Colin." Dillon stepped

around him and grabbed some shirts from his closet. He was traveling light, not just because he didn't require many creature comforts, but because he had no idea where he was headed or what he would need when he got there. Dillon only knew one thing: he had to leave his pack. Every day he remained at the pack headquarters, he was reminded of his parents. Daily, hourly, every minute, he saw their faces, heard their voices. Like ghosts hiding in the shadows, they haunted him. It was beginning to drive him mad, and his wolf couldn't heal when every time they got near his parents' home on the pack compound, he smelled their scent. It was like continually reopening a wound.

"Where are you going to go?" his friend asked, with anxiousness lacing his voice.

"South." Dillon zipped the duffle and pulled the straps onto his back. "I've already told our alpha. He understands, though he doesn't like it. And he's asked that I check in periodically."

"Will you come back?"

The worry in Colin's eyes gutted Dillon, but it was nothing compared to the pain he felt at the loss of his parents. Stupid humans hunting wild wolves. That's how his parents had been killed. Shot by a greedy hunter who cared nothing for the animals he murdered.

"I don't know," Dillon answered honestly. "I have no family left. My grandparents were killed by rogue wolves. There's no one else."

"You have me. And you have your pack."

His friend wasn't a dominant wolf. He was kindhearted and gentle. And though their alpha didn't put up with dominant wolves giving the less dominant ones crap, that didn't mean it didn't happen. Dillon had kicked a few of their asses for picking on Colin. "You may not be dominant, brother, but you're still a wolf. Let your beast release that pent-up anger inside of you, and I promise those idiots won't mess with you again."

Dillon pulled Colin into a hug and pounded him on the back with his fist. "You're going to be fine, C." It was the nickname Dillon had given him when they were children.

"Promise you'll keep in touch." Colin patted Dillon and then released him.

"You know I will."

Dillon marched out of his house with his friend on his heels. He tossed his bag into the back of his truck bed and then climbed into the cab. He rolled down the window and lifted his chin at Colin. "Take care."

Colin's eyes glimmered with unshed tears. Dillon understood his pain. Pack was family. Losing a pack member was like losing a piece of yourself, no matter how it happened.

He backed out of the driveway and drove swiftly to the entrance of their pack's property. He couldn't say any more goodbyes. Colin wanted to go with him, and while Dillon would have enjoyed his company, Dillon needed some alone time. He felt as if his pain was going to overwhelm him, and he didn't want reminders of the life he had previously shared with his parents—not even Colin, because he was a part of those memories.

Without even looking in the rearview mirror, Dillon drove through the gate and out onto the highway. He'd never before considered facing a future that didn't include his parents. They'd never meet his future true mate, hold their grandchildren, or get to watch them grow up. He'd never hear his mother's boisterous laughter or listen to his father tell the same stories over and over again because he loved to relive his past. There would forever be a hole inside of Dillon where they belonged. Dillon didn't know how to cope with his pain. Perhaps he was running, as his alpha had suggested. But running away was still better than staying at home, waiting for his loved ones to come back, and hoping that it was only a nightmare from which he would eventually awaken.

"Screw that." He rolled down the windows and let the roar of the wind fill the silence. Dillon had no plan except to drive until he was tired of driving. Maybe that wouldn't be until he reached the ocean, in which case he may or may not just drive right into it. If he couldn't find some purpose in his life, some meaning other than living with the grief that filled him, then Dillon couldn't promise he wouldn't take his truck for a dive into the depths of the sea.

With those dark thoughts filling his mind, he drove into the night.

Some months later, Dillon reached a campground called Wolf Lake Park. It was nine minutes from a small town called Coldspring, Texas. As far as he knew, there were no packs in the area. On his journey, Dillon had quickly learned he didn't like motels with their overwhelming strange smells. And sleeping in his truck got old. So he'd purchased a small travel trailer and stayed at campsites when he needed to rest.

"A fitting place to end my journey." He was tired of running and tired of driving, not to mention, too much farther and he'd just hit the ocean. He parked his truck and camper in the assigned spot. Dillon climbed out of his truck and walked over to the picnic table that was near a firepit. He sat and then stretched out on his back on the bench and closed his eyes, soaking up the afternoon sun. He sighed. It had been months since he'd left his pack, and the pain still hadn't eased. Maybe it never would. Maybe he'd build a life here, away from other packs. He'd leave the dangers of being a *Canis lupus* behind and just live like humans did. A lone wolf. And no doubt the only actual wolf in Wolf Lake Park.

Dillon took a deep breath and let it out slowly before sitting back up and then standing. He stretched his back, his vertebrae popping as he did. His wolf itched beneath his skin, hoping to phase and go on a run, but Dillon told the beast no. He didn't know if he'd ever take his wolf form again. His final memories with his parents were of their last hunt together, running through the forest with the wind whipping through his fur. Pushing those thoughts away, he went to work setting up the camper as he'd done dozens and dozens of times. Only this time, maybe it would be the last time.

Tomorrow, he'd go into Coldspring and see about finding a job. Preferably hard labor that would exhaust him every day so he'd pass out when he came home. Considering what he was, it might take two jobs to do the task. He'd work as much as he could to accomplish that goal and continue to wait until thoughts of his parents no longer felt like a knife to his heart.

💧

1985

. . .

DILLON EFFORTLESSLY TOSSED ANOTHER SACK OF CATTLE FEED INTO his friend's trailer. It was the fiftieth one he'd loaded in an hour.

"How can you do so much work and not break a sweat?" Steve asked, as he hooked his thumbs into his front pockets. "Especially in this heat?"

The man shrugged. *"I'm a werewolf. I have superhuman strength, and the heat doesn't bother me as much as it does humans"* is what Dillon wanted to say. But he didn't want his friend to think he was an escaped mental patient, so instead he leaned against the side of the truck and crossed his arms. "I work out a lot. Guess I'm just in good shape."

Steve eyed him skeptically. His wrinkled face was tanned from working in the sun, and despite his advanced age, the man had a spryness about him that Dillon found endearing. "Well, whatever you're doing, it's working. And people are noticing, especially the womenfolk. The missus swears every single woman in this town suddenly has something they need from the feed store." The old man chuckled. "I told her they were probably coming in to check the corkboard to see about finding studs to breed their heifers. She said they were some heifers looking for a stud alright, but it had nothing to do with livestock."

Dillon shook his head. "I've noticed. Tell Gladis it's not just the single ones. I may be big, but I still don't want to fight off any jealous husbands. Especially around here, where everyone has a rifle hanging in a gun rack of their pickup truck."

Steve's eyes twinkled with mirth. He waggled a finger at Dillon and smiled. "I'm going to tell her. It will tickle her and give her some gossip to share with her Bunco group."

Dillon's brow furrowed. "Bunco?"

Steve leaned in and in a conspiratorial whisper said,

"It's really a ladies poker group, but they don't want to call it that on account that it might offend some of the folk who think gambling goes against the Good Book."

"Ahh." Dillon nodded. "Got to keep up appearances." He understood that more than Steve could possibly know.

"Something like that." Steve climbed into the cab of the truck and leaned out the open window. "I'll see you next week, Dillon. You let me know if *my* bride comes in here looking for a stud."

Dillon tapped the side of the older gentleman's truck and laughed. "I'll do that. You take care, Steve." Before he could close the door, Dillon added, "Hey, are you having any more problems with coyotes getting your calves?"

Steve shook his head as he stuck it out. "Not since we talked about it last week."

Dillon nodded. "Let me know if you do. I'm always up for a good coyote hunt."

"Will do." Steve waved again and pulled away.

Dillon headed back toward the large bay door that opened into the feed room of Coldspring Feed Co-op, his place of employment since his third day in town, back in 1980. Dillon enjoyed his job. He was constantly busy, and he worked from sunup to sundown, even though the owner, Bobby Banks, told him not to. Dillon didn't care if he didn't get paid for the extra hours. He just wanted to stay busy. When he wasn't working or sleeping, he spent his time guarding local herds from coyotes for the farmers. It gave his wolf time to run and hunt, which kept it in a somewhat less cranky mood. To say Dillon's wolf was unhappy was an understatement. His wolf craved a pack. Wolves weren't meant to be lone creatures. But Dillon wasn't ready to go back to his pack or be a part of any pack, for that matter.

He glanced at his watch. One hour til closing time. This time of day, there seemed to be an influx of female customers. At first, the women coming in would only surreptitiously glance at him. But as the weeks passed, they started getting bolder until some of them walked right up to him and handed him their number on a piece of paper. After that, Dillon started staying in the back. Bobby didn't mind, although he said it was amusing to watch the women make spectacles of themselves. Dillon didn't find it funny in the least. And his wolf was flat out offended—females throwing themselves at him like dogs in heat.

The wolf only thought of their true mate, even though they'd not met her, and who knew if he ever would? It was offensive to his beast to even think of being with another female. Dillon just wanted to survive. He didn't care about any relationships. Caring about someone meant losing them would eventually be painful. He didn't want to go through that again. Five years after his parents' deaths, he could finally think about them without feeling raw. He missed them fiercely, but he didn't feel like he was drowning anymore. He was actually beginning to have hope that maybe it wouldn't always hurt so badly. Maybe someday he could be happy again.

By the time Dillon returned home to his camper, which he'd been living in for the past five years, he was exhausted. Not necessarily physically, but mentally. The constant stress of pretending that he was human, that he was no different from the people around him, wore on Dillon.

He pulled off his clothes and took a quick shower. Dillon didn't like cooking, especially only for one person, so he made himself a protein shake. Even after all the time he'd been gone, he still hated eating alone. When he was with his pack, there was always someone to dine with, whether it was Colin, his parents, or eating at the alpha's home, where many pack members gathered every night. Dillon missed that. He sighed, downed the drink, and then climbed into bed. He turned on a loud fan to drown out any noise that his wolf's hearing might detect. The beast in him was on constant alert because there were no other pack members around to have his back. He was a lone wolf without protection. And that kept his inner beast on edge.

Dillon flicked off the light and told his wolf to chill the hell out. Then he closed his eyes and hoped that he wouldn't see his parents' faces—the faces of them in death, lifeless and blank. They haunted him in his dreams. "Maybe tonight will be different," he said, just as he did every night.

FALL 1990

DILLON STOOD WATCHING AS THE CASKET WAS LOWERED INTO THE waiting grave. He had been with Steve when he suffered the massive heart attack that took his life. Steve's wife had passed away a year earlier for no apparent reason, and her death had driven Steve crazy. He had told Dillon many times that if he had known what was wrong, maybe he could have prevented it.

"You can't prevent death, Steve," Dillon had told him. "It comes for all of us. No amount of knowing when or why can stop the eventuality of it."

Dillon and his wolf both mourned Steve, who had become a dear friend over the years. Dillon had known Steve wouldn't live forever, but even so, he was unprepared for this. He stepped back and sat down on one of the chairs that had been set out for guests, most of whom had already left. He leaned forward, resting his forearms on his knees, and closed his eyes, taking several deep breaths to get his emotions under control. He wanted to throw back his head and howl.

"Be at peace, my friend," he said softly. He continued to sit there, not paying attention to anyone who was left, even as the cemetery workers began to cover the casket with dirt. Life and death were so undignified. You enter the world naked and screaming and end it by being put in a box and covered in dirt. "Damn, Steve, this sucks."

"Did you know him well?" a woman's voice said from just to his right.

Dillon forced himself not to sigh and give a biting answer. Even after all the years he'd been in Coldspring, women still asked him out, though it was pretty well known in the small town that the guy who worked at Coldspring Feed Co-op didn't date. There was all kinds of speculation, from maybe he had a wife who died and he never got over her to the possibility that he preferred men. Some said he was celibate because of his religion, despite the fact that he'd never stepped foot in one of the churches. He'd been invited at least a hundred or more times over the years, but his creator wasn't found in a human church. And he'd been unable to bring himself to reach out to the Great Luna because of his anger.

Finally, when he was sure he wouldn't growl at the woman, he answered, "I did. Steve was a good friend."

She sat down one seat away, thankfully, and made a

humming sound. "I knew him and his wife, Gladis." She chuckled. "They were a pair, but Steve was never the same after she died. I always thought he'd die of a broken heart. And I guess, in some ways, he did. A heart attack is essentially a broken heart. That's why I've decided that love sucks."

It was the first thing a woman had said to him in the past decade that he agreed with. Love definitely sucked. "Can't disagree with you there," he muttered.

"I'm sorry for your loss. The town won't be the same without either of them."

Dillon finally turned to look at the woman. Her gray eyes shimmered with unshed tears. She was lovely, in a very understated way. Perhaps it was because she was at a funeral, but she didn't have any makeup layered on her face or an excessive amount of perfume on her. Those were common themes with the women who came into the feed store, which annoyed Dillon and his wolf senses.

The woman's face flushed, and Dillon realized he had been staring at her without saying a word. He cleared his throat and introduced himself as a polite gesture. "I'm Dillon."

Her lips turned up slightly. "I know. You've been the talk of the town for quite some time. I get to hear all about you in the bookstore from the women who come in looking for a good romance to read."

Dillon rolled his eyes. "Don't believe everything you hear."

"I form my own opinions." She looked back at the grave.

Dillon glanced at her left hand and saw no sign of a ring to indicate she had a mate. *Husband*. He reminded himself that humans didn't call their significant others' mates. He didn't see a tan line, either, indicating that she had taken off any rings. Her skin was smooth and unlined with age, suggesting that she was in her early twenties. He stared at her profile, noting her delicate features. She had brown hair that shimmered in the early morning sunlight, just long enough to brush her shoulders. Her jawline was soft and feminine, and her lips were not thin, but not overly plush. She had a cute nose that turned up slightly. He couldn't help but find the woman quite lovely.

Her cheeks flushed even more, and Dillon forced himself to look away. She wasn't his true mate, yet he felt drawn to her. She was human, and he didn't sense any sort of gypsy healer magic in her. That was the only way a human could be mate material. He shifted in his seat and leaned a little closer, no longer looking at her, and took a deep breath. There was something different about her scent that he hadn't noticed on other people in town. Her perfume was messing with his nose, making it difficult to figure out what it was. That was intriguing, and even his wolf perked up. It was a hunt of sorts, and his beast loved a good hunt.

She started to stand, and Dillon reached up and touched her arm. "You never told me your name."

She smiled down at him. "I know."

Dillon couldn't help but let out a low chuckle. He memorized her scent as he watched her walk away without another word. She had caught his attention, and it had only taken her less than five minutes. Women had been coming into the feed store for a decade, but none of them had ever managed to make him want to take a second look. Yet this female had grabbed his attention with her gray eyes and understated beauty, not to mention her obvious compassion for Steve and Gladis. Dillon could see in her eyes that she was a genuine person. She was also quick-witted. For the first time in a very long time, he was interested in something other than work, killing coyotes, or shooting the breeze with Steve. He'd be able to find her easily enough, and that was the only reason he didn't follow her like a weird stalker.

Two days passed before Dillon finally gave in to his curiosity to find the female from the funeral. He had thought he would have to use his wolf senses, but then he remembered she had mentioned working at the bookstore. Considering there was only one in town, it wouldn't take a detective, or a werewolf, to hunt her down.

IT WAS EARLY EVENING, AND HE'D ACTUALLY LEFT WORK AT closing time. He stood opposite the store, staring at Book Lover's Den. He chuckled at the name. Wolves loved a good, cozy den. It was oddly appropriate. None of the sheep inside had a clue the big bad wolf was about to enter the store. Dillon shook off his ridiculous thoughts and walked across the street. It was early September, and the sun set earlier and earlier with each passing day. The lights inside the store lit up a large room filled with a rainbow of books. The shelves were no doubt packed with adventures, romances, and anything the human imagination could come up with. There would no doubt be a few books about his own kind, inappropriately filed in the fiction section.

DILLON PULLED OPEN THE DOOR, AND THE SCENT OF BOOKS, perfume, and body odor overwhelmed his sensitive nose. He tried to restrain his wolf to prevent the scents from taking over. However, his inner beast was captivated by Dillon's thoughts on the woman. Dillon's interest in the female intrigued him, and he wanted to know more about her. As for himself, he found her attractive, which was surprising since he had never been attracted to a human before. Though he had noticed beautiful women, he had never been drawn to them beyond that. As he took a few steps forward, he caught her scent and followed it until he found her talking to a young boy in the children's section, where the tables were decorated with brightly colored books and toys. She spoke softly to the child and pointed at the book he held. The child smiled and hugged her before walking away. Dillon had the urge to follow the child and ensure his safety. *Canis lupus* pups were precious to the packs and so rare that they were always well guarded. The child was walking unattended through the store, oblivious to the possibility of an evil human taking advantage of him. Even after living among humans for so long, Dillon still found it strange how naive they could be about the dangerous world around them. He was about to step forward when he saw a woman emerge from behind a shelf and hold out her hand to the child, who took it without hesitation, speaking animatedly while holding the book.

"Dillon?" His name drew his attention away from the boy, and he looked at the female he'd been hunting. She wore jeans and a black shirt with the words Book Lovers Den across the front. She also wore a name badge that read, *Lilly*. A lovely name for a lovely woman.

"Hello, Lilly." His voice held a slight growl that surprised him. He'd been victorious in his hunt, and regardless that he wore human skin, he was still a wolf and liked to find his prey. Dillon hoped the woman didn't notice it.

"How do you know my name?"

Dillon pointed at her chest, where the name badge sat just above her right breast. *Stop looking at her breast.* He was surprised to find himself admiring her physical form. She had full hips, shapely legs, and a small waist. His eyes returned to her face, and he saw once again a flush in her cheeks. The sight made him smile. Wide-eyed, she stared back at him.

"Right." Lilly gave a sharp nod. "Is there something I can help you with?" She wrung her hands in front of her and shifted from one foot to the other.

Dillon enjoyed the fact that he flustered her. It was endearing. Though she held her chin high and her shoulders back, she didn't come across as haughty like many of the women who came into the feed store. "I'm looking for a book." He glanced around the store.

"As you can see"—Lilly cleared her throat and gestured around her—"you've come to the right place. Do you have a specific book in mind?"

Dillon tried to keep a straight face as he spoke, but it was difficult, especially with her looking so serious. "Something about wolves."

"Fiction or nonfiction?" Her voice steadied, and the flustered appearance left her. She was slipping back into her element, answering a customer's question about books.

Well, that won't do. Dillon liked her flustered.

"Which do you recommend?"

She shrugged. "I guess that depends upon whether you want to learn something or you want an escape."

He shrugged. "I guess I need an escape. I spend a lot of time alone when I'm not at work. I can only spend so much time working out and running before it starts to get boring."

He saw Lilly's eyes move down, taking in his body. Her lips pressed together until her eyes moved back up and she met his gaze again. "Exercise looks good on you, I mean, it's good for you. Running is good for you. Not just you, but everyone."

Dillon lifted his hand and rubbed it across his mouth to hide his grin. She was cute. His wolf growled inside of him. He didn't approve of where the man's thoughts were heading. Dillon ignored his beast and focused on the lovely Lilly. He stared at her, watching her squirm under his scrutiny.

"Okay." She brushed her hands down her thighs and turned on her heel. "Let's check out the paranormal section. There are loads of books about werewolves, and they're quite entertaining."

"You read about werewolves?" He followed close behind her, trying not to notice how her backside swayed back and forth when she walked. He was failing miserably.

"I like to read just about anything." Lilly's tone was confident again. "As I said before, reading is a way to escape. You get to travel to different worlds, meet new people, and forget about your own problems for a little while."

She stopped in front of a section of books, but Dillon's gaze remained on her. "Do you have a lot of problems you need to forget about, Lilly?" His voice sounded more serious than he'd intended, but he suddenly found that he didn't like the idea of this woman having to suffer through any hardships. *What the hell, Dillon? She's not ours.* His wolf growled at him. *Maybe not,* he answered. *But that doesn't mean I can't be her friend and help her if she needs it.*

Lilly bit her lip and looked as if she was contemplating how to answer. Finally, she looked up at him. "No more than anyone else, I'm sure."

Dillon narrowed his eyes on her, and he saw the pulse in her neck increase. Her scent changed, telling his wolf she was nervous. He could tell it wasn't the same kind of nervous she'd experienced when she'd first seen him in the store. *Canis lupus* learned that emotions had distinct smells. Even variations of the same emotion smelled differently to the nose of a wolf. The nervousness she felt right now told Dillon she wanted to get away from him. He was asking questions she didn't want to answer.

"So." She blew out a breath and motioned to the shelves. "Here's our paranormal section. Lots to choose from. I'm sure you will find something that intrigues you."

"I already have," Dillon said softly. He continued to look at her, ignoring the books at which she was gesturing.

Lilly swallowed and crossed her arms in front of her. She glanced down at the ground, and Dillon wondered if she was hoping a hole would open up so she could escape him.

"Am I making you uncomfortable?" He already knew the answer.

"You know you are."

His lips stretched into a wide smile, and he stepped closer to her. He liked her scent. It was driving him crazy that he couldn't tell what about it was so different from a human's. But it was definitely different. Perhaps she was a dormant? If so, maybe the bond between true mates wouldn't respond the same way as between two full *Canis lupus*. *She is not our mate,* his wolf grumbled. Dillon ignored the sulking beast and focused back on the lovely Lilly. "Would you let me take you out on a date so I can continue to make you uncomfortable?"

Her eyes snapped up to his face. "You enjoy making me nervous?"

Dillon shrugged one shoulder and slipped his hands into the pockets of his jeans. "It makes you blush. And that makes your skin turn a soft, rosy red. It's very becoming."

She quickly dropped her arms and glanced around as if someone might have overheard him. There was no one near them, not that Dillon cared if someone was listening.

"You are quite forward, Mr...." She paused, waiting for him to fill in the blank.

"To you, just Dillon." He tried not to smirk at her obvious frustration, but she was too dang cute.

"Okay, Mr. Just Dillon. I've got to get back to work." She started to turn away from him.

"Hold up." He reached out and wrapped his hand around her arm, making sure to keep his grip gentle. She was human and much more fragile than he. "You didn't answer my question."

Lilly stopped and turned slightly so she could look at him. Several seconds ticked by before she replied. "Why would you ask me out?" He saw confusion in her eyes, and her brow wrinkled. "Women have been chasing you for as long as I've been in this town. And as far as I know, you've not accepted any of their advances. So why me?"

"Because you smell good." That hadn't been what he meant to say, so he quickly followed it up with something he hoped was a little less creepy. "And you intrigue me."

Lilly's eyes went wide. "I ... *smell* good?"

"I'm sorry. I guess if I had said you looked good, you wouldn't have thought that was as creepy, huh? But think about it. The sense of smell is just as important, isn't it? At least to some species, anyway." His attempts to sound less creepy were not going well.

"Some species? Um, I guess so." She shook her head and grinned. "Are you some kind of dog, judging me based on my smell? I guess I should be thankful you haven't tried to sniff my butt."

He smiled as he saw humor in her gray eyes. She was

enjoying the fact that he was the one who was uncomfortable for a change. "It's just a date, Lilly. We both need to eat. I'm tired of eating by myself. Do you have anyone to eat with?" The thought of Lilly dining with someone else bothered him. *Weird. Why the heck would that bother me?*

It shouldn't, his wolf said. *It doesn't bother me. She can eat with whomever she wants. She is NOT ours.*

Again, Dillon ignored the wolf. He watched Lilly's eyes dart away, and she shook her head. "No, I don't have anyone to eat with."

"So eat with me." He sounded more nonchalant than he felt.

After what felt like an eternity, she gave a curt nod. "Okay. I'll eat with you. When?"

"Do you work tomorrow?"

She nodded. "I get off at five."

"I'll meet you here at five-thirty." He grabbed a random book from the shelf and started to back away, his eyes fixed on her. "Don't chicken out on me."

Her gaze sharpened, and she smirked. "I'm not scared. Especially of a man who reads werewolf romances."

Dillon glanced down at the book in his hand and shook his head as he chuckled. The cover was of a half-dressed male with clawed hands wrapped around a wanton-looking female. "Don't judge a man by what he reads, wild Lilly."

"I've found it to be a pretty good standard." She held his gaze until he winked at her. The blush came back, and she dropped her eyes immediately.

Dillon turned and walked to the register and paid for the book. The woman at the register looked at the cover and then at him. The gossip mill would be in full working order within the hour about what the weird bachelor reads.

Dillon shook his head as he took the bag and left the store. He wanted to look back and see if Lilly was watching him, but he forced himself to have a little dignity. He'd practically begged her to eat dinner with him. And she'd said yes. Dillon took a deep breath of the warm night air. For the first time in a long time, he was looking forward to waking up the next day.

CHAPTER
TWO

"It's possible to experience the highest levels of joy and deepest depths of sorrow simultaneously. The experience is not something I'd wish on my worst enemy." ~Dillon

S ummer 1991

DILLON STARED UP INTO THE GRAY EYES OF HIS WILD LILLY. His head rested in her lap as her fingers ran through his auburn hair. Clouds scattered across a blue sky framed her face. Despite seeing Lilly as nothing more than a female he cared for, Dillon's wolf rumbled. The beast loved being touched. She'd been the only touch he'd experienced since leaving his pack, and both the man and wolf craved it. Did it hurt that the woman doing the touching was beautiful? The wolf refused to answer.

He stared up at her and noticed she seemed deep in thought. Though her eyes were looking at him, he could tell her thoughts were far away. "What are you thinking about, beautiful? You look sad."

"I need to tell you something. And it's going to be hard to believe."

Dillon chuckled. "I'm pretty sure there's nothing you could tell me that I wouldn't believe." *Considering I'm a werewolf.*

Lilly clenched her fists. He could tell she thought what she was about to say was very big news. She inhaled deeply, as if mustering enough courage to speak. She told him that for as long as she could remember, she had gut feelings. Her voice shook as she spoke, and she cleared her throat several times. She continued to share with him about the foreboding sensations that always came in regard to someone she knew and something that would soon happen to them. They were never wrong.

He sat up and turned to face her. "Have you ever told anyone about this?" He took her hand and rubbed his thumb across her knuckles enjoying the feel of her silky skin.

"Um, no." She laughed. "I don't really want people thinking I'm crazy."

His heart felt heavy in his chest as he considered what she'd dealt with for so long. "It must be a huge burden. Knowing something bad is going to happen to someone you know, but being unable to tell them."

She swallowed hard, and he could practically see the weight of it on her shoulders as they rolled forward. Dillon wanted to take that burden from her. He wanted her to know that she wasn't alone, that she wasn't the only one with peculiar abilities. "I'm sorry," he said softly. "If I could bear it for you, I would."

She tilted her head and gave him a curious look. "There's another reason I'm telling you this. I get the feeling about you, but it's a little different. It's good and bad. I don't understand it. I just know you're not quite what you seem to be."

Dillon's gut twisted as his heart beat painfully in his chest. It was a conversation he needed to have with her nearly a year ago before their emotions grew so strongly for each other. But up until now he didn't know how to tell her and expect her to believe him. With this new information she'd just shared, perhaps there was a chance she wouldn't tell him he needed to be on some meds. But, then there was all the baggage that went along with his race. He didn't want to lose Lilly, but he owed her the truth. "Your feelings aren't wrong." His lips turned up in a sad smile.

"Care to elaborate?" Her words were soft, but she lifted her chin as if to brace herself for what he would tell her.

"I've been thinking about this for some time." *Like since the day I asked you on that first date.* His wolf snarled inside of him, as it often did since he'd begun dating Lilly. What Dillon was doing was not unheard of in the *Canis lupus* world, but it was definitely taboo. Because all *Canis lupus* had a true mate— the one who held the other half of his soul—and being in a relationship with anyone else was doomed to failure. A wolf's true mate was the only one who could keep the darkness inside of him at bay. "I wasn't entirely sure how much, if anything, I would tell you about my ... own ability." He looked down at the grass and picked up a blade, wrapping it around his finger and then unwrapping it. He repeated the motion over and over until the blade tore in half.

"I'm all ears."

He looked up and met her eyes. "I won't lie to you. I will never lie to you." He filled his voice with the authority of his wolf because he wanted her to hear the conviction in it. "This will sound crazy, Lilly." She started to say something, but he held up his hand. "No, this is going to make what you told me sound sane." Dillon took a shaky breath as sweat broke out on his neck and back. He didn't want to do this. He didn't want things to change between them, but it wasn't fair to her. "Since your own ability is obviously supernatural, even though you may not realize it, I feel safe telling you about myself now that you've confided in me. What I'm about to say will seem impossible, entirely fictional." He wanted to tell her to take every idea she'd learned from the paranormal books she loved so much and throw them out the window.

Dillon ran his hand through his hair. His wolf was growing more agitated. His beast wanted the female to know so that she would understand they could not be what she needed. She was not the other half of his soul, and there would be a gaping hole inside of him that Lilly could never fill, even though he loved her. Dillon inwardly snarled at his wolf. The man didn't need to be reminded. His jaw clenched, and suddenly Lilly's warm hands cupped his face, drawing his attention back to her and away from the thoughts of his wolf's disapproval.

"You can trust me, Dillon. I will believe you."

He nodded at her. He knew she would. Lilly was trusting to a fault sometimes. It made him want to protect her from those who would take advantage of her. Bile rose in his throat as he considered that he could be considered one of those. She had no clue, and yet he'd fallen in love with her and allowed her to fall in love with him. He was the lowest of the low. "I'm what's called a *Canis lupus,* otherwise known as a werewolf." His words came out in a rush. "I told you it would sound crazy, but I swear to you it's the truth. There's a whole supernatural world that lives in the shadows of the human world. And I'm one of them." His hand gripped hers tightly, as he silently implored her to trust him.

To his surprise, she didn't burst out laughing. Instead, Lilly sat quietly, appearing to process the information he'd just given her. Dillon wanted to know what was going on in her head. If she'd been his true mate, he would have been able to hear her thoughts. He would feel her emotions. The thought hammered home the reality that she wasn't his—not really.

"So you can actually change into a wolf?" she asked after several agonizing minutes.

He nodded. "Yes, but we call it phasing."

Her eyes held his. "Will you show me?"

Lilly's reaction wasn't what Dillon expected. But he'd gotten used to Lilly surprising him in unexpectedly pleasant ways. She was different. That was one of the many things that drew him to her. His wolf pushed forward, though he wasn't sure if it was in challenge to her possible disbelief or because he wanted to show off. "On one condition." He knew his eyes were glowing because his beast was close to the surface, scratching just under his skin to get out.

"I can't tell anyone, right? That's the condition?"

Dillon smirked and shook his head slowly. "You have to promise to pet me."

THE DRIVE TO LILLY'S APARTMENT WAS A QUIET ONE, FILLED WITH anticipation. The air was thick with not only his own eagerness but it seemed to be rolling off of her in waves as well. Her breathing increased and she kept rubbing her palms up and down her legs. Dillon's skin rippled with the need to phase. Now that he'd told her it felt as if a giant weight had been lifted off his shoulders. *You haven't told her that she's not ours,* his wolf reminded him. And just like that the weight was back, only this time it was a hundred pounds more, threatening to crush the breath right out of him.

"Are you okay?"

Dillon kept his eyes on the road and nodded. "Nervous," he answered honestly. "There's more I need to tell you."

"I figured." She shifted in her seat. " 'I'm a werewolf' can't possibly be the end of the conversation."

He parked her car in front of her apartment and climbed out. As he walked around to open her door he wrestled with the conflicting emotions that boiled inside of him. It was as if a hurricane had taken up residency and was wreaking havoc on his insides. He opened her door, and she took his offered hand. As they walked to Lilly's door, Dillon held onto her like a lifeline. Everything was about to change. It possibly meant that she would tell him they couldn't see each other anymore. The thought of that was nauseating, but staying with her when he might have to leave her one day was just as sickening. She deserved better.

Once they were inside, Dillon took a deep breath, soaking in her familiar scent. His was mixed with it, and the possessive part of him liked that. His beast did not approve.

"Okay." She sat down on the couch and dropped her purse beside her. "Let's see it."

"I sort of feel like I'm about to give you a strip tease," he joked, trying to relieve his anxiety. "Maybe you should wave some cash around for me."

"Is your wolf form going to be wearing a G-string?" Her nose scrunched up. "Because I don't think I can pet a wolf wearing a G-string."

Dillon laughed, loud and long because his wolf was thoroughly offended. He took a deep breath as the humor died down. "I have to strip or I'll ruin my clothes," he warned her.

She grinned, a wicked gleam in her beautiful eyes. "It's nothing I haven't seen before."

It was just another thing to add to his list of transgression in regard to his wild Lilly. They weren't married or mated, and yet he'd taken her and given himself to her. He shoved the guilt into the box he kept it in and focused on the here and now. Tomorrow wasn't promised, and today he was with her, the woman he'd fallen in love with. Dillon began to undress and ignored his nose which picked up the scent of her desire. When he was completely naked, he phased and stood in her living room taking up a considerable amount of space. He gave himself a good shake and then looked at Lilly. His wolf was so large that he was eye to eye with her where she sat on the couch.

"Wow," she whispered softly, eyes wide with amazement. Her breathing quickened, and the smell of excitement mixed with that of her fear, although the latter was quickly replaced by curiosity. Lilly extended her arm, and Dillon stepped closer so she could feel his fur. It was as pleasant to be touched in his wolf form as it was when he was in his human form. His beast longed for contact; he missed that part of being in a pack.

"You're breathtakingly beautiful," she said, her voice achingly soft.

Dillon's heart beat faster as he watched her, mesmerized. Once back in his human form and dressed, he sat down beside her. Dillon took her delicate hands in his rough ones, tracing the blue veins beneath her porcelain skin with the tip of his calloused finger. He moved closer, his skin growing clammy with fear as he struggled to find the right words to tell her. Dillon knew that with just a few words the tremors of destruction would begin, and there would be no going back; they could never recover from the truth he had to tell her.

"The fact that you are a werewolf isn't what you were afraid to tell me, was it?" Lilly's voice cracked, and her shoulders began to quake. Her eyes glistened with unshed tears. Lilly's anguish was palpable, and he wanted to rip himself apart for being the root of her misery.

He closed his eyes and shook his head. *Be a man, Dillon.* Then, like a coward, he started spouting trivial facts. Or trivial in comparison to the bomb he needed to drop on her. "Our race is different from yours, obviously. We live much longer for one thing. We heal quickly. It is difficult for the females to carry their pregnancies to term. Unlike your government, our packs aren't a democracy. There is an alpha in each pack, and he and his mate maintain order between dominant males that would otherwise cause havoc with challenges of dominance." He paused. *Get to the damn point*, his wolf snarled.

She looked confused as she watched him. "As interesting as all of those facts are, Dillon, they're not what's got you agitated. What aren't you telling me?"

A growl rumbled up from his chest, and he didn't try to hide it now that she knew what he was. "We're also different in the way that we mate, or"—his words faltered—"what you call marriage."

Lilly's hands tightened in his. "Different how?"

"Dammit." The breath whooshed out of him. "I should have told you. In all honesty, I should have never asked you out."

"What?" She recoiled as if he had struck her. "Why would you say that?"

"This isn't fair to you, and I know it." His voice was a pained whisper as he looked into her eyes. "I had no right to fall in love with you, let alone allow you to fall in love with me. Both of our hearts will be broken when the inevitable happens."

"You cannot *allow* me anything, Dillon. I'm a grown woman." She rubbed her forehead. "What do you mean when the inevitable happens?"

"Us. The end of us."

She shook her head in confusion, her forehead creasing. Dillon knew he was causing her pain, and he hated it. "Are you breaking up with me? Is that what you're saying?"

Dillon leaned his head far back and studied the ceiling. He couldn't vocalize the thoughts that were clogging his mind as every muscle in his body tensed. Never had he wished that he were human, but in that moment, it was the only thing he wanted. He cursed under his breath, then with a swift motion, he rose to his feet and let go of her hand. He walked to the center of the room and shoved his hands in his pockets. "You don't understand. *Canis lupus* have true mates." He forced himself to look her in the eye. She deserved that, and so much more. "Or soul mates, for lack of a better term. They are two halves of one whole. Each has the other half of their mate's soul."

Lilly fixed him with a puzzled stare as he spoke, her face slowly twisting with despair as the full weight of his words sunk in.

Dillon swallowed hard as he continued. "The true mate of a *Canis lupus* must be another *Canis lupus*. The males of our race have a darkness within them. It comes with having a beast that lives inside of us. The darkness slowly grows, and without our true mate's light to keep the darkness at bay, it will consume us. Males that do not find their true mates become feral wolves, eventually having to be put down."

"Have you met your true mate?" It sounded as if she'd forced the words from her mouth.

Dillon gave a sardonic grunt. "No," he bit out. "I wouldn't be with you if I had. The pull between mates is undeniable."

"You love me." It wasn't a question, but he responded anyway.

"Yes."

"But I'm not your true mate." Her eyes dropped, and her shoulders fell forward.

"No," he mumbled. "It can take decades or longer for a wolf to find their true mate. When or even if I find my true mate, I will not be able to stay with you. That is simply a fact. It's the nature of my species. I wouldn't be able to fight the pull to her, and I wouldn't want to. And even if I don't find her, I will eventually go feral. I would be a danger to you and anyone else around me." He clenched his fists tightly and stared at the ground. "I don't know how much time I can give you. But I will understand if you want to break this off. In fact, we should."

Lilly's head snapped up, and her eyes widened. "I don't want that. I love you, Dillon. I can't imagine my life without you."

Dillon pulled his hands from his pockets and ran them through his wavy hair. Her words were like a knife twisting in his gut. "That's the problem, wild Lilly. Whether you can imagine it or not, a life without me will eventually be a reality. I wish I could promise a life with you, but I can't." He pointed his finger at the door. "If my true mate walked through that door right now, no matter how I feel about you, my soul would choose her. My wolf would choose her."

Tears tracked slowly down Lilly's face. Her glassy eyes were filled with both anguish and hope. "And the man?"

Dillon felt as if he was being ripped in half. Tendon, bone, and muscle viciously separated as he told her the truth that he wished he could spare her. "The man would be divided." He stepped toward her and then kneeled, taking her face in his hands. "I am sorry. I'm so, so sorry."

Lilly leaned forward until their foreheads touched, and he felt her warm breath on his face. Her voice shook. "Today, right now, you are mine. And I am yours."

Since his parents' death, Dillon had not felt so helpless. The part of him that was *Canis lupus* longed for his true mate. No matter how he felt about Lilly, the darkness inside of him grew daily, and she could not keep it from spreading. That didn't mean there wasn't a place in his heart that had been carved for her.

"I understand what you're telling me."

He jerked his head back. "Do you?" he demanded. "Are you truly telling me you comprehend the fact that you could lose me any day?"

"I do. But unless you walk away, I'm not going anywhere." Her hands gripped his biceps, her nails sinking into his skin as she pinned him with a fierce gaze. "I want any amount of time that you *can* give me. It's my choice."

Staring into her eyes, Dillon contemplated the events of the past year and felt the internal struggle. These were memories he had never intended to make with anyone other than his mate. He'd made a mistake in allowing her into his life when there was another who was destined to hold a claim to his heart. Dillon knew he ought to stand up, leave, and never look back, but his selfishness was preventing him from doing so. The decade he'd spent working with no one in his life had drained his soul, sucking it dry. All the while the darkness had spread like a rapid disease. Lilly gave him hope. She brought light into his life, though it was much different from what his true mate could give him. For Dillon, it was enough. If only he'd acted sooner, maybe then he wouldn't be in too deep. But now it was too late. *"You're a fool,"* his wolf snarled. *"She will never be enough."* The truth of those words was a dagger to his heart. Even so, he ignored them.

"Don't go," she implored him. "Not until you have no other choice."

The air felt heavy in his lungs as he ran a thumb across her soft lips. "One day, you will hate me. All that will be left of me are memories that will make your soul ache with bitterness. I could never wish that upon you."

"I will never hate you," she whispered, her voice ripe with sincerity. "Will it hurt to lose you? I imagine it will be a pain that will devastate me. But I would rather have those memories of you than nothing at all."

"Okay, wild Lilly, okay." He breathed out as desperation took over, and he resigned himself to the moment, allowing his lips to find hers. An electric shock surged through his veins as they touched, and Dillon was suddenly aware of every tiny sensation. Her scent filled his lungs, and his spirit ignited as the heat and passion emanating from her overwhelmed him and melted away the icy chill that had begun to numb him. He knew he'd already been trying to protect his heart from the pain of leaving. His desire for her engulfed him, threatening to consume him completely. He effortlessly swept her off the couch and stalked toward her bedroom.

Dillon laid Lilly on the bed and lowered his body over hers. Their mouths crashed together again, and their tongues began a passionate, timeless dance. His skin felt oversensitive with excitement, and his heart raced. Every follicle on his body stood to attention in anticipation, and his senses were in a heightened state of arousal, ready to explode the moment she touched him. He ignored the voice in the back of his mind that told him he had no right to take or give anything to this female. He and Lilly had made up their minds. For better or for worse, they would be lovers until death, or until his fate came knocking.

December 1992

Dillon waited for the gas station pump to issue his receipt after filling up his truck. He'd just finished delivering a trailer full of square bales of hay to a farmer outside of town, and now Dillon was headed fifty miles back to Coldspring. The land was nearly entirely flat and mostly devoted to the grazing of cattle. The occasional grouping of trees offered small slivers of shade in the summer, but now they were bare and stood out like a sore thumb in the dead grass of the large pastures. It was chilly, but nothing like the winters he remembered in Montana. As he pulled open his driver's side door, Dillon felt his wolf suddenly come howling to attention.

"Focus." His wolf growled, and Dillon made a slow circle, his eyes scanning their surroundings. There was only one other vehicle, a passenger van, parked in front of the gas station. It had been there when Dillon pulled up, but he hadn't seen anyone get in or out. Now there were three males leaned up against it talking amongst themselves. They kept looking back at the door as if waiting for someone.

"I can't believe they expect me to eat gas station food. Okay, so the nachos aren't that bad, but that's not the point. Do they seriously expect me to eat this disgusting, cholesterol-packed, gas station death food all the way back to Colorado? Not happening."

A voice invaded Dillon's mind. It was like a warm caress, and his beast roared with recognition. *Mate*, the wolf rumbled. Hearing that word sent a wave of initial shock through him. When it finally dissipated, Dillon was elated, relieved, and utterly destroyed simultaneously. He felt the connection between him and his mate. It was uniquely theirs, and though he'd heard the experience of finding a mate described many times, Dillon still found himself unprepared. He frantically erected walls around his thoughts and feelings. Pain radiated through his skull. He clamped his teeth together, and his legs weakened beneath him. He could feel his pulse hammering in his chest as he gasped for air, and sweat beaded on his forehead. The woman—his mate—prodded against his mental shield, trying to gain access to what he held inside. But Dillon wasn't about to let her in, not like this.

If she saw the memories and thoughts that he'd stored over the past two years, she would be devastated. He was hers. And he'd shared himself with another. Dillon would be lucky if she didn't kill him, or worse, reject him as her true mate. Even as he considered how painful that would be, Lilly filled his mind. He knew he was going to do exactly what he warned her would happen. Dillon was going to leave her, and all they'd built together, and it would crush her. It would crush a part of him, as well. Regardless, he had to at least tell her goodbye. He couldn't just disappear. He'd go back to Coldspring. Then once his goodbye was taken care of, he'd hunt down his mate.

His mate mentioned that she was traveling to Colorado. She must be a member of the Colorado Pack. He would be able to track her once he put things in order in Coldspring. His attention was drawn to the chime of the door, and Dillon looked up just as *she* stepped outside. Their gazes met, and she studied him with narrowed eyes, confusion shading her caramel-colored irises. Was she confused about the fact that she had just found her true mate out in the middle of flatland Texas? Or confused because her mate wouldn't allow her access to his mind, a right that was hers alone?

She moved toward him, and he couldn't help but take her all in. The gray sweater, black leggings, and ankle boots that still made her feet look small showed off her petite body. He didn't let his eyes linger on her form, though he and his wolf were both highly intrigued by the brief glimpse of curves. He forced his gaze back up where long, light brown and golden strands of tousled hair cascaded down her shoulders. Dillon ached to touch it, to feel how soft the silk-like locks were. Her face was heart-shaped, with lips so full and red that they reminded him of a ripe apple. His mate's skin was porcelain-perfect with the exception of a beauty mark above her right lip. Her delicate neck swept into a petite frame that he once again had to stop himself from examining further.

"Tanya, what gives?" One of the males pushed away from the van where he'd been leaning and reached out, placing his hand on her shoulder.

Dillon growled before he could censor his reaction. It was loud enough that the other males heard, and they turned glowing eyes on him. His wolf zeroed in on the hand that still rested on his mate's shoulder. He wanted to rip it off. The visceral reaction caught him off guard. Dillon took a step back, forcing himself not to attack someone that was obviously her friend, or maybe even a relative. *It better be a relative.* Dillon tried to wrestle his beast under control.

"Who are you?" the largest of the males asked. His blond hair was pulled up into what Dillon had heard called a man-bun, but the local farmers around Coldspring called them twat knots. He had a close-trimmed beard, and his golden, hawklike eyes were zeroed in on Dillon. "I don't know of any packs in this area."

"And yet here stand four wolves," Dillon pointed out. If there are no packs in the area, then what in the world were these four doing?

"Five," the shortest of the males said.

"I belong here," Dillon's wolf growled. Although he was a lone wolf, he had claimed Coldspring and its surrounding areas—where he had developed relationships with people he cared for—as his territory. These four, including his mate, were trespassing. "You do not."

"So you admit you're not part of a pack?" the man with the bun asked.

Tanya's eyes remained on Dillon, though she had stopped trying to break through his mental barriers. Her body appeared tense, and he noticed her knuckles turning white from gripping the drink and food in her hands so tightly.

"Take your eyes off her and answer the question."

"Austin," Tanya snapped at the one who hadn't spoken before. His white-blond hair was striking against his tan skin, creating an incongruent appearance. His eyes were a vivid green, and his build was similar to Dillon's, as was his height.

"What?" Austin asked. "He's staring at you like you belong to him."

Dillon's gaze returned to Tanya, and his brow rose. His wolf was challenging her to see how she would respond to Austin's comment. Dillon disapproved, considering he didn't want to deal with this unexpected development. Moreover, having not encountered another *Canis lupus* in over a decade, he never thought he would meet his true mate, at least not in Lilly's lifetime. *"We wouldn't have survived. You know this is what's supposed to happen. This is our path. You chose to veer from the path,"* his wolf told him. The words were harsh, but his beast tempered them with as much understanding as possible.

Tanya lifted her chin, clearly rising to his challenge.

The man with the bun, now identified as Trevor, stepped forward, glancing from Dillon to Tanya. Dillon could practically see the gears turning in Trevor's head as he processed Austin's words. Then realization struck him. He placed his hand on Austin's chest and pushed the other male back.

"What are you doing, Trevor?" Austin questioned.

"This isn't our business," Trevor growled, sounding less than pleased. "At least not unless we need to make it our business." His eyes met Dillon's and narrowed.

Dillon growled. His wolf wasn't about to back down to another. He felt the tension escalating between them and noticed beads of sweat forming on Trevor's forehead. Maintaining Dillon's gaze seemed to require considerable effort, but Trevor hadn't looked away yet. Dillon's wolf pushed forward, and Dillon felt his teeth lengthen. He stalked toward Trevor, intending to put the less dominant male in his place. However, Tanya stopped him in his tracks when she suddenly appeared right in front of him. He'd been so focused on Trevor that he hadn't even seen her move.

She was only a few steps away, her hands outstretched as if to prevent him from advancing further. Dillon noticed she had let go of her food and drink to approach him, and he mentally promised himself to buy her new ones before leaving.

"Don't," she said softly. "They're my pack."

Dillon leaned down; although he was just shy of six feet tall, he still towered nearly a foot over her. "And you are my mate." Voicing the words provided a satisfying surprise.

She lowered her hands and straightened her shoulders as she looked up at him. Her boldness impressed Dillon, and unlike Trevor, Tanya held his gaze effortlessly.

"That's yet to be seen," she replied, her voice as soft as his had been.

"Tanya, let's go," one of the three males called, though Dillon wasn't sure which one. "We can let your father know there's a lone wolf running around these parts."

Dillon's eyes shot up to the speaker, and he bared his teeth. "What business is it of his?"

"He's the alpha of the Colorado pack," Trevor replied. "It's any alpha's business to know if there are wolves running around without a pack, no matter where they are located." He crossed his arms and rocked back on his heels. "You should know that unless you've never been part of a pack."

"Were your parents rogues?" Austin's sea-blue eyes shone with his inner beast.

Dillon acted swiftly, wrapping an arm around Tanya's waist and pulling her behind him. A moment later, he had Austin by the throat and slammed him against the truck. Dillon lifted his arm until the younger wolf's feet no longer touched the ground. He heard the snarls of the other two males, but the power radiating from him stopped them in their tracks. Turning his head, he saw Trevor still trying to move, but when Dillon's eyes met Trevor's, he dropped to the ground and bowed his head. Why on earth had Tanya's father sent her so far from their pack with three males who couldn't even stand up against a lone wolf?

"Dillon, let him go," Tanya's voice almost soothed his wolf enough to obey, but then he remembered Austin's mention of Dillon's parents, speaking as if they were insignificant rogue wolves with no pack, undeserving of respect from these self-righteous pricks.

"You speak of something you know nothing about, pup." Dillon growled through wolf teeth. "You talk about my parents as if they didn't matter, even if they had been rogues, which they weren't. Not that it's any of your business. Perhaps you should get off your high horse before someone knocks you down. I can assist with that, if necessary."

Austin's face turned a disturbing shade of purple. Dillon knew their mate would likely be upset if they killed her friend, so he released him. Austin crumpled to the ground, gasping for air as he touched his neck.

Dillon panted heavily, his breathing affected by rage rather than a lack of air. He took several steps back until he could see all three males. "You can tell her father you met me, and you can tell him I am Tanya's true mate. I will come to claim her once my affairs are in order here."

As Dillon reined in his power, the males managed to stand, though none dared to meet his eyes. He turned to see Tanya walking toward him, her face red, lips thin, and anger burning in her eyes. She reached up and slapped him. He didn't flinch, which seemed to infuriate her further. She pulled her hand back to strike again, but Dillon caught her wrist just before her palm could make contact. Then he pressed her hand against his face. The effect of her touch, skin to skin, was immediate. His wolf settled, his heart slowed to beat in tandem with hers, and the urge to mark her surged like a tidal wave.

Tanya inhaled sharply, and Dillon felt her fear and curiosity through their bond. She stepped closer, her body heat radiating onto his. He gazed at her red lips, imagining how good she would taste, like the scent of a spring morning and air just after the rain. A scent only he could detect. Without his conscious thought, Lilly's face flashed in his mind, and guilt wrenched his gut.

Tanya frowned and yanked her hand away. She'd seen it. His walls had been weak enough, distracted by her closeness, that she'd glimpsed Lilly's face. "Tell me she's a family member," she demanded, her hands curling into fists.

Dillon simply stared at her, unable to do anything other than accept the emotions pouring into him from his mate.

"Tell me," she snarled. "Is she related to you? Is she a

rogue? Tell me she's not what I think she is." The betrayal in her voice threatened to crush his heart.

"*I can't*," he finally answered, opening the bond enough to speak to her.

She took a step back, her eyes boring into him as she shook her head. "Do not come after me. You are not claiming me. You have obviously already laid claim to another."

"Tanya," Dillon's voice rumbled as he started toward her, but she snarled at him.

"No!" She continued to shake her head slowly, as if unable to believe his admission. "I will kill you if you come to Colorado."

"Or we could just do it now," Daniel interjected, as if they had any chance of taking Dillon on.

"He is mine to deal with," she told her companions. The claim she made was not that of a mate but of someone with a vendetta against another, allowing no one else to deal out punishment.

Dillon wanted to argue with her, but now wasn't the time. He would go after her no matter what she wanted. She was his, and he was hers. Regardless of their pasts, their future was meant to be together. *"Go,"* he said gently through their bond. *"But you know that as your true mate, I will never stop coming for you. You are mine."*

"I don't want you." Her words cut him to the bone.

"That may be, but I am yours, and I do *want you."*

He took his eyes off of hers and looked at the three males. "Keep her safe. If anything happens to her, I will kill each of you, slowly."

Dillon turned on his heel and stalked to his truck before he did something like steal her away, which is what his wolf wanted to do. Dillon started the engine and peeled out of the gas station as if death itself were chasing him. Perhaps it was, considering his mate wanted him dead. *"Dammit, Dillon."* He mentally snarled as his hand slammed against the steering wheel until his palm hurt. *He'd* done this. He'd broken his mate's heart and was about to crush the heart of the female he'd come to love. *"I warned you."* His wolf rumbled in his mind. Dillon ignored his beast and focused on not having a wreck. He drove back to Coldspring, trying to figure out how he was going to tell Lilly goodbye.

CHAPTER
THREE

"Every beat of my heart was aimed at finding my true mate. I longed to know the sound of his laughter, to feel his skin, and touch his hair. I wanted to create a life with the one who was as eager for that as me. But in one terrible moment, those dreams evaporated like smoke. I glimpsed a woman in my mate's thoughts, and the emptiness that filled my soul was like a gaping chasm that threatened to devour me and everything I ever wanted. In a single moment, our futures had been forever changed. Instead of being one and completing our bond, we would live half lives." ~Tanya

TANYA GRABBED THE EMPTY BAG FROM DANIEL'S HAND AND covered her mouth with it as her stomach expelled its contents. This was not how she had envisioned meeting her true mate. She had never imagined that he would be involved with another woman. How could he do that? Not to her specifically, she supposed, because Dillon didn't know her. But how could he do that, knowing he had a true mate out there in the world? Was the woman a *Canis lupus*? A human? Or another kind of supernatural? How old was Dillon? Had the darkness consumed him so much that he simply tried to replace the true mate he hadn't found? She had heard of some older males doing that. But not *her* mate.

"Why don't you want him?" Trevor asked, his voice still guttural with his wolf. "Other than the fact that he seems like an ass."

Austin chuckled. "He really does."

If only that was all. Tanya could deal with him being an ass. What she couldn't deal with was a cheating ass. *"He is ours,"* her wolf said softly in her mind. Her wolf was a gentle soul. Though she could be fierce when necessary, mostly, she was a lover, not a fighter. Tanya tried to gauge her beast's feelings about Dillon. She knew what Tanya knew— that their mate hadn't been faithful. The feelings she had sensed through the bond when the woman's face had appeared in his mind made it clear that she meant a lot to him. *"We don't know the whole story."*

"Aren't you the least bit pissed off?" Tanya asked her wolf.

"I do not think as you do. He is our mate. We have found him. Our souls can be complete."

"Mates don't cheat," Tanya snapped.

"Without us, the darkness inside him will continue to grow. He needs us."

"He should have thought about that before," Tanya said out loud. She wiped her mouth with the napkin Daniel handed her.

"He should have thought about what?"

Tanya sighed. "Nothing, Austin." She sat in the passenger seat while Daniel drove, and Trevor and Austin sat in the back seat. The three males were some of her father's fiercest warriors, yet her mate had put all three of them on the ground like pups, simply from the dominant power that lived inside him. His wolf was obviously extremely dominant, probably to the point of being an alpha. Maybe he had been one and his pack had cast him out for being an ass. She almost laughed because it didn't seem that far-fetched. And that would just be her luck. Not only had her mate been in a relationship with another woman, but he was a disgraced alpha, as well. "Of course," she muttered under her breath as she wiped her eyes with the back of her hand. Tanya loathed crying. It didn't help anything. It actually made things worse because not only did she feel upset, but now she had snot running out of her nose. Ugh, not cool.

"Talk to us, T," Daniel urged.

She shook her head. "I don't want to get into it, not right now." She tied off the bag and set it on the floor, planning to toss it at their next stop. Tanya leaned her head against the warm window, watching the flat country of Texas pass by. The hum of the tires on the road lulled her to sleep, but even in her dreams, she couldn't escape the pain that squeezed her heart. His face filled her mind. He was handsome in a rugged, devil-may-care sort of way. She hated that she already loved his auburn hair and wondered if they ever had a child, would they inherit his hair or her blonde hair? There was no point in going down that road. It wasn't happening.

She and her pack mates had been on what should have been a simple mission to Louisiana. The Missouri pack alpha had asked for help finding and dealing with a pack of rogue wolves in Louisiana, which had been reported by other supernaturals. Their mission had not been a success as they didn't find the rogue wolves that supposedly had been running amuck, so once they headed home she asked the guys if they could go on a sightseeing detour through Texas. Instead of finding the pack of rogues, they found one rogue—her mate. Her cheating jerk of a mate.

Tanya attempted to push the thoughts away and prayed to the Great Luna that she could sleep peacefully. She didn't want to arrive home and unload everything to her mother and father. Mostly because her father would go berserk. He was incredibly protective of her. There was a reason her father was the alpha—not only because he was so dominant, but also because he had no problem putting a wolf in its place. He loved his pack fiercely, and that love was magnified a hundred times when it came to Tanya and her mother.

Something warm covered Tanya, and she was immediately enveloped by Trevor's scent from his jacket. She knew he had brought it specifically for her, though he hadn't told her that. But every time she slept in the vehicle, she woke up with the jacket laid over her. Tanya ignored the affection he had for her. She knew he wished they were true mates. But he had never treated her as anything more than a dear friend. Yet she knew, simply by the look in his eyes, that he had feelings for her. *"Is that any different from what our mate has done?"* her wolf asked. Tanya inwardly groaned. She didn't want to think, and yet her mind wouldn't turn off.

"Trevor hasn't acted on his feelings," she pointed out.

Her wolf growled. When her wolf got irritated, Tanya found the beast was quite articulate, and she wondered if it was borrowing the more humanlike speech from Tanya's mind to convey her irritation. *"Regardless, one day he will meet his true mate, and she will have access to his memories. She will see that he has had romantic feelings toward you. How will that make her feel? Do you want her to feel what you feel now?"*

Tanya knew her wolf had a point, but policing Trevor's feelings wasn't her responsibility. He was a grown man, and he knew his true mate wasn't Tanya. But meeting Dillon had triggered a powerful reaction in Trevor. Certainly that was because he knew Dillon was her true mate. Maybe now that he knew without a doubt that Tanya wasn't his, it would put an end to Trevor's emotions. She couldn't understand how he hadn't realized it before. Emotions seemed irrational, making a sane person act insane. This made Tanya question whether true mates were actually a blessing or a curse.

Enough. She mentally scolded herself. Tanya cleared her mind and took slow, deep breaths, focusing only on the sound of the wind and the road. She would deal with her emotional turmoil once she was back home. There was nothing to do about it now, anyway. He had said he needed to get his affairs in order. Who knew if he would even come for her? What did his word mean if he couldn't even remain faithful to his future true mate? *Nothing,* she whispered in her mind. *His word meant nothing.*

DILLON SAT AT THE TABLE IN HIS SMALL CAMPER, PAPER BEFORE him and pen in hand. He stared at the blank page, thinking about the woman who had held a piece of his heart for nearly three years. How was he supposed to say goodbye without crushing her? It would certainly crush a part of him. Why had he let this happen? Why had he been so foolish to think that things would work out between him and Lilly? He supposed the biggest blessing in all of this was that they hadn't had a child together. Earning back his mate's trust would be hard enough, considering what she already knew. If he had to tell her he'd had a child with another woman, she would likely follow through on her threat and kill him, regardless of the consequences to herself.

He sighed and took a deep breath. His wolf howled within him, urging him to get his act together. With every passing minute, their mate drew further away. He could feel her through their bond, although she wouldn't let him inside her mind. Her emotions were so strong that she couldn't completely block him out. Dillon wasn't sure he wanted to be in her head at the moment. The dominant side of him would want to force her to submit to their bond, but Tanya seemed quite headstrong and would only resist that kind of order. He would have to coax her, woo her, convince her to see that they belonged together, regardless of their pasts.

Finally, he pressed his pen to the paper and wrote.

My Sweet Lilly,

What can I say? Words are not adequate, nor is this letter. The truth is, I couldn't face you. I am too much of a coward. I couldn't tell you goodbye without falling at your feet and begging you to forgive me. I wish I could explain to you in a way that would make you believe me. The love I felt for you was real. It wasn't infatuation or some silly crush. If I were a human, I would have married you in an instant. But I am what I am. My future is mapped out by the Great Luna. We've already talked about all of it, and I know you said you were willing to deal with it when the time came. Looking back, I shouldn't have let you. I should have argued, put up more of a fight. I should have walked away then so that now the pain might have been less. But neither of us could have realized it would happen so soon. There are no words to fully express how sorry I am. I never wanted to hurt you, or at least that's what I keep telling myself. But what kind of man does this? What kind of man falls in love with a woman and lets her fall in love with him in return, knowing he can't give her the world? What kind of man allows a woman to give herself to him in every way, knowing he cannot do the same? There was always a part of me that wouldn't belong to you. Maybe I should have explained that better. Then maybe you would have been pissed off and told me to take a hike, which would have been for the best. As possessive as my kind are, I wanted all of you, and I demanded all of you. Yet, I couldn't reciprocate. I wanted your attention. I wanted your time. I wanted my scent all over you, which always made you laugh. I will miss your laugh. I will miss a lot of things.

You're strong, Lilly Pierce. You're probably already kicking my memory to the curb, which is what I deserve. I know you will bounce back, and some lucky SOB will sweep you off of your feet. Then I will be but a pleasant memory, if that. I hope that for you. I hope you will be happy. You deserve more than I could ever give you.

I have cleared out all of my stuff. I didn't want you to have to deal with it. I'm an ass for not saying goodbye. But I know I would have wanted to hold you. I would have wanted to kiss you one last time. And I couldn't. I couldn't because, well, you know why.

I've dragged this out long enough. Be happy, beautiful Lilly. I know you will curse me, throw things, and scream. Knowing your temper, you might even try to track me down and kick the shit out of me. I wouldn't blame you. Hell, I'll lay on the ground and let you. But that doesn't change what is, what has to be.

Thank you for the time you gave me. Thank you for giving me you. I had no right, and yet you gave anyway. Two nights ago, you told me you'd given me your heart. I nearly demanded you take it back, but the selfish part of me wanted your heart. I wanted you to be mine, even though I could never be yours. There aren't enough sorrys in the world. You gave me everything, and I gave you nothing in return. I am truly sorry.

Be well, my wild Lilly.

Dillon's hand trembled as he set the pen down, his gaze fixed on the salty tear that landed on the paper below. His heart felt as though it had imploded inside his chest, crushing his soul as a wave of conflicting emotions surged through him. The pain was beyond anything he had ever felt before, even more than when his parents passed away. His breath grew shallow, and tears filled his eyes. He was certain he would succumb to a heart attack right then and there, despite his kind supposedly being impervious to such human ailments. How had he let it come to this? It was a question he would never stop asking himself and one he would never truly have an answer for.

He folded the letter and put it in an envelope. Dillon checked his watch and saw that Lilly would still be at work. He felt like a coward, but he was also protecting them both. He had no idea what kind of woman his true mate was and didn't want to give her any more ammunition that might cause her to hunt Lilly down. The final nail in their coffins would be if Dillon had any physical contact with Lilly after having met his true mate. He couldn't do that to either woman.

Dillon parked outside her apartment and entered with the key she had given him over a year ago. He placed the envelope on the mantel and stepped back as if it might attack him. Then he hurried through the apartment and grabbed anything he had left: a sweatshirt of his she liked to sleep in, a toothbrush, a pair of shoes, and some clothes he kept for when he stayed the night, which had been most nights.

Dillon had never brought Lilly to his camper. Not once. He didn't want her to show up unannounced, in case he somehow met his true mate. How foolish he had been thinking that would never happen in Coldspring, Texas. Dillon hadn't wanted Lilly to come face-to-face with the woman who held the other half of his soul. Something Lilly could never do. She couldn't chase away the darkness that had continued to grow inside him, even though it had seemed to slow down over the time he had been with Lilly. Regardless, it had never stopped growing.

His mind was a blur. He fled the apartment as if the devil were on his heels. Dillon practically flung himself, along with the armful of belongings, into the cab of the truck. His hand shook as he put the key in the ignition and started the engine. He threw the truck into reverse, and as he drove away from her apartment, Dillon didn't look in his rearview mirror. It was a part of his life that he had to lay to rest. Dillon couldn't undo it, but for the sake of his future, he had to forget it.

"Would you be interested in buying my camper?" Dillon asked Pat, the gentleman who oversaw the campsite. Dillon was there to pay the final month's rent for the spot where he'd been living.

Pat's white hair stuck out from under the cowboy hat that he always wore. He leaned back against the counter behind him, and stuck his weathered hands in his pockets. Pat chewed on a toothpick that seemed to be as much a part of him as his hat. The wrinkles on his face shifted and deepened as he frowned, appearing to scrutinize Dillon. "I take that to mean you're leaving us for good?" Pat asked in a low drawl, his voice hoarse from years of smoking. His eyes narrowed slightly as he waited for Dillon to answer. The air was thick with the scent of coffee beans and cigarette smoke, both smells Dillon had come to associate with the older man and probably always would.

Dillon slipped his hands into his pockets and rocked back on his heels. "Afraid so. Life's taking me in a different direction."

Pat nodded and let out a deep sigh. "Just going to pick up and go despite having built a life here?"

"I've got some fences to mend elsewhere." Tanya's devastated face flashed in his mind. Mending fences was putting it lightly.

"Mm-hmm." Pat hummed. "Well, I can appreciate that." The toothpick bobbed up and down with the movement of his lips. "Life is short. You don't want to leave this world with burned bridges."

Dillon didn't respond. He just shook his head and stared at the ground.

Pat leaned forward. "You look like you think the bridge you burned can't be rebuilt."

"I think I burned it pretty good. I'm not sure."

"You might be surprised. When something burns down, you find out what caused it, see if there's a way to keep it from happening again, and then build it back better." He pulled the toothpick from his mouth and tossed it in the trash can, then slipped the pack of cigarettes out from his shirt pocket.

"What if the bridge can't be rebuilt? What if there is no material that could possibly reconstruct it?"

Pat stuck the cigarette in his mouth but didn't light it. "I'm just gonna take the whole bridge analogy to mean a woman. The only bridge a man burns that he feels completely hopeless about is a woman."

Dillon didn't respond. He simply stared back at the elderly man.

Pat pushed off the counter and pulled a lighter from his pocket. He flicked it until a flame ignited and then held it to the end of the cigarette still in his mouth. "If she's worth it, then forget the damn bridge and figure out another way to reach her. Scale a wall, swing on a vine like Tarzan, buy a plane to cross the chasm between you. You do it all over and over again until she is finally willing to listen, if for no other reason than to get you to leave her alone. You fight for her." Smoke flowed from his nose as he spoke. The passion in Pat's voice surprised Dillon.

Dillon tilted his head slightly and narrowed his eyes. "Who'd you lose? Who didn't you fight for?"

Pat's eyes took on a faraway look as he answered. "My daughter, Maggie." He pulled the cigarette from his lips and tapped the burned ashes into the ashtray on the counter. "I never got to make it right before she was killed in a car accident." Pat shook his head. "I'd give anything to go back and fix it."

Dillon didn't ask what "it" was. That wasn't his business, and deep loss still filled Pat's voice. "I'm sorry for your loss, Pat."

"Don't make the mistake I made, Dillon. Whatever wrong you've done, make it right."

After an exchange of money for the camper Dillon was leaving behind and the wisdom Pat had bestowed, Dillon climbed into his truck and set the GPS on his phone for the middle of Colorado. Come hell or high water, he would do whatever was necessary to claim his mate and earn her love.

CHAPTER
FOUR

"Home used to be a place I loved. But now, knowing that he will be coming for me, I find it a prison. Yet a part of me loves the idea that my mate will hunt me down. Damn werewolf instincts. The other part of me wants to keep a pair of fae blades in hand, ready to throw at his cheating face as soon as it comes into view. Sure, it's also a handsome face; don't remind me. I think I might be having a personality crisis. That's a thing. If it wasn't, it is now." ~Tanya

"I want to make a detour," Tanya announced as they stopped at yet another gas station for provisions and a bathroom break, courtesy of her small bladder.

"We're already on a detour, and look what happened," Trevor pointed out. "You found the one thing every *Canis lupus* hopes for and told him to take a hike."

"A detour to where?" Austin ignored Trevor and pushed the door of the van open.

"Missouri." Tanya hopped out and shut the door behind her. "I haven't seen Lisa in forever, and since we're still a ways from home, we might as well."

Trevor sighed. "It's in the opposite direction."

Tanya didn't look his way. "Not completely, just a few hours out of the way."

Daniel held the door to the gas station open and gave Tanya a questioning look as she passed through. "Not to mention, the alpha told us to come straight back when we were done."

"I'll call him." She waved her hand dismissively. "He'll be fine with it."

Trevor followed closely behind. "Will he be fine with it when he finds out you met your mate and rejected him?"

Tanya whipped around, her finger already pointed, ready to jab her packmate in the chest. "You will not say a word to my father." She jabbed him three times. "It's not your place." She jabbed another three times. "And if you do, I'll take you out."

Trevor held up his hands and took a step back. "There's no need to get violent, T."

Austin stepped up beside her, and Daniel next to him. "Can we just get what we need, do your business, Tanya," —he glanced at her—"and then talk about this in the van?" He ran a hand through his hair, his jaw clenched. As beta to her father, Daniel had the right to flat-out deny her request. The fact that he hadn't simply done so gave her hope that he'd allow them to make the trip.

She gave a sharp nod and headed for the bathroom. Regardless of what Trevor said, Tanya wasn't going home.

Not yet. She wanted to talk to Lisa. She knew her friend could help her process her emotions.

Tanya hurried over to a pay phone and shoved in some coins before she dialed her mother's number. Rose Ellis answered on the second ring, and Tanya couldn't help but smile at her mother's warm voice.

"Hello, darling. Your father told me that Daniel reported in just a couple of hours ago and said you all were on your way home. You didn't find anything?"

"Oh, she found something," Austin muttered standing only a few feet away from her.

Stupid werewolf hearing. It was challenging to have a private conversation with a *Canis lupus* around. Most were polite enough to simply ignore what they heard. Austin was not.

"What did he say?" her mom asked.

Tanya rubbed her hand across her forehead. "Nothing, Mom. Austin is just being his usual charming, obnoxious self."

"Can I file a complaint with the alpha for emotional abuse?" Austin said a little louder, as if he needed to speak up for Rose to hear him.

"Now you're just being ridiculous." Tanya huffed, then focused her attention back on the conversation with her mom. "We started a detour through Texas because I can't remember the last time I came through here. But then I thought, we're so far away already, why not go visit Lisa?"

"You've been gone—" Rose began, but Tanya cut her off.

"She's not getting any younger, Mom. Please. We'll be safe. I've got the Three Stooges with me. What could possibly go wrong?"

"Please refer to my earlier comment." Austin snorted,

prompting Trevor to smack him on the back of the head. "What was that for?" Austin grumbled, rubbing the back of his head.

Tanya glanced between the two males as she continued to speak to her mom. "We'll only stay a few days and then head straight home."

"I really don't like it when you're so far from home, and there are rumors of rogues out there." Concern filled her mother's voice.

Tanya clenched her free hand into a fist, allowing her nails to bite into her flesh. She was on the verge of blurting out that she had met her true mate, but she knew that would lead to a barrage of questions she wasn't prepared to answer. "Please, Mom. I really want to see her." She wasn't lying. It had been a long time since she had seen Lisa, even though they talked on the phone frequently. She missed Lisa's face, warm hugs, and calming demeanor that always seemed to put her at ease. Tanya could use some of that peace right about now.

Her mother sighed. "Alright, I'll take care of things with your father."

Tanya closed her eyes and inwardly relaxed. Her father, Jeremiah Ellis, was extremely protective of her. The only reason she had been allowed to join his top three wolves on this mission was because her mom had convinced him. Tanya was no longer a child. She had trained in fighting techniques in both her human and wolf form. She might have been the child of the alphas, but she didn't want to be treated like a princess.

"Thank you."

"Call me as soon as you arrive at Tyler's pack."

Tanya nodded, although her mom couldn't see her. "Of course."

"I love you, Tanya."

She smiled. Rose Ellis was one of the most caring people Tanya knew, and not just because she was her mom. Tanya had watched her mother over the years care for others, giving her time and energy to meet the needs of other pack members. Tanya's dad always told her that his mate was the only reason he wasn't a complete tyrant. She was just impressed that he actually recognized that he was, at least in part, a tyrant. "I love you, too. I'll call later to let you know no rogues have run us off the road and dragged us to our doom."

She could practically hear her mother's eye roll. "You think that doesn't happen? You're not immune to bad things."

"I know, Mom," Tanya huffed. "I was kidding. But seriously, we'll be fine. Won't we, Daniel?" she hollered to the beta.

"Absolutely, Alpha," he called from where he stood beside the other two males. "I'll keep her out of trouble."

"I'd say it's too late for that," Austin said.

Tanya turned her body as she heard a scuffle. Trevor had his arm wrapped around Austin's neck and was attempting to cover his mouth with his hand.

"Okay, Mom," Tanya said quickly, "I've got to go. You know Daniel can't navigate a map." Total bull. Daniel could use a GPS device they had in the van just fine without Tanya's help. But she needed to get off the phone before Austin could say something more revealing than his already intriguing questions. He wanted to pique Rose's interest enough that she would speak with Jeremiah about it, in hopes that he would call Daniel and try to get information out of him.

"Tell those boys not to roughhouse in the van," her

mother admonished, obviously picking up on the grunting coming from the guys. "They could distract the driver."

"I'll get on it," Tanya assured her. "Love you!"

"Love you, too, darling."

Tanya ended the call before her mother decided to ask some questions regarding Austin's odd comments.

"Could you be any more of an ass?" Tanya glared at Austin.

Austin pushed Trevor's hand away. "Absolutely." He smiled. "This is low-level ass-ness. I can take it up several notches if you'd like."

Tanya turned back to the phone and put more coins in. "I'd like you to keep your mouth closed about something that I will discuss with my parents when I'm ready to."

Austin was quiet for several minutes before he finally spoke. "I just want you to be okay, T. You're like a sister to us. When you hurt, we hurt."

Her heart squeezed in her chest, and she had to focus hard to keep the bond locked down, which was hard to do when emotions were running high. And Tanya's were definitely up there. She dialed the number she had memorized and waited for Lisa to answer.

"Your father let you off the leash?" Lisa's voice was playful and warm.

"Ha, ha, the dog jokes never get old," Tanya said dryly. "How'd you know it was me?"

. . .

"Your mom just called. She said, 'Tanya's headed your way. Find out what's wrong.'"

Tanya rolled her eyes. She should have known her mother wouldn't leave well enough alone. "Nothing is wrong. I just figured I'd take advantage of my brief freedom while I can."

"Fair enough." Lisa didn't sound like she believed Tanya at all. "How long till you get here?"

"Ten hours," Daniel called out, still eavesdropping on her conversation. Rude.

Tanya sighed. "Twelve with bathroom breaks. Trevor has a small bladder."

"I know where you sleep, T," he called back. "You should be kinder to me."

"Tell him he should have that checked out. It seems abnormal," Lisa teased.

"He's a *Canis lupus*, Lisa. We don't get bladder issues," Tanya reminded her, even though she knew the human was well aware.

"Yes, but can you imagine the look on his face if a pretty nurse told him to pee in a cup?" Lisa cackled. "Would he have to lift a leg to do so?"

"I can hear you, old woman," Trevor called out. "You're not funny."

Tanya grinned. "You're totally funny, Lisa."

"See you soon, little wolf," Lisa told Tanya and then hung up.

She headed to the van with her three guard dogs in tow and tried to tamp down her excitement of seeing her friend. Even with the looming knowledge about Tanya's true mate, she was happy she'd get to spend some time with Lisa.

Daniel glanced over at Tanya, who had fallen asleep after another stop for gas and food. She had been quiet since she talked to her mother, which was not like Tanya. Typically, she had lots to say about anything and everything, but the woman sitting next to him wasn't the one he knew. Whatever had happened between her and the wolf named Dillon had shaken her up. Daniel didn't want to pry, and he didn't want to go behind her back and talk to her father about it. But as beta of the pack, he answered to the alpha first, not the alpha's daughter and his friend.

Daniel heaved a deep sigh and refocused on the highway. The sun was setting, painting the sky with streaks of light blue, pink, and yellow, dotted with cottony white clouds hovering in the air. He could see the moon becoming more visible and noticed it was full. His lips turned up as he thought about the fact that humans had the lore of his kind all wrong. They didn't have to turn on a full moon, or only turn on a full moon. The *Canis lupus* could phase, as they referred to it, at will. For which he was profoundly grateful. His wolf was as much a part of him as the air he breathed. If he was cut off from his beast and only able to interact with him once a month, it would feel like a slow death. His wolf growled at his thoughts. *"You need to contact the alpha,"* his beast said. Daniel didn't disagree, and he was avoiding it by letting his thoughts wander.

"You're doing an awful lot of sighing up there," Austin said.

Daniel briefly looked at him in the rearview mirror. "Have you ever seen her like this?" He motioned with his head toward Tanya.

"She met her true mate. He turned out to be an ass," Austin said as if they were just talking about the weather and not the fate of one of their pack mates. "How do you expect her to act?"

"Why won't she talk to us about it?" Daniel's hands gripped the steering wheel. "We've grown up together." He shook his head. "Why doesn't she trust us?"

"Dude," Trevor spoke up. "We're not female. She's not going to talk to us about this."

"Hence why we're driving ten hours in the opposite direction of home," Austin added. "She wants to talk to Lisa."

"Why would she want to talk to a human about true mates?" Daniel's mind was running around in circles as he attempted to figure out what Tanya could want to ask Lisa that a wolf wouldn't know. Especially about true mates.

"Lisa has been with the Missouri pack for a long time," Austin pointed out. "Maybe she has some insight that a female she-wolf doesn't."

"Even Tanya's own mother?" Daniel frowned and forced himself to loosen his grip on the steering wheel.

"I stopped trying to understand the female mind a long time ago." Daniel saw Austin shrug in the rearview mirror.

"Let's just take her to her friend, and maybe she will be able to work things out, and then we can head home and see if Dillon shows up, even though she threatened to kill him."

"He'll show up." Conviction filled Daniel's voice and heart. He knew it as sure as he knew his own mind. A male who had met his true mate would follow her to the ends of the earth, even if she was throwing rocks at him the whole time while cursing his very existence. There was no way in hell Dillon would leave Tanya alone. And Daniel couldn't blame him, even if his first impression was less than impressive.

He sat back into the seat and rested one hand on his leg while he used his other to steer the van. Night slowly took over the sky, which was barely visible because of the brightness from the full moon. It was almost as bright as the sun, but with a softer glow. He might not need to phase during a full moon, but the forest bathed in the beautiful light called to his wolf. When they arrived, he'd have to let his beast out for a good, long run. Then, after he could give himself a little more time to see how Tanya acted after speaking with Lisa, he would decide if he should contact Jeremiah. And he'd have to put on his metaphorical armor because Tanya was going to kick his ass when she found out. Daniel rested his head back. *We'll cross that bridge when we get there.*

CHAPTER FIVE

"There were few things worse than being divided in my loyalty. Living with a wolf inside of me, harmony between us was a necessity to sanity. As an unmated male I lived on the brink of darkness. My heart was divided in multiple ways. The human I'd loved, the pack I'd left behind, and the mate I desperately wanted. How would I ever feel whole again? Did I even deserve it?" ~ Dillon

Dillon pulled away from the curb, his tires squealing. He glanced over at the duffel bag in the passenger seat. One paltry bag of belongings. Thirteen years in Coldspring, and that was all he had to show for it. That and the shattered heart of a woman he loved.

"Stay focused." His wolf spoke in his mind.

Dillon growled back at his wolf. *"You cannot understand."*

The man felt like a loved one had passed. In essence, that's exactly what had happened. He knew he would never see Lilly again. How can you love someone, practically live with her as a husband and wife would, and then leave her at the drop of a hat? Every day for the past three years, he'd gone home to Lilly's apartment. That was more his home than his camper had ever been. Now, in the blink of an eye, she was gone. No, she wasn't gone. He was. Dillon was the one that had left. This wasn't Lilly's doing.

He gripped the steering wheel and pushed the pedal to the floor, thankful that no police were around to pull him over. If they had, he wasn't sure he would have stopped.

"I understand what I need to understand. You are a fool. You've hurt our mate."

Another wave of guilt crashed over Dillon. The wolf was right. But there was nothing he could do about it now. He couldn't go back and change his life with Lilly. And if he were honest, he wasn't sure he would. *"What a coward I am."*

The wolf huffed its agreement.

Dillon decided to test the bond. While he was gathering his things and writing the note to Lilly, he'd kept his mind tightly closed. Given her reaction, Dillon didn't think his mate would be trying to communicate with him, but still. Better to be safe than sorry. The last thing he needed was Tanya to appear in his mind as he was pouring his soul out in a letter to another woman.

He pushed against the bond a little, nothing too strong. Dillon didn't want to invade his mate's mind. He hit a wall as solid as granite.

Relief and frustration washed over Dillon in equal measure. Though he wanted to reach out to Tanya, he knew that he wouldn't be able to entirely hide his memories of

Lilly. They'd been together for three years, and his feelings toward her were strong. That kind of thing couldn't just be shunted aside. He couldn't just forget her, as much as he wanted to. And just like at the gas station, he knew Tanya's reaction wouldn't be good.

"I told you so."

"You're not helping," Dillon snarled back at his wolf.

What kind of life am I going to lead? Dillon wondered. *I cannot open my mind to my mate for fear of what she will see.* He swore and slammed his hand down on the steering wheel.

Mile after mile passed in a blur. Dillon drove like a maniac, tearing up the miles north to Colorado. He wasn't sure what he'd find when he got there. It had been some time since he'd visited the Colorado pack. He remembered the Alpha being a tyrant, but not much else.

Dillon's pager beeped, jarring him from his thoughts, mostly because he hadn't heard it beep in so long. For a moment, he panicked, thinking it must be Lilly. He'd been expecting to hear from her, gone over and over what he would say to her. He'd try to be as gentle as he could but firmly tell her he couldn't return. They'd talked about this at length. She'd always known this day would come. But having the pretend conversation in his mind and having to actually form the words to speak to Lilly was entirely different. He pulled over to the first gas station he found and headed for the pay phone. He steeled his courage as he looked at the number. It wasn't a Texas area code.

He quickly dialed the number. "Hello," he choked out.

"Hello, old friend." A male's voice came through the phone. For a moment, Dillon was so surprised at hearing his friend Colin's voice, he couldn't speak.

"Hello? You there?" Colin asked.

"Um, yeah. Sorry, I dropped the phone." He cleared his throat. "Yeah, I'm here. What's up, Colin? So good to hear from you." Dillon couldn't remember the last time he'd talked to Colin. Dillon checked in periodically, and Colin caught him up to speed on the news of the pack. But after he'd found Lilly, Dillon and Colin had spoken less and less.

"You don't sound happy to hear from me. You sound like you've just found out that someone died."

His gut twisted at the accuracy of his friend's observation, considering a part of him had died and needed to. "I'm sorry. I've just got some stuff going on here."

"Anything you want to talk about?

"No." Dillon breathed. "Not really."

"Okay, I understand, I guess. I've got some stuff of my own going on here." Dillon heard worry in his friend's voice.

"What's going on?"

"Two of our pack mates have been killed."

The words were like a gut punch. "Killed? How?"

"Shot. We're assuming by hunters. When Jagger went missing, the Alpha sent out a search party. We found traces of blood spatter in the woods, tire tracks. Looks like someone shot him in his wolf form, then hauled him off. Same with Link."

Dillon knew both of the wolves. They were men he considered friends. He wasn't as close to them as Colin, but still. Knowing they'd been murdered, especially in the same way his parents had been, hit harder than he would've guessed after all this time. For a moment, he wondered why he hadn't felt their deaths through the pack bonds. Then a realization hit him, another hammer blow to his already battered soul. He was no longer a member of the Montana pack. He'd been living as a lone wolf for so long, the pack bonds had severed themselves. Tears formed in Dillon's eyes. He lifted his hand and pinched the bridge of his nose, attempting to pull his emotions together.

"Dillon, you there, man?" Colin's voice came through the phone.

"Yeah, yeah, I'm here. The news just hit me wrong."

"Everyone here is up in arms." Colin's voice was agitated. "Some of the pack wants to start going door to door, dragging humans out until they find out who did it. Others are a little more levelheaded, but the alpha is having a hard time keeping everyone calm."

"I can imagine." The Montana pack alpha was a just man, but losing pack members could cause serious unrest and, without strong leadership, a mutiny.

Colin breathed out a heavy sigh. "I know you've been gone a long time, Dillon, but I was hoping you might come and help us find out who did this. You were one of our best hunters. And"—he paused—"it's time you came home."

Dillon bit the inside of his cheek. It wasn't until this moment that he realized how much he missed his old pack. Living as a lone wolf had left him calloused, and more darkness than he'd known had spread inside of him. Lilly had been the only bright spot. He desperately wanted to be back with his old pack now, seeing familiar faces, hearing the stories around the fire pit again. He couldn't just refuse to help after two of his friends had been murdered.

A noise came from within him. Almost a feral whine. For the first time in thirteen years, he and his wolf were in agreement on something. The wolf, too, hungered to be back with their pack. It was essential that he help his brothers in need. But he also knew they had a bigger priority. Probably the only thing that would make him refuse such a request.

"I'm sorry, Colin," Dillon said in a quiet voice. "I can't come back right now. I have to go somewhere else first."

"What?" Colin practically growled. "What could possibly be more important than this? Where are you going? I know you've been gone a long time, man, but c'mon. You're still a part of this pack."

Dillon didn't bother to tell him that that wasn't exactly true. "Listen, I want to help, but—"

"But what?" Colin asked, concern and frustration filled his voice. "What's your problem?"

Dillon hesitated, unsure of how much to tell his friend. Finally, he took a deep breath and let it out slowly. "I've found my true mate. I'm on my way to Colorado."

Colin was silent for several breaths. "Colorado? How the heck did you find your mate in Colorado? I thought you were in Texas."

Dillon shook his head and stared out the pay phone window "It's a long story, Colin." He knew his old friend could probably hear the defeat in his voice.

"One it sounds like you are in no mood to tell."

"It's not pretty, so no, not right now." He didn't know if he ever wanted to tell it considering how he'd been living the past few years went completely against the ways of their kind.

"Well, I guess congratulations are in order, though I'm really not sure considering the sound of your voice. But I can certainly understand why you don't want to help."

"No, it's not that I don't *want* to help. Not at all," Dillon assured him. "As soon as this business is finished, I'll be there. Hopefully with my mate in tow."

A few seconds of silence ticked before Colin finally spoke. "Fair enough. Good luck. You know I got your back if you need me." Click. The line went silent.

CHAPTER SIX

> "It amazes me that supernaturals think that being a human is so simple. They think we can't possibly understand what it's like to experience emotions as strongly as they do. I often have to remind them that they didn't coin love and all that goes with it. Choosing to love is universal for humans and supernaturals alike." ~Lisa Owens

Tanya tried not to react as she stared at the elderly woman who stood in the doorway. Her friend, Lisa, lived in a house located on the Missouri pack compound. Tanya thought back to when she'd last seen Lisa and realized it had only been a little over one year since they'd seen one another, but Lisa looked as if she'd aged a decade. The woman who'd been so full of life when Tanya had last seen her now appeared fragile and withered, like a piece of paper that had gotten wet and then dried, leaving it wrinkled and delicate, easily torn.

"Stop looking at me like that," Lisa said, her tone sharp as a whip. "I can still spank you if I need to."

Tanya's lips turned up slightly, even as her heart broke at the reminder that her friend's life was shorter than her own. One day, Tanya would have to say goodbye, watch Lisa be shoved into a casket, and then lowered into the ground, covered with dirt in her eternal resting place. *Damn, my thoughts are morbid.* She walked toward the woman who held her arms open, always ready for a hug. Normally, Tanya would have run to her, but she was sure if she did that, she would knock Lisa over and break several of her bones. "Be gentle," she told her wolf, even though she didn't need to. Her wolf adored the human woman as much as Tanya did.

Lisa's arms wrapped around Tanya, and her familiar scent enveloped her. She breathed deeply as the comfort and peace that Lisa wore like a well-worn piece of clothing flowed over her. "Oh, how I've missed you, crazy girl." Lisa gave her a weak squeeze before letting her go. She grabbed Tanya by the shoulders and pushed her back a bit, running her eyes up and down her. "You're more beautiful every time I see you."

Tanya rolled her eyes. "You have to say that. You love me."

Lisa scoffed. "I'm perfectly capable of loving ugly people. Though I will admit that it can be harder if they're jackasses. Loving ugly jackasses is harder than loving pretty jackasses."

Tanya laughed. "And why would that be?"

"Because at least pretty jackasses are nice to look at." Lisa motioned for Tanya to follow her as she walked toward the front door of her home.

Tanya glanced back at the van where the three males still sat. She gave them a wave. "I'll talk to you later."

"How long are we staying, T?" Daniel asked, no doubt reporting back to her father.

"I don't know." *Until Dillon forgets about me, or I forget about him,* she amended in her head. But the answer she gave the beta was the truth. She had no idea how long she would need to be somewhere where Dillon wouldn't find her. Maybe forever. She turned back and left them, closing the door behind her.

The scent of cinnamon and vanilla filled the air, and she nearly squealed. "You made me cookies?"

"No. I made them for the squirrels. They have particular tastes and will no longer eat nuts."

"Smartass," Tanya muttered as she followed Lisa's voice into the kitchen, where at least two dozen cinnamon vanilla cookies were stacked on a large platter. "How did you know I would need comfort food?"

"Psht," Lisa scoffed. "This isn't comfort food, and you know it. This is 'my heart is hurting' food, and I want to fill it with cookies so it won't feel empty. You made me make them for you when your dad made you get rid of your cat." She opened the fridge and pulled out the milk, then a glass from a cabinet. As Lisa poured a large amount, she continued, "And it was a total dick move for your father to do that. Your heart was shattered. I didn't think you'd ever stop crying."

Tanya remembered that, and though the pain had eased a decade later, it still made her sad to think about. She had been so miserable that her mother had allowed her to come stay with Lisa for a couple of weeks. Their friendship was unlikely, considering Lisa was human and much older than Tanya. But from the moment she had met Lisa when she had visited the Colorado pack, they had hit it off. Kindred spirits, Tanya's mother called it.

Tanya took the offered glass and snagged four cookies from the stack before heading for the table. She slipped into a chair and set her goodies down. "I still don't understand why I couldn't keep her. No one would have eaten her. She was someone I could talk to without it getting back to my dad. I love him, but I swear he tries to control every aspect of my life, even though I'm a freaking adult. That he let me go on this hunt is a miracle."

"Why did he?" Lisa gingerly sat down across from Tanya.

"Mostly because Daniel went." Tanya took a bite from one of the cookies and hummed. "So good," she said as she chewed.

"The loyal beta." Lisa nodded. "And yet, he brought you here, with something bigger than a lost cat tearing you up inside."

"I have no illusions that he won't contact my father." Tanya took a gulp of the cold milk. "He may be my friend, but he's the beta of our pack first."

Lisa nodded as she took a bite of her own cookie. "Mm-hmm," she said as she chewed. Once she'd swallowed, she added, "That may be true, but he brought you here when, I'm guessing, he was told to come straight back to the pack. Which means he cares, and whatever has you all tied up in knots is bad enough that he wanted to do whatever he could to help." Lisa continued to eat her cookie but remained quiet, leaving her words to hang in the air.

Tanya knew her friend was done talking and would now simply wait her out until she finally spilled her guts. She finished two more cookies before deciding to give in. She had, after all, come to Lisa for this reason. That, and she really had missed her friend. Talking on the phone was a poor substitute for the real thing. Might as well rip the band-aid off. "I met my true mate." There. She'd said it and managed not to puke. That was something, right?

Lisa's face lit up, and her eyes filled with joy, but a moment later, it was gone, and her smile dropped, the creases in her eyes falling along with it. "Alright, I've been in the pack life for quite some time, and I'm pretty sure this is something we're supposed to be celebrating. Yet you look like you'd rather have your fingernails pulled off."

Tanya bit the inside of her cheek. She hated crying. And she wasn't about to shed a tear for that cheating punk. Good grief. Couldn't she come up with some better insults? She could, but her wolf was holding her tongue, even her mental one.

"Go on." Lisa motioned with her hand. "Let it out. I will not let you have any more cookies until you get it off your chest."

Tanya narrowed her eyes. "Holding cookies hostage is not what BFFs do."

"It is when said BFF is acting like a hardheaded toddler."

She flopped back against the chair and folded her arms across her chest, suddenly feeling very defensive. Tanya knew she had every right to be angry. *Didn't she?* Yes, she most definitely did. "It *is* supposed to be something that we celebrate. It's supposed to be amazing." Tanya's stomach twisted into knots as a fresh wave of disappointment crashed over her. She felt something pushing at her mind and knew it was him. The strength of her emotions was making her walls weak. She quickly reinforced them. Tanya wasn't ready to deal with Dillon. She didn't know if she ever would be. "I met him at a gas station in Nowhere,

Texas. I mean, what a bizarre place to meet your mate. And" —she held up her finger—"he's not even in a pack. He's rogue."

"Is that what he told you?" Lisa's brow rose.

Tanya pursed her lips. "Not in so many words. But—" She quickly continued when Lisa opened her mouth. "He made it clear that there were no other wolves around."

"That doesn't mean he's a rogue." Lisa rested her hands on the table. Tanya noticed the dark spots on them and hated that her friend was aging.

"Are you okay?" Tanya smelled something on the woman other than Lisa's usual scent, but couldn't put her finger on it.

Lisa shook her finger at her. "Oh no, you're not getting out of this. We're not talking about me. This is all you. Keep going."

"Ugh, this is a disaster." Tanya gritted her teeth. "I heard his thoughts. His mind was in mine, and it was this intimate connection I've never felt before. Goosebumps ran all over my arms, and I felt like electricity lit me up from the inside out. It was amazing." Tanya heard the awe in her voice and wished that she could end the tale there. "But then, I saw something I wish I could unsee." She closed her eyes and allowed the female's face to fill her mind. But it wasn't just her face. "There was a woman in his mind. Not just any woman." She bit her lip again, holding the tears back. "The emotions he felt when he thought of her made me want to throw up. Even just remembering them makes me nauseous." She shuddered.

Lisa reached across the table and rested her hand on top of Tanya's. She pulled it away from her, uncrossing her arms until their joined hands rested back on the table. "You feel betrayed."

Her eyes snapped up to Lisa's. "Of course I feel betrayed. He *did* betray me. I'm his true mate. There is nothing more sacred in our race. We're taught this from childhood." She shook her head as she felt her hand tremble beneath Lisa's. "To seek out someone else when you know you have a true mate out there, the one person who will complete your soul? It's... Well..." She pinched the bridge of her nose. "It's wrong! It's just wrong. I feel like a part of me has been shredded. Like my heart has been ripped apart, and I didn't even know it could be so thoroughly devastated." She was breathless as she finished her emotional word vomit. Tanya wanted to find a deep hole to crawl into and hide. She felt exposed, and dammit, she had tears running down her face.

Lisa squeezed her hand but didn't say anything right away. She simply sat there, giving Tanya quiet support as she tried to gather herself. But the longer she sat there with Lisa's tender eyes staring at her, the more her chest seemed to rip open. She felt as if a hand had pushed past her ribs and wrapped around the beating muscle, attempting to squeeze it until she couldn't breathe. Tanya sucked in large breaths, needing to get air into her body, but it was as if her windpipe had completely closed. How had this occurred? This wasn't supposed to happen, not to *her*. "I don't know what to do." Her voice cracked as she swiftly wiped at the tears that simply continued to flow. "I don't want him and yet "

"He's yours." Lisa's gentle tone of her voice gutted Tanya all over again.

"But I don't want him," Tanya said again, her voice rising with her agitation and anger. "How could he do that to me?"

"I wish I had wisdom to give you, but as a human, it's

hard for me to relate to the *Canis lupus* true mate bond." Lisa told her. She patted Tanya's hand and pulled hers away. "We don't have soulmates. At least not how you all do. There are many people who love deeply, lose their spouse, and then find another and love them just as fiercely as the first one."

Tanya's eyes widened in horror. "How could they disrespect their first mate that way?" Tanya couldn't comprehend the human way of mating. Their feelings seemed so finicky. One minute, they declare their love, and in the very next breath, they tell the person they no longer love them and want to separate. They court one another in this ridiculous ritualistic way where they dress up for one another, always attempting to look their best, only to then stop doing that once they are mated. Why are they so changeable? Don't their pre-mating rituals still matter? If you cared enough to do it while you're courting, then why would you not care enough once you're mated? Tanya would never get it. She'd watched tons of human television shows and still couldn't understand their emotions and how they shift like an unstable foundation. The rumblings of a volcano were more reliable than the emotions and commitments of a human. How could anyone live that way? Why would anyone want to be in a relationship if there was such a high chance that the other person would one day decide they no longer wanted you?

"To love another after your spouse has passed away is not disrespecting them. It doesn't change the fact that you loved them in life. Your love doesn't die just because they did. Our hearts are very big things with lots of room for love, Tanya. Love for people, love for animals, love for creation, love for life and even death."

Tanya frowned. "How could you possibly love death?"

Lisa suddenly looked very weary. "Death is what makes life so beautiful. Even your species can die, and eventually will, though your long life might make you forget that at times." Lisa turned and looked out of the window that her table sat beside. It was nearly noon, and the winter sun shone brightly on the lightly snow-covered ground. Tanya had barely noticed the bite of the cold air—another difference between their two species. "One day, much sooner than you, I will die," Lisa continued.

Tanya shook her head. "No... I don't..." She paused as the tears that had finally stopped welled up in her eyes again. "That's not something I can think of."

"It doesn't matter if you can think of it or not, Tanya." Lisa turned her brown eyes back on Tanya. "You have to accept it. And understand that our relationship, what we have now, is all the more precious because of it."

Tanya suddenly wanted to jump and run. She wanted to shed her human skin and let her wolf take over and just run until her legs would no longer carry her. She didn't want to think about her cheating mate, her controlling father, the torn beta who was loyal to both her and his alpha, or her friend who was mortal, every day moving closer to death. Isn't that what humans were? From the moment they took their first breath, they began to die. Tanya shoved away from the table and stood up so fast that her chair nearly toppled over backward. Her quick reflexes allowed her to grab it and slam it back to the ground. "I need some air." She wiped her face with the bottom of her shirt.

"Take some clothes." Lisa pointed to a cabinet by the front door. Tanya knew that the woman had learned long ago that it was good to have clothes on hand when you lived around werewolves. "Come back when you're ready. I'll be here."

Tanya clenched her fists. "Will you?"

Lisa stood slowly. "Sweet girl." She walked over and pressed her hand to Tanya's cheek. "My time in this world is not yet over."

"You look older than the last time I saw you," Tanya said before she could censor herself. "You move so much slower, as if you might break if you fell."

Lisa patted Tanya's cheek. "Yes, I have aged. But I still have things to do before I go home to my maker. And the top of that list is helping you in your time of need." She walked toward the door, opened the cabinet, and took out a stack of clothes from a shelf with Tanya's name on it. "When you get back, I will be here. Waiting. Maybe I'll even make you dinner."

Tanya took the offered clothes and pressed a kiss to Lisa's cheek. "Thank you," she whispered and then hurried out the door before she collapsed and begged the Great Luna to somehow spare Lisa's life. She headed for the woods, in the opposite direction she'd seen Daniel drive off. She didn't want company. As soon as she was under the cover of the trees, Tanya found a place to tuck the clothes away and then she gave control over to the wolf. In a blink, she went from two feet to four.

Her wolf shook out its fur and then threw back its head and howled. There were so many emotions in the wolf's song, Tanya was sure that even her beast would be shedding tears when she opened her eyes. She pawed at the ground, sinking her claws past the snow and into the cold ground. Her wolf drew in a deep breath, enjoying the bite of the cold air in her lungs. Without another thought she lunged forward, taking off in a dead run. A part of her wanted to keep running and never stop. But she knew eventually she would have to face her mate. And her wolf looked forward to it. *Stupid wolf.*

After Tanya disappeared from her sight, Lisa remained in the doorway of her home, her heart aching for the young woman who was learning the painful side of love. Many people, including the *Canis lupus* at times, believed love to be just an emotion. However, it was much more than that. Love encompassed facets that some might never experience in their lifetime. Love went beyond a feeling, beyond the flutters in your stomach or the excitement of a new relationship. Throughout her lifetime, Lisa had heard so many people say they had "found" love. But love was not something to be found because it was not a tangible object that one searched for. When people claimed they were "in love," what they really meant was they were "in infatuation," which wasn't a bad thing unless it became the foundation of their relationship. If that were the case, they would fail from the start.

Love was what made a relationship last, especially on the bad days when your partner was at their worst. In those moments when their words were unkind, their temper short, or their choices selfish, that was when love was crucial. It was then that you chose to love that person even though they were unlovable. Love was hard, often ungrateful, until that person, or even yourself, recognized that your actions or words had caused pain. Love was forgiving, even when it wasn't deserved. It was about giving grace when you would rather have revenge. In short, love was a choice.

It was an action, not just a feeling. Even between the powerful connection of true mates, the bond was not enough to ensure a healthy relationship. They could remain loyal and faithful to each other, but they were still imperfect beings who, like humans, could be selfish and cruel.

Lisa closed the door behind her, her movements stiff with pain. The winter months only exacerbated her discomfort, although that was not the main reason for her bodily aches. As Tanya had pointed out, Lisa was aging and no longer a spring chicken. What Tanya didn't know was that Lisa's agony stemmed from the disease that was slowly killing her. It was a recent diagnosis, and Lisa was still grappling with the reality of it. The idea of having to reveal her condition to her sweet friend, especially after the emotional blow she had just endured, made her stomach twist. Despite these thoughts weighing on her mind, Lisa pushed them aside and rummaged through the cabinets to find something to cook for dinner. Comfort food was the order of the day—a meal that would hopefully make her friend feel loved, even though she doubted whether she could love or be loved in return. Although she knew Tanya would not feel the cold due to what she was, Lisa still hoped that the warmth from the stove would offer some comfort—perhaps not the same kind of warmth as a human would feel, but warmth, nonetheless.

As Lisa prepared the meal, her mind wandered back thirty years earlier to the time when she first learned about the *Canis lupus*. She remembered how shocked she was when she discovered that a supernatural world existed around them.

As a nurse, Lisa often worked late nights, and the drive home to her house in the country was filled with long stretches of road with nothing around. It wasn't uncommon to see a dead deer on the side of the road or even a coyote. However, on that particular night, as her headlights pierced through the dark night, it wasn't either of those two things that she encountered. The form in the middle of the road was much larger than both deer and coyote and had a lot more fur. At first, Lisa thought it was simply a massive dog, but as she drove closer, she noticed its legs moving. She couldn't believe the animal was still alive. Even though her medical training was in human care, her heart cared for all living beings. She couldn't leave it to suffer while waiting to be hit by another car that might not be paying attention.

Lisa pulled her car over to the shoulder, ensuring that she kept it far enough back so that her headlights illuminated the animal, allowing her to determine the extent of its injuries. As she climbed out of the car, the sky overhead suddenly lit up with lightning, even though there had been no forecast for a thunderstorm that she had heard on the radio or news. Thunder boomed as she approached the injured creature, which was the only way she could describe it as she drew closer. It was huge. Once she was only a couple of feet away, Lisa froze. Thunder rolled overhead, and more lightning flashed, adding an even more surreal feeling to the already impossible sight. The creature had distinct parts that were not animal-like. Where giant paws should have been, there were hands—human hands. The chest was not covered in fur as it should have been; in fact, it wasn't an animal's chest at all. Fur surrounded flesh that appeared to be that of a human man. Lisa didn't know what to think. It wasn't Halloween. Could it possibly be someone dressed up in an incredibly well-done costume for some bizarre reason? Were the fur and head that were absolutely canine in appearance elaborate pieces to what appeared to be a Hollywood-quality getup?

Suddenly, the animal groaned, and its back legs moved. Lisa jumped and nearly screamed but quickly covered her mouth. What if this person was a weirdo with a sick fetish, using this ruse as a way to abduct people who were bleeding hearts for injured humans or animals? When the creature made noise again, it no longer resembled a growl. In fact, it didn't sound like an animal at all. Lisa's eyes ran back over its form, and she took a step back as she watched the head, which had been completely canine, begin to morph. Her breathing sped up, and her heart beat so painfully in her chest that she was sure she was going to have a heart attack on the spot. It would be her luck, and then this man-beast would probably eat her, leaving her bones for the carrion to pick the leftover rotting meat. "Good grief, Lisa," she said breathlessly. "Pull yourself together."

To be fair, Lisa had every right to be freaking out. Unless there was some other explanation for what she was seeing. Maybe one of her coworkers slipped her some sort of antipsychotic because they were feeling vindictive over having to do an extra bed bath. That's because Lisa had been pulled aside by a surgeon to be yelled at over something that wound up being his own fault. Yes, that definitely had to be it. There was no way she was watching a wolf turn into a man, a very naked man, right before her eyes. Or maybe she was simply having a mental breakdown from the stress of her job. Nurses had one of the highest burnout rates in the country. It wasn't easy to care for people who were sick, in pain, or dying. Family members could be verbally abusive, doctors were verbally abusive, and patients sometimes got physically abusive. All in all, it was a pretty challenging job, but she still loved it. That didn't mean it couldn't be taking a toll on her mental health.

"I'm going crazy." More lightning struck, the crack of it so loud that she jumped. "That's what it is. There's probably not even a storm happening. I'm just imagining it, too. Yep." Lisa nodded. "I'm actually driving down the road, and all of this is in my head. If I don't pull myself together, I'm probably going to have a wreck and not even realize it."

"You're not going crazy," a deep voice came from behind her. Lisa screamed and turned as the sky opened up and drenched her. It rained so hard that she could barely see the person who spoke. He was tall, seriously tall. He wore jeans and a black T-shirt, without a jacket. In late November, evenings in Missouri could get quite cold, but this man didn't seem bothered in the least. His body appeared relaxed, but she could see his hands clenched into fists at his side. She squinted to see more of his appearance, but the lights from her car behind him cast him mostly in silhouette.

"Wh-who are y-you? And wh-where in the world di-did you come from?" She looked around and didn't see another vehicle. They were miles away from even the nearest gas station. All around them was the forest.

"That's not important," the man said.

"Umm, I disagree." Lisa decided she preferred anger to fear. "I think it's pretty damn important. I am a woman alone in the middle of the night. I have come across a dog-man and another man who appeared virtually out of nowhere. Do you think this is some sort of friendly meetup in a grocery store? If who you are and where you come from aren't important, then what is?"

"I think you need to chill out so I can help my friend who is in a bad way," the man said gruffly.

He began stalking toward her. Lisa backed up so quickly that she didn't pay attention to where her legs were taking her. She felt her heels hit something, and her arms pinwheeled as she fell backward. The man grabbed one of her flailing arms and pulled her forward, managing to keep her from falling backward over the dog-man and onto her butt. He pushed her to the side, not gently, but not hard enough that she fell. Then he kneeled down and rolled the wolf over—nope, not a wolf.

"What in the hell is that?" She gasped and knew her eyes were so wide she probably looked like a cartoon character. The rain eased up, and she pushed her wet bangs from her face. "That wasn't there when I stopped. That was not there."

"He's a person, not a 'that,'" the large man barked at her. "He's injured, and I need to get him help."

As Lisa approached, she noticed a river of blood running from under the naked man's body. The part of her brain that needed to help people battled with the part of her brain that said there was no way what she'd just seen was possible. The man groaned again and then began to cough. He tried to get air in his lungs, but the more he tried to breathe, the harder he struggled.

"He's got a punctured lung." The nurse in her won out. "And we need to see where he's bleeding and get that under control." She walked around to the other side of the two men and kneeled down. Her eyes met the green, glowing ones of the large male across from her. "I'll help, but you have to promise not to hurt me." She was sure she was crazy; there was no other explanation.

"You have my word as the alpha of my pack that no

harm will come to you." Lisa shook her head and muttered, "I'm not touching that with a fifty-foot pole." She returned her attention to the naked man and saw that he had a bad chest wound. Quickly pulling off her jacket, she put it over the wound. "Push down on this hard. The wound needs pressure to help staunch the bleeding. Can you pick him up?" The man on the ground seemed just as big as his friend, and she didn't see how he'd be able to lift someone so solid. But the large man had muscles that Lisa knew she really shouldn't be noticing in the midst of such a crisis.

"I can carry him. My name is Tyler." He slipped his arms under his friend and lifted him as if he weighed no more than a child.

Lisa blinked and stood. She followed him to her car and muttered, "Still not touching it. Just going to pretend this is all completely normal. Nothing is weird about this. Just a hit-and-run victim that needs help. No naked wolf men or men who appear out of nowhere."

"Are you able to drive, or are you too busy losing your shit?" Tyler asked her.

She shot him a glare. "I can always leave you here in the middle of the road."

His lips turned up in a small smirk after laying the unconscious man in the back seat. "That's good."

Lisa frowned. "What's good?"

"That you've got claws." He walked around to the passenger side and somehow folded his large body into the small vehicle. "You're going to need them where we're going."

She climbed into the driver seat and shoved the keys into the ignition. "I'm going to need claws at the hospital?" She shrugged and started the engine. "You're not wrong, actually. A bunch of female nurses working together for thirteen to fifteen hours straight—claws definitely come out." She put the car in drive and started to turn the vehicle around to head back to the hospital where she worked.

Tyler put his hand on the steering wheel, stopping her motion effortlessly. "Not the hospital. We take him back to the pack. You have medical training?"

No, no, no, she chanted in her mind. *Say no.* "Yes." *Dammit, why did I say yes? Because I'm wearing scrubs, genius. With a damn hospital badge.*

"If you get him stable, he will heal on his own."

Her eyes widened. "He has a massive gash in his chest, and he's lost a lot of blood. There was a river of it on the road, in case you didn't notice."

"I promised you that no harm will come to you, and I keep my word. I will also compensate you well if you will do this." Tyler glanced over his shoulder to the man in the back. "He can't go to a hospital. If he phased in the middle of being sewn up, it probably wouldn't go over well."

"I have no idea what the hell phasing is unless it's something he's going through that he's going to grow out of," she muttered. "Fine. Where to?"

Lisa's mind returned to the present when she heard her phone ring. She walked over to where it hung on the wall and picked up the receiver. "Hello?"

"Lisa, it's Rose."

Lisa sighed. "Hi, Rose. It's good to hear from you."

"Is my daughter there?" The female alpha's voice was filled with worry. "She was supposed to call when she arrived, but I haven't heard from her."

"Yes, they got here safely. Tanya has gone for a run. She said she needed to stretch her legs after such a long journey in the van. Not to mention, she probably needed fresh air after being stuck in there with those three males."

Rose chuckled though it sounded forced. "Yes, I imagine she did." She cleared her throat, and Lisa knew what Tanya's mother was going to ask. "Is she alright? When I spoke to her before, she sounded like something was off. She usually talks to me. It's not like her to keep stuff from me."

"You know it's not my place to share what Tanya tells me, Rose," Lisa said gently. "She's a grown woman. It's her decision if and when she talks to you if there is something bothering her."

"I know." The alpha sounded completely helpless. Lisa hated that she couldn't share. She cared about Rose, even if she was mated to an asshat. "I just worry about her."

"As a good parent should. But you've got to let her grow up." Lisa felt a little strange giving parenting advice, considering she didn't have any children. Not to mention, Rose Ellis was a hell of a lot older than her, even if she didn't look a day over forty.

"Will you remind her to call me? Tell her I won't meddle. I just want to hear her voice."

"I can do that," Lisa assured her. They said their goodbyes, and Lisa put the phone back on its cradle. Her arm felt so tired just from holding the phone to her ear for that brief conversation. The rest of her felt just as exhausted. Her medical treatments took more and more of her strength every time she went in. Tyler had cussed a blue streak when she'd told him about the cancer. Over the years, they'd become as close as family. She looked at him as an older brother, though she looked much older than him than when she met him thirty years ago. She'd come to the pack mansion that dark night and helped a man named Eric—a man who wasn't just a man. She'd learned all about the *Canis lupus*, and Tyler had trusted her with that information. He'd let her leave without so much as a threat, knowing that she could have told someone. But she didn't. And Tyler called her again when another of their pack was injured. Eventually, Tyler insisted she just work for the pack. He made her an offer she couldn't refuse, and she'd been there ever since.

Lisa looked over at the food she'd laid out on the counter. She wanted to cook for Tanya, but she needed a little rest before she could do it. She'd just lay down for a half hour to regain her strength. As she walked slowly to her room, she thought about Tanya and the pain she'd seen in her eyes when she'd told Lisa about her true mate. She'd known the man all of ten minutes, and already she'd written him off. Lisa didn't fully understand the true mate bond, but she understood human relationships and human emotions. She understood that people could love more than once whether that was "romantic" or not. The case was that regardless of Tanya and Dillon's fate, they were going to have to choose to be together and not just rely on the mate bond. Their relationship had begun with pain, and it would take time to heal. Lisa just hoped Tanya wouldn't give up before she even gave it a chance.

CHAPTER
SEVEN

"When life gives you lemons, squeeze them in your enemies' eyes." ~Dillon

Dillon had stopped racing toward Colorado. After speaking with Colin about the recent killings of two of his former pack mates, he'd slowed down to think. His top priority was still Tanya, but he couldn't shake the feeling of dread that haunted him after hearing about the fate of his old friends.

As Dillon made the last leg of his journey, his anticipation grew. Heading north up the winding mountain road, he looked for familiar landmarks. It had been some years since Dillon had visited the Colorado pack, but he was pretty sure he still knew the way. The sun was beginning to set, casting shimmering hues of orange and pink across the sky. Rolling down the window, he took in a deep breath of crisp mountain air as he drove past towering pine trees lining either side of the highway. The air was thinner than in Texas, and despite the fact that it wasn't Montana, it felt closer to home than he'd felt in a decade, no matter the life he'd built in Coldspring.

Finally, after what seemed like an eternity of driving, Dillon spotted the Colorado pack mansion. It was a majestic structure built to look like a giant ski lodge, with tall, pine pillars along the entranceway. A grand stone fountain bearing a pair of howling wolves with jets of water shooting from their open mouths sparkled out front. Dillon could see multiple balconies protruding from the upper levels and windows that glimmered in the fading sunlight.

He pulled his car into one of the many parking spaces on site, and his heart began to race. Though he'd turned it over and over in his mind during the drive, he still didn't know what he was going to say to Tanya. There was nothing he could say to fix what he'd done. He'd broken her trust. He'd given to another what rightfully belonged to her. It didn't matter that he hadn't known Tanya at the time. Wolves were supposed to be patient hunters. And his wolf was. But the man was not. The man was weak. How he wished he would have listened to his wolf and waited. But even as he thought this, images of his life with Lilly flashed in his mind. Before, they would have brought him joy. Now, each one was like a piece of himself being ripped away. There were a few times during the drive that he'd tried to put himself in her shoes, but even the idea of her with another male enraged him and his wolf. *What a hypocrite.* *"And an ass,"* his wolf added.

Dillon took a few moments to compose himself before getting out of his truck and walking up to the mansion, head down and shoulders slumped. With heavy feet he trudged up the steps to the entrance. Just as he reached the top step, the massive door to the mansion opened with a loud creak, and two men stepped out. Dillon thought he might've recognized them from previous visits to the pack, but he couldn't be sure.

"A lone wolf on our doorstep?" one asked. "Are you lost?" They both studied him intently.

"Not at all," Dillon replied. His wolf felt uneasy as he attempted to search Tanya out through the bond. He figured once she got home and told her parents about him, her emotions would get the best of her, and he'd be able to sense her. But there was nothing. He'd decided to go with as much truth as he could. But before revealing his hand completely, Dillon wanted to feel out how Tanya's father would react. His reputation as being an egotistical ass was well known. "My name is Dillon Jacobs, I was hoping to speak with your alpha."

The second man narrowed his eyes. "If you're not a lone wolf, and you've not indicated an affiliation to a pack, that would make you a rogue."

Dillon straightened himself up and looked at the second wolf, holding his gaze. It took a few seconds, but the man eventually lowered his eyes. Dillon didn't feel the need to stare down the first wolf. He could tell that one was less dominant than his partner. Seeing his pack mate drop his gaze, the first wolf would understand a challenge was futile. "I am *not* a rogue, and if I was, I certainly wouldn't give your alpha the courtesy of knocking on his door. Perhaps I wasn't clear. I said, 'not at all', but I was referring to you asking if I was lost. I didn't deny being a lone wolf. Lone wolf and rogue wolf are two very different things. I will explain myself to your alpha, not you."

The two males growled but didn't argue.

"Shall we?" Dillon motioned to the door.

The two guards looked at each other briefly before gesturing for Dillon to follow them inside. They led him down a long ornate hallway lined with framed artwork from generations past.

Dillon's wolf growled within him. *"I smell her, but not strongly."*

The man's heart raced. He knew what the wolf meant. He expected to smell Tanya's scent the moment they walked into the door. Since the gas station, her scent—like a field of wildflowers just after a thunderstorm—was imprinted on his brain. And both the man and wolf longed to smell it again. Yet he was only detecting traces of her. He couldn't imagine that she'd have her own home. Not with a mansion this size. And especially not with her father being the alpha and she being unmated.

They passed through several plush sitting rooms before finally entering a grand hall filled with members of their pack. As soon as Dillon walked into the room, all eyes fell upon him, accompanied by low murmurs and hushed whispers. Though they may have been whispering about Dillon's presence, no one approached him or addressed him directly. Dillon quickly scanned the room. Tanya was nowhere to be found.

"Where is she?" Dillon heard the frustration in his wolf's voice. The man felt the same way, but he dared not let it show on his face. At least not until he fully understood the situation into which he was walking.

An older male wolf stepped forward from deep within the crowd. He cleared his throat loudly, and the room went silent. Though Dillon had difficulty placing most of the Colorado pack members, he had no trouble remembering the towering alpha. Jeremiah Ellis was not a man easily forgotten. The alpha had a wide chest and broad, blocky shoulders. Should the United States ever need to go to war and run out of armored vehicles, they'd need only to add tracks to Jeremiah's feet, and he would pass easily as a Sherman tank ... and probably do just as much damage. Jeremiah leveled a calculating gaze at Dillon through hazel eyes. His face, bearing a thick nose, broad cheeks, and thin lips, betrayed no emotion.

Dillon made it a point not to lock eyes with the man. He didn't know yet who was more dominant, and it didn't matter. Dillon wasn't here to challenge anyone. He just needed to find his mate as quickly as possible.

He swallowed hard. Dillon wanted to tell Jeremiah the truth, that he was here in search of his mate, Tanya, that he knew she was a member of this pack, and that he needed to know where the hell she was ... now. But he knew he couldn't come into another wolf's territory and start making demands, especially not under the conditions in which he and his female parted. Jeremiah would be extremely suspicious that Dillon showed up without Tanya at his side if they were true mates. He had to be careful. His last encounter with Tanya's pack mates hadn't exactly earned him any friends. And he had no idea what Tanya had told her alpha or her other pack mates.

The alpha took a step toward Dillon. Everyone in the room seemed to simultaneously suck in a breath. "Well, who do we have here?" His deep voice rumbled through the space. "You look familiar to me, though I cannot remember your name."

"I'm Dillon Jacobs." He raised his chin, careful not to meet the alpha's gaze. "A former member of the Montana pack."

Jeremiah folded his arms in front of his muscular chest. "Former? What made you leave your pack? And why have you chosen my territory to come into unannounced?"

Dillon glanced around. "No disrespect, but I feel this is a

conversation I'd like to have in private." He looked back at Jeremiah, his eyes dropping to the alpha's chin. "If you'd be so inclined."

Jeremiah narrowed his eyes. He seemed to be measuring Dillon's words and perhaps his intentions. Dillon wasn't lying. This *was* something he wanted to discuss in private. There would be no scent of deception about him. Finally, the alpha nodded. "Follow me." He turned and headed in the direction he'd come.

Dillon kept his eyes on Jeremiah's back as he walked.

At the end of a long hall, Jeremiah opened a door and stepped inside. He didn't bother to invite Dillon in; he just kept right on moving until he reached his desk. Dillon stepped into the office and shut the door behind him. He took a deep breath and gathered his thoughts, reminding his wolf that they'd have to tread carefully if they didn't want Jeremiah to give them the boot, or worse, decide that Dillon was a threat and attempt to kill him. He turned to face the alpha and placed his hands behind his back, his shoulders pulled back. Though Dillon didn't want to look overly dominant, he didn't want to appear weak either. He had to walk a fine line.

"Now," Jeremiah rumbled, "you're a lone wolf."

"Yes." It wasn't a question, but Dillon wanted to make sure it was abundantly clear that he wasn't a rogue. "I left my pack, but not because I was forced out. I was dealing with some things and needed to be on my own for a while."

Again, Jeremiah seemed to study him. Dillon refused to squirm under the alpha's scrutiny. He wasn't a pup to be intimidated, but he would remain respectful, at least until he had Tanya. Then all bets were off. "Why not go back to the Montana pack? Why come here? If you left on good terms, then they should accept you back and welcome you as a prodigal son." His tone had a slightly mocking tone to it. As if Dillon would be *crawling* back to his pack while licking his wounds.

"Pompous ass," Dillon's wolf muttered. The man didn't disagree. "Sometimes the past needs to stay exactly there—in the past." Dillon shrugged. "Returning to Montana doesn't feel like the right thing to do."

"So you're looking for a new pack?" Jeremiah folded his arms across his broad chest.

Dillon nodded. "Yes. I'm asking for a trial period." He cleared his throat. "I know there's always a possibility that I might not be a good fit. I'd ask that you, please, give me a chance." Dillon's wolf was balking at the permission he was asking for, which made Dillon begin to think his beast must know that they were dominant to Jeremiah. Dillon focused closely on his power and made sure it was tamped down tight. He did not need the alpha to see him as a threat. "*We could just kill him and take over the pack,*" his wolf said coolly. Dillon mentally rolled his eyes. "*You need to check yourself, wolf. Our mate probably wouldn't appreciate us killing her father.*" Okay, so maybe letting his wolf lead wasn't going to be the best idea, even if Dillon had gone against his beast's wishes in regard to Lilly.

After several tense moments of silence, Jeremiah finally lifted one shoulder as he tilted his head to the side. "Okay. I'll let you stay as a probationary member. However"—he took a step toward Dillon, and he felt the alpha's power fill the room—"this is *my* pack which means my rules. If you cannot obey me as your alpha without question, then you're out." The alpha's wolf showed itself in his glowing hazel eyes, and Dillon knew when he said, "You're out," he didn't mean a swift kick to the backside on his way out the door. This was an all-or-nothing deal. The power in the room bore down on Dillon's shoulders, and he knew he needed to kneel, but his wolf was fighting him. "Any dominance fights," Jeremiah continued, "and you're out. This isn't a democracy. I keep my wolves under control, and that keeps infighting from causing chaos." There was a final burst of power, and Dillon forced his wolf to submit even though, in reality, Jeremiah's wolf was *not* more dominant than him. He fell to his knees and tilted his head, bearing his neck in submission.

"If I could rip out your throat right now, I would." Dillon's wolf snarled at him. Dillon didn't respond to the beast. He knew this had to happen.

"You understand that in order for a pack to thrive, the hierarchy must be known and abided by. Male wolves, unmated especially, are volatile when they don't know their place. Order must be kept. Am I clear?" Jeremiah began to rein in his power, most likely due to Dillon's submissive pose.

"Yes, Alpha." Dillon wouldn't argue with him on any of those matters, though he might disagree on *how* Jeremiah enforced his orders. He'd have to see for himself just how bad the alpha's assholery was.

Jeremiah stepped back. "Stand."

Dillon pushed to his feet and fought the urge to shake off the magic that had washed over him. He straightened his spine and let his eyes land on Jeremiah's eyes momentarily before moving away, then back to the alpha's. *"Brief eye contact,"* he told his wolf. *"Nothing more."*

"Would any of this have to do with those markings on your neck?" Jeremiah's eyes dropped to the flesh in question and then met Dillon's briefly before Dillon dropped his own.

Dillon had noticed that his markings had changed. But

he'd expected Tanya to have been here when he arrived. Her absence had thrown his plans all to hell. "In part, yes." This is where he would have to be very careful. He couldn't lie—Jeremiah would smell it and possibly attempt to gut him. But he could give him a little kernel to appease him, and also ask for some understanding on the alpha's part.

"Those are mate markings," Jeremiah continued. "Did you leave the Montana pack because of your mate?"

Dillon shook his head. "No." He brought his arms to his sides and then slipped his hands in his pockets. "I've met my mate one time. That was enough for the markings to change." Dillon didn't want to say more about it. He'd be treading on thin ice to keep from telling a lie.

"She's not with you, nor do I smell a female on you."

"True mates are a very private matter." Dillon kept his tone respectful. "As you're mated, I'm sure you can appreciate that. While this is a trial period for me in your pack, it is also a trial period for your pack. Building trust takes time. I'm asking that you allow me to build that trust before I discuss something as sacred as my mate." Dillon felt sweat rolling down the middle of his back as he waited for Jeremiah's response to his request, which, though bold, wasn't entirely out of line.

"I suppose that is fair enough of you to ask. But before you can become a Colorado pack member, you will have to divulge that information, at least to me."

Dillon nodded but kept his jaw clenched tightly closed to keep from telling the male to go pound sand. He'd forgotten what it was like to take orders. Living as a lone wolf had made his beast an alpha unto himself. This hierarchy was definitely going to take some getting used to.

"When we bond with our mate, he should be removed. He is no leader," his wolf declared. *"He is a despot. I can smell the*

fear of his wolves. They should respect him and follow him for that reason. Not because he's a tyrannical ass." Dillon's wolf was feeling very articulate. And Dillon found he agreed with him completely but knew they *had* to play the game until they knew more and until Tanya returned and could shed her own opinion on the matter. As it was, she might show up and ask her father to kill him.

Jeremiah picked up the phone on his desk and dialed a number. "You are welcome to stay for a few weeks. That should give us both plenty of time to see if this is the pack for you." He then put the phone to his ear and began to speak to someone on the other end. "I need you to come and take Dillon Jacobs to one of the guest rooms." He hung up the phone and only a minute later a wolf walked in. Jeremiah glanced at the new male. "Robert, this is Dillon. I will fill the pack in tomorrow regarding his situation." Jeremiah turned back to Dillon. "I'm afraid dinner has already been served this evening. I'll have someone bring you something up shortly. Anything in particular you would like to eat or drink?" Jeremiah wore a pained expression, and it looked to Dillon as if the alpha was forcibly swallowing a glass of poison. Apparently, hospitality was painful for the man.

Dillon inclined his head. "Thank you, Alpha. I'm not picky. Anything will do."

"That's obvious. Otherwise, you wouldn't have settled for a woman who was not our mate," Dillon's wolf spoke up again. *"I could do without the constant commentary,"* Dillon growled back.

Dillon followed Robert down the hallway, up a flight of stairs, and then down another hallway. As they walked, Dillon found himself appreciating the beauty of the mansion. There were many wood carvings in fine detail on the posts and banisters of the stairs and columns. The colors were warm and inviting, rich browns and lush greens made it feel forest-like which appealed to his wolf. "This is a beautiful home," Dillon said to Robert.

"Mm-hmm," the other man offered, but said nothing more.

"Have you been a member of the Colorado pack your whole life?"

"Mm-hmm."

Okay, not the most talkative man in the world. After another hike down yet another hallway, Robert stopped at a door that, like the others, had ornate carvings of wolves howling and playing in the woods. He pointed. "This is you."

"Three words," Dillon told his wolf. *"That's progress."*

His wolf growled at him. *"You're pathetic."*

"Thanks," he told Robert, who simply waved a hand over his shoulder as he walked away. The man seemed bored, but Dillon hadn't missed the tension in his shoulders.

Once behind the closed door, Dillon began to pace. Tanya wasn't here. He would bet his life on it. "Where are you?" he asked the empty room. A large bed stood in the middle of the room, and there was one window on the right side of the room framed by a set of thick curtains. The walls were brown, and the floor was covered with rustic wood and a deep green rug in front of the bed. Sparse but clean. Dillon couldn't detect any smell other than a tad muskiness which meant that no one had stayed in this room in quite a while.

His feet ate up the space as he walked to one end of the room, turned, and walked back the way he'd come. There was no way he'd get any sleep, especially since he had no clue where his mate had gone. She'd had plenty of time to get home, which meant she hadn't come home. He growled, his teeth elongating as his wolf's frustration grew. "Pull yourself together," he said to his beast out loud. "Snarling about it isn't going to make her suddenly appear."

"What if something has happened to her?" his beast challenged. *"What if rogue wolves attacked or they were in a car wreck?"*

"We would have felt the emotions something like that would have emitted," he reminded his wolf. *"She wouldn't have been able to keep the bond shut so tight in either of those traumatizing situations."*

His wolf didn't like the fact that Dillon had a point. He was angry that they'd hunted her and failed. The man was proving to be quite a shitty mate. Then again, she'd told him not to come after her, and he'd made it clear that he would. So, it was most likely that she'd not come home by choice in an effort to avoid him.

"Think, Dillon." He ran his fingers through his wavy hair and gripped it before releasing it and dropping his arm to his side. A knock sounded at the door, and his feet froze. Dillon should have heard the person approaching, but he'd been so caught up in his thoughts of Tanya that he'd let his guard down. Stupid in a place where the alpha wasn't exactly trusting or trustworthy.

Dillon walked to the door and pulled it open, revealing a young woman standing on the other side. She clutched a tray of food in her hands, and her smile seemed nervous as she held it out to him. Dillon saw her hands shaking. He quickly grabbed the tray, afraid she might drop it, and wondered why she was scared. Despite her tense smile, he could smell and see her fear.

"I figured a hamburger was a safe bet since you didn't tell Alpha Jeremiah anything specific."

Dillon tilted his head. "Thank you..." He let the words hang in the air, waiting to see if she would give her name.

"Oh, I'm Penelope. Nell for short." She pointed at herself as if he wouldn't know who she was talking about.

Dillon took a breath through his nose and frowned. "You're a dormant."

She dropped her eyes and seemed to shrink in upon herself. The woman's voice shook when she replied. "Yes." Dillon detected the scent of shame filling the air.

"Why on earth would that embarrass you?" Dillon was puzzled, and he hated to see the woman feeling ashamed of who she was.

She lifted one shoulder and bit her bottom lip, her eyes still cast down and to the left. "I'm nobody. You shouldn't even concern yourself with me."

Dillon stepped to the side and put the tray on the small table near the door. He didn't invite her in as that would be inappropriate, but he wasn't done speaking with her. "Who the hell told you that you're nobody?" Her eyes widened at his tone. "Being a dormant doesn't make you any less valuable to a pack than a full-blooded wolf. Surely you know that."

Nell still didn't lift her head. "It's fine. I have my place here, and it's better than being vampire fodder or living without the protection of a pack."

Dillon placed his hands on his hips and considered her words. She shifted on her feet and turned slightly away from him. It was then that Dillon saw the bruises on her neck, which looked suspiciously like finger marks from where she'd been held too tightly. "Do you have a mate?"

She paled. "No." Nell shook her head. "Of course not.

Dormants don't have true mates. I don't even pretend to think of something so wonderful happening to me."

Dillon had to fight down a growl as he took in this female with such a beaten-down countenance. She'd been cut to the quick by a sharp tongue and firm hand. Neither of which was needed for one so submissive. "Listen, Nell, and listen good."

She nodded and clasped her hands in front of her.

"Nobody has the right to put their hands on you in a hurtful way or any way that you don't want, for that matter." He sighed, his heart feeling sorry for her knowing this had most likely either happened at the hands of Jeremiah or, at the very least, someone he'd ordered to do it. They'd beaten her down until the woman had become a she-wolf who didn't know her value. It seriously pissed Dillon off.

"Can I get you anything else?" She suddenly changed the subject. It was obvious Nell wasn't comfortable with the conversation, but Dillon wanted to press her for more information. He wanted to know for sure who had allowed this to happen.

"You can." Dillon nodded and watched as her shoulders relaxed. He lowered his voice as he said, "You can tell me who put their hands on you, and you can tell me where Tanya is."

Nell looked left and then right. Dillon stuck his head out and followed her gaze. It took him a minute, but using his wolf's eyesight, he saw the small black dot on the ceiling about five feet down the hall. *Fantastic. Cameras.* He saw more of them farther on. Dillon pulled himself back into his room and looked around the ceiling. He saw no cameras, but that didn't mean they weren't there.

Looking back at Nell, he mouthed, "My room?"

She shrugged, showing she didn't know. "You don't need to worry about me." He saw her eyes flicker once again to the camera, and then she said, a little louder than necessary. "The alpha took care of it."

Dillon bit back all the words that wanted to spew forth about Jeremiah Ellis. No alpha would allow any member of their pack, dormant or otherwise, to be treated in such a way, especially a female. His mind briefly jumped to the thought of Jeremiah putting his hands on Tanya violently, and he felt claws push out of his hands as his wolf shoved forward. The man and the beast were on the same page. If Dillon found out that Jeremiah had laid a single finger on his mate, he would kill him.

"If you need anything else, you can just pick up the phone and dial 4695." Without another word, Nell turned and rushed away.

Dillon sighed and closed the door. He looked at the hamburger and found that after his interaction with Nell, he no longer had an appetite. He picked up his bag and headed into the open door, where he could see the bathroom beyond. Dillon needed a shower and sleep. He also needed to figure out how the hell he could find his mate without anyone becoming suspicious. That is, of course, if no one saw and heard the conversation he'd just had with Nell. Guess he'd know soon enough if Jeremiah came knocking on his door. Part of him wished he would. His wolf could use a good fight. But he wasn't sure how Tanya would feel about Dillon killing her father. It might not go over too well, especially since she hated Dillon.

He dropped the bag on the white countertop and looked in the mirror. "Then again, *since* she *already* hates you, what's one more little thing, like taking daddy dearest out?" He ran a hand down his face. Bloody hell, now he was talking to himself in the damn mirror. He'd officially lost his mind. Thinking about taking out an alpha when he'd been a lone wolf for a decade? *"You need rest,"* his wolf reminded him. *"We are useless to protect her if we are not strong."* Dillon agreed, but then again, how the hell did he protect his mate when he had no clue where she was?

JEREMIAH HUNG UP THE PHONE AND TURNED TO FACE THE WINDOW of his office. He scratched his chin as he thought back on the conversation he'd just had with the Montana alpha. Dillon, the *lone* wolf staying in one of his guest rooms on the second floor, had indeed left his pack, but it had been over a decade ago. The male hadn't bothered to offer up just how long he'd been a lone wolf. And the Montana alpha admitted that at this point, they didn't think he'd ever come back.

"So why do you suddenly want to be a part of a pack again, Dillon?" Jeremiah said out loud as he stared out over the grounds of the compound. "And why *my* pack?"

There was a knock on his door. "Come in." He turned to see his mate step in. She was every bit as beautiful as the day he met her. "You're a vision, Rose."

She walked over to him, and he pressed his lips to her forehead. Then he ran his hands down her arms until their hands clasped. She didn't smile as she usually did when he complimented her. Her face was pensive, and her eyes seemed lost. "What's wrong?" When she didn't answer right away, Jeremiah gave her a little shake. "Rose?"

She seemed to come out of her stupor and looked up at

him. Her pink lips turned up into a small smile though her eyes remained dim. "I'm just worried about Tanya. And Lisa, as well."

His brow drew low. "Why? I thought when you talked to Tanya and told her she could go to Missouri, she sounded fine. And why would you be worried about Lisa?" Jeremiah knew how fond both his daughter and mate were about the human that Tyler had taken into his pack decades earlier.

"I called and spoke with Lisa." Rose stepped out of his grasp and wrapped her arms around herself. "She sounded frail."

"She's aging, love," Jeremiah reminded her. "We will be here long after she is gone."

Rose covered her mouth, and her eyes watered. Maybe he hadn't needed to be so blunt.

"Why are you worried about Tanya?" he quickly asked, hoping to get her mind off of Lisa.

She shrugged and waved him off. "It's nothing really. Just a mom missing her daughter and hoping she is well. You know how I get."

Jeremiah searched their bond for anything she wasn't telling him, but all he found was exactly what she said. Rose did tend to worry about their daughter, and he tried to keep that to a minimum by keeping a tight leash on her. He and Tanya had had a knockdown drag-out fight over her going with the three males to hunt in Louisiana. It was Rose who'd actually talked him off the ledge. If it were up to him, Tanya wouldn't leave the pack territory. She was an adult, technically, but she was his only child and a female at that. *Canis lupus* females were protected because their birth rates were so low. But he also wanted Tanya to be able to stand on her own two feet if there came a day when she needed to fight. Peace wasn't guaranteed, unfortunately. So he was having to learn to let go. A little. He wasn't about to get crazy about it. She'd always have his beta and third and fourth dominant males with her when she wasn't in pack territory.

"You have something on your mind, love." Rose drew him from his thoughts. "Or someone, I should say. Who is this Dillon I'm seeing in your thoughts?"

Jeremiah slipped his hands in his pockets. "He's a wolf that showed up at our door. He's asked to go through a trial period to see if our pack is a good fit for him. He was a member of the Montana pack at one time but said he didn't feel like that's where he belonged anymore."

"Hmm." She nodded. "And judging by your tone of voice, I'd guess you don't trust him?"

Jeremiah's jaw clenched. He trusted few people, and his mate knew it.

"What are you going to do?" She cocked her head to the side.

"My first instinct was to send him back to Montana. Let them deal with him." Jeremiah's ire at the wolf had simmered while he'd discussed his daughter and Lisa with Rose, but now it began to grow again. "But I agreed to let him stay. I called Mathew, in Montana, and he made it clear that Dillon has been gone from their pack for a lot longer than Dillon let on. The alpha wouldn't divulge why he left, said that was Dillon's story to tell." He sighed. "A wolf who hasn't been a member of a pack for *that* long might not have the ability to follow orders because they've been out of the pack hierarchy. Not to mention, the darkness in lone wolves grows faster than those within a pack. He might be on the verge of going feral."

Jeremiah had considered those things before granting

him the probationary period. But the truth was, he was intrigued by the man, especially after asking about the mating marks. The chance that Dillon would go feral was lower since he had the markings, but not much. Being separated from his female, no matter the reason, would drive him crazy and might just push him over the edge. If he was a wolf on the verge of going feral, or creeping that direction since he wasn't with his mate, it was better to have him close where he could be put down quickly then to turn him loose and be responsible for the deaths of innocents. Jeremiah would never let himself look like an alpha that didn't have control of his wolves. And a wolf leaving his pack and killing people would give that appearance.

She held up a finger. "If that's the case then he's a wolf in need of help, that doesn't make him a bad male."

He chuckled. "You always want to see the best in people, Rosey."

"And you always want to assume that everyone's intentions are bad."

"And I'm usually right. I have good instincts, and I follow them." He walked back over to the window and looked out at their territory. "We have a good thing here, Rose. I've been pack alpha for over a decade. This pack was a mess under the leadership of the previous alpha. He was weak. Look what we've built."

"And you think this one wolf will compromise all of that?"

There was a voice in the back of his head that was screaming "Yes!" It wasn't just Dillon's lie by omission that troubled the alpha, but the potential disruption he represented. "My wolves fear me and obey me without question. There is no infighting in my pack because none can hold a candle to my dominance, and each knows their place."

Apart from the random vampire encounter every so often, Jeremiah hadn't had to deal with many problems in his position of alpha. "We've had peace, especially in the middle of North America. I aim to keep it that way."

"So you let him stay. Why?" Rose stepped up beside him and rested a hand on his back. Her warmth seeped through his shirt and into his skin.

"Because if he is on the verge of going feral, I can put him down quickly. Although I will have to be sure to make him understand that I don't like liars, even those by omission. He should have been honest about how long he'd been a lone wolf."

"Surely it won't be necessary to put him down. He must have seemed stable enough for you to let him stay." Her voice was soft. His Rose didn't like violence. A first impression of his mate would lead some to believe she was a submissive wolf. And though she preferred to deal with things in a more diplomatic manner, his mate could tear out the throat of someone threatening those she loved and not lose sleep over it.

"True. Only time will tell. And I've given myself time by allowing him to stay."

"Maybe give him the opportunity to share more about his past as that time passes instead of jumping on him about not being completely transparent," she suggested. "You catch more wolves with fresh meat than rotten roadkill."

"Perhaps." He admitted to himself the idea had merit.

Her arms wrapped around him from behind. He ran his hand over hers. "Think about it," she encouraged. "If you want to keep peace, then start with a peaceful approach." With a final squeeze, she released him. "I'm going to bed." Exhaustion filled her voice. "Don't be too long, okay?"

"I won't, love," he said absently as his mind worked over what she'd said and what he'd already been thinking. As he heard his office door click shut, his wolf rumbled in his mind, *"We need more information."* Jeremiah agreed with his beast. Knowledge was power, and the more he had on Dillon, the more power he had over him.

Jeremiah picked up the phone and made a quick call. Five minutes later, two wolves filed in. He would have preferred to have his beta, Daniel, and two of his other stronger members, Trevor and Austin, handle these jobs, but they were otherwise engaged thanks to his flighty daughter and her continual detours. They wouldn't be back for a few days.

"Huck, Orson." He nodded. "You two are going to visit the Montana pack. Be discreet. I want you to find out everything you can about Dillon Jacobs. Report back to me as soon as you learn anything."

The two wolves nodded and left.

Jeremiah sighed as he watched them go. Maybe he was making a mistake by letting the male stay. He ran a hand through his hair and thought about the interaction he'd had with Dillon. He'd not smelled any deceit on the wolf, nor had he felt any large amount of dominance. He wasn't a submissive wolf, but he wasn't more dominant than Jeremiah. So was there really any worry for the wolf to possibly become a member of the pack? He'd know more once Huck and Orson gained further information, and until then, he'd just keep a close eye on Dillon. If the new pack member stepped out of line, then Jeremiah would follow through with his threat.

CHAPTER
EIGHT

"No matter how fast or how far you run, your troubles are faster and have far more endurance than you."
~Tanya

Tanya sat in her wolf form next to a stream that ran through the large forest surrounding the Missouri pack territory. It was no easy feat to tire out a *Canis lupus*, but she had run for four hours straight. Whenever she began to slow, *his* face would fill her mind, and she would feel anew the pain that had crashed through their bond before he had slammed it shut. The pain would spur her legs to pick up speed again. Tanya did not want to see him again, and yet she wanted to throw herself into his arms. She longed to know what it felt like to be held by him, what he smelled like, whether he laughed easily or kept his emotions close to his chest. What were his dreams, goals, and desires? Her heart desired so much, but she didn't know if she would ever have it. She didn't know how to get over his past.

Lisa's words filled her mind. "Our hearts are very big things with lots of room for love, Tanya. Love for people, love for animals, love for creation, love for life and even death."

Could her mate love her even if he had loved another before? Did Tanya still want his love, even though he had feelings for someone else? She growled as her claws extended and retracted. She wasn't getting anywhere. Tanya's mind was racing in circles. The only way to find out if she could try to have a relationship with him was to go to him. *I'd rather eat dead fish.*

Her wolf huffed. *I only eat live fish, freshly caught.*

Tanya stood and shook out her fur. She turned and prepared herself for the long run back to Lisa's house. Her heart warmed at the idea of spending more time with her friend. Lisa would help talk Tanya down from the "run away to another country" ledge upon which she found herself. Lisa was levelheaded. She was ruled by her mind, not her emotions. And since Tanya was only running on emotions at the moment, that's exactly what she needed.

The trees passed in a blur as her paws ate up the ground. By the time she reached the bag where she'd left her clothes, it was full-on dark. She phased and quickly slipped back into her clothes. When she reached Lisa's house, she didn't detect any scents of food. But then she'd been gone for hours, so perhaps Lisa had put whatever she'd cooked in the fridge, or just gave up altogether. Tanya wouldn't have blamed her. Lisa looked like she was exhausted and needed some rest. She'd rather her friend take care of herself first. Tanya was perfectly capable of cooking her own food.

Tanya headed for the door and turned the knob, knowing it wouldn't be locked because such precautions were unnecessary. Lisa lived on pack territory, and nobody would come into her home without permission. Tanya knew how protective Tyler was of Lisa. Anyone who messed with her would be on the receiving end of his very sharp teeth.

As she stepped into the small house, Tanya noticed it was chilly. She frowned, wondering why Lisa hadn't turned the heat up. The pack paid for her bills, and the electricity was completely covered. There was no reason for her to keep it down, as if she needed to save money.

"Lisa?" Her friend wasn't in the kitchen or the living room. Tanya headed down the hall and noticed that the bathroom door was open, and the light was off. She continued on until she reached her friend's bedroom. The door was ajar, and there was a small light coming through the crack. Tanya knocked gently.

"Lisa? Can I come in?" She waited, then used her wolf's hearing to see if she could pick up the woman's breathing. If it was slow and deep, then Tanya would know that Lisa was asleep, and she wouldn't disturb her. Tanya frowned when she heard nothing. She stepped closer to the door and pressed her ear close enough that she was nearly touching it. Tanya closed her eyes and focused her wolf hearing even more. Tanya realized her heart was beating so hard that it would likely drown out any other sound she might have heard. "Focus," she snarled at her wolf. Tanya lifted her hands and let them rest on the door before pushing it slightly open. "Lisa?" she whispered.

Finally, Tanya heard something—a small wheezing sound. Now she didn't wait to see if her friend would answer her. Tanya shoved open the door and hurried to the bedside. Lisa lay on her back, her hands resting over the top of the blanket that was pulled up just below her chest. Tanya kneeled down beside her and pressed her hand to Lisa's forehead. Her skin was cold and clammy. Tanya's eyes dropped to her friend's chest, and she saw that it still rose, barely.

"Lisa." She gently shook the woman. "Wake up. Please." Tears filled her eyes to see her longtime friend so frail and weak. She'd known something was wrong, but the stubborn woman wouldn't tell her. Now that Tanya paid attention, she could smell the sickness on her. "Lisa," she growled. "Dammit, open your eyes, you strong-headed goat." After a couple of seconds, Lisa's eyes blinked open. She turned her head slowly, and it seemed to take every ounce of strength she had.

"Why are you crying?" Lisa's voice was barely a whisper.

Tanya's eyes went wide. "Why am I crying?"

"That's what I asked you, child. Has your hearing gone?"

Tanya's lips turned slightly. "What's wrong, Lisa? What can I do for you?" She took her friend's frail hand in hers, careful not to squeeze too tightly because Tanya knew she'd be able to snap the brittle bones easily.

"I'm sick, little wolf," she said affectionately. "And there's nothing you can do."

"Can I call a human doctor? Doesn't Tyler know? Surely he will get you help. You can't—"

"There's nothing anyone can do. Tyler knows. He's not too happy."

"Why?" Tanya frowned. "It's not like it's your fault that you're sick."

Lisa patted Tanya's hand. "He's upset because I waited

to tell him. I thought the doctors could get rid of the cancer. But they couldn't. That's when I told him." She sighed. "He marched himself straight up to the hospital and demanded they fix me. But that was an order no one could follow."

Tanya chuckled, even as tears ran down her cheeks. "Sounds like something an alpha would do."

Lisa's smile was slow, as if even that small action pained her. "He cares deeply for those he considers his."

"All alphas do." Tanya pushed up until her elbows rested on the bed, Lisa's hand still in her own.

Lisa took a breath, and Tanya heard wheezing in her lungs. Lisa's face was pale, and her lips showed a bluish hue.

Tanya sucked in a sharp breath when she felt her friend's heart skip a couple of beats. "Lisa, please tell me what to do." Tanya's insides churned and terror overwhelmed her, making her afraid she was unraveling at the seams... This wasn't the way things were supposed to be. Lisa and Tanya should've been cooking and laughing in the kitchen while Lisa scolded Tanya for stealing food off the countertop. Not this. Not Lisa lying in bed barely alive. Because that's what she was, clinging to life.

"Listen to me, little wolf," Lisa said, her voice dry and rough. "We didn't get to talk more about this, but you need to hear it before I go."

"No," Tanya snapped. "You're not going anywhere. You can't." She could barely see Lisa through the tears filling her eyes. "I need you here. With me. Tyler needs you. This whole damn pack needs you."

Lisa scoffed. "I put bandages on wolves that heal in two minutes. They only do it to humor me." She chuckled and then coughed. Tanya slipped an arm behind her small shoulders and lifted Lisa to help her catch her breath. After a couple of minutes, Lisa nodded, and Tanya lowered her back down.

"Could you get me some water?" Lisa said as her head hit the pillow.

"Of course." Tanya jumped up and hurried to the kitchen. She pulled down a glass and filled it with water. As she headed back, she saw the phone hanging on the wall. She picked it up and dialed Tyler's number.

"What do you need, old woman?" The Missouri alpha's voice was filled with humor and fondness. He also must have caller ID since he knew who was calling.

"Tyler, it's Tanya."

The strain in her voice must have been quite clear because the playfulness immediately evaporated. "What's wrong?" The voice on the other end of the phone was no longer just Lisa's friend, but her alpha.

"Lisa is sick. She's lying in bed, and she can barely breathe. It's bad. You need to get over here, please. Help her." Tanya felt like a child asking for her father to fix her favorite toy that had broken. But Lisa wasn't a toy. She was a dear, precious friend.

"On my way." *Click.*

Tanya hurried back to the bedroom. She had to help raise Lisa upright again so her friend could take a sip from the glass. After what Tanya felt was entirely too small a sip, Lisa nodded. Tanya set the glass aside and once again laid Lisa back down.

Lisa cleared her throat, but when she spoke it still sounded so thready. "I know you're hurting over your true mate."

"We don't need to tal—"

"Yes, we do." Lisa's voice was a little stronger. "And you're going to listen."

"Yes, ma'am," Tanya said automatically to the authoritative tone of the wise woman.

"Part of love is pain. One cannot exist without the other. Love means taking a risk that the other person might not love you back. It's giving all of yourself, even though the other person might not do the same. Love is maturity because it is a tough, tough choice." Lisa coughed again, but held up a hand when Tanya went to lift her. "If you want a future with this man, then you have got to find it in you to forgive him. You're going to have to pray to the Great Luna to heal your heart and allow yourself to see past his mistakes and to the man he is. Don't let go of something that is rightfully yours because of pride. It's never worth it."

"But," Tanya began, but then snapped her mouth closed. She realized how foolish it would be to argue with her friend, who was dying before her very eyes.

"Promise me, Tanya." Lisa narrowed her eyes and patted Tanya's cheek. "Promise me you will at least hear him out. Let me leave this world knowing that you haven't given up on a chance to be happy with your true mate."

"You're not playing fair." Tanya sniffled.

"Never have." Lisa smiled. "Now, promise me. Neither of you is perfect. Neither of you is going to be perfect. You're going to get mad at each other, and you're going to want to kick him in the shins more often than not, but it's worth it. Even if he loved another woman, it shows you he's capable of love and loyalty. He was both of those things, even with a woman who wasn't his mate. Just because he cared for her doesn't mean you can't have a place in his heart. I'm sure it will be a much bigger one than she holds."

Tanya wanted to scream that this was not the time for them to be talking about this. She wanted to growl at the old woman and tell her to focus on breathing instead of wasting her breath on Tanya's relationship issues.

"Promise me," Lisa repeated.

"Ugh, fine, you old bat." Tanya huffed. "I'll hear him out."

Lisa's cracked lips spread into a much bigger smile. "Thank you. That makes me happy." She settled back and relaxed, as if she'd accomplished what she needed to.

"Where is she?" Tyler's voice came from the hall, along with the sound of many footsteps. Along with the alpha, Tanya picked up on the scents of Austin and Daniel.

The door pushed open, and Tyler hustled inside. His eyes immediately landed on Lisa and softened. "Damn you, woman." He shook his head and went around to the opposite side of the bed and sat beside her. Tyler's much larger hand enveloped the one Tanya wasn't holding. "Why didn't you tell me it was getting worse?"

"Didn't want to worry you, obviously. Don't ask silly questions, Alpha." Her voice was weaker, and her chest rose and fell much more slowly. Somehow, her skin seemed even paler.

Tyler lifted his other hand and cupped Lisa's wrinkled cheek. The look on his face was filled with love. He looked at her the way Tanya's dad had looked at her many times over the years. She realized that Tyler saw Lisa as more than a pack mate. He saw her as a daughter. Lisa was his, and his heart was breaking. Tanya could see it in his eyes and the broken look on his face. He seemed helpless, and Tanya knew that was a feeling that no alpha liked to feel. Tyler started to speak, but his voice broke. He paused and closed his eyes, seeming to compose himself. Tanya bit back a sob as she watched a tear roll down the large alpha's face.

"It's not time yet, Healer," he whispered.

Tanya knew Lisa wasn't their kind of healer—a gypsy healer—but Tyler often called Lisa a healer as a sign of respect. The woman's skills as a nurse had helped many of their injured wolves over the years.

"You are a strong alpha, but it's not your will that holds me to this earth or takes me from it." Lisa gave him a loving smile. "My maker calls us home in His time, just as your maker calls you to Her when it is *your* time."

"I don't much like your maker right now." Tyler growled.

"We've talked about this, Ty," Lisa said affectionately. "I cannot live the life of a *Canis lupus*. It is not my path. I was created to do exactly what God wanted me to do, and I believe I have accomplished that."

"But we still need you," he argued. "*I* still need you."

Tanya covered her mouth as she tried to keep herself from completely breaking down. This was not how this trip was supposed to go. She wasn't supposed to meet her mate and run from him. She wasn't supposed to visit her friend, only to lose her. What the hell was happening? How had everything spiraled out of control?

"I'll always be with you." She leaned her face into his palm. "I have loved you as a sister loves a brother, and then as a mother loves her own. For I have been both to you. Even if you are technically older than me." She huffed out a small chuckle but seemed too weak to give more than that. "Tell this one that she has to keep her promise, or you'll turn her over your knee and bust her bottom like a spoiled child."

Tyler's brow rose, and he cut his eyes to Tanya.

"I met my mate. He's an ass. It's a whole thing." She waved a dismissive hand. "Not important."

"It's very important," Lisa barked at her and then coughed.

"Save your strength, you mule," Tanya bit back.

Tyler met Tanya's eyes. "I promise, Lisa. I will make sure she gives the stupid male a chance. We men all tend to be a little dense when it comes to females. Surely, she can find some grace in her heart."

"I'm sitting right here." Tanya rolled her eyes and then looked back at Lisa. The woman's eyes were closed, and Tanya panicked. "Lisa." She shook her, probably a little more roughly than was necessary.

Lisa's eyes opened. "Calm down. Just resting my eyes. I'm tired."

Tyler pushed her gray hair back from her face. "You rest if you need to. We're not going anywhere."

Tanya heard shuffling behind her. She turned and saw pack members filing into the room. One by one, they kneeled, giving this woman, who had dedicated so much of her time to them, the respect they would show a pack member. Then they bowed their heads and placed hands over their hearts—the respect they would only give their alpha. Tanya had to choke back a sob. This human woman meant so much to all of these wolves. They were hurting just as much as Tanya was.

Tanya held Lisa's hand as she watched the old woman's chest rise and fall. She found herself trying not to blink. Tanya felt that if she took her eyes off of Lisa for even a split second, her friend would slip away. She swallowed hard and let her eyes roam over the contours of her friend's face. How was it that only hours ago they were sitting in Lisa's kitchen laughing and joking? Now Tanya knew this was it. Soon, she would never hear the woman's voice again. The voice that had given her advice and guidance so many times over her life would be no more. She took deep breaths as tears slid down her face, and she prayed to the Great Luna for a miracle.

The phone on Jeremiah's desk rang. He snatched it up and held it to his ear.

"What?" he growled.

"Alpha." Huck's voice came through the phone in a deep rumble. The two males he'd sent to Montana had driven the twelve hours at a ridiculous speed and had called Jeremiah once they'd arrived in the wee hours of the morning. It was only a few hours since then and they were calling again. That was good news.

Jeremiah sat forward and rested his elbows on the desk. "What have you got for me?"

"We know where the lone wolf has been living, Alpha. There's a bar that caters to the supernaturals in this area, and we managed to run into some of the Montana pack. Some of the wolves were a tad pissed about Dillon bailing on them. There's a wolf here called Colin who is apparently Dillon's best friend. With a little bit of pressure"—Huck's voice deepened to a growl—"we got some info out of him. He said Dillon traveled the country for a while after his parents were killed by human hunters. Eventually, he settled in a place called Coldspring, Texas. He stayed there for some time."

Some time my ass. Try over a damn decade. "Hmm, what made him leave Coldspring? And why the hell did he come here?"

"Colin told us he called Dillon a few days ago to report his old pack needed his help. They've found two dead wolves. Looks like the human hunters are still active up there."

"Sucks for them," Jeremiah answered dryly. "And what did Dillon say to his friend? Why wouldn't he go back to his former pack to help them out?"

Huck cleared his throat. "Here's the kicker, Boss. Colin told us that Dillon refused to come back to Montana and help. Dillon said he had found his mate, and he was headed to Colorado. I'm guessing she must be one of our pack."

Jeremiah went still. The mating marks on Dillon's neck flashed in his mind. "Here?" That was something Dillon hadn't bothered to mention. Though, to be fair, he had asked Jeremiah to give him some time to share more about his true mate. But why not just tell Jeremiah that he thought his mate was among the Colorado pack? He thought back again to their meeting and reminded himself that he hadn't scented any deceit on the male or in his words.

"That's what this Colin person said," Huck answered.

The alpha's mind went back to the living room when Dillon had first arrived. Now that Jeremiah thought about it, he *had* noticed Dillon looking around the room. But that could have been because he was in a room full of unknown wolves. It didn't necessarily mean Dillon had been looking for his mate.

Though it had been many years since he had found his Rose, Jeremiah could still recall the intense feelings that had come over him when he first saw her, when he first heard her voice in his mind. It was like a dam breaking, releasing a torrent of emotions that swept over him like a tidal wave. He could admit it now, so many years later, but

Jeremiah had been almost feral when he'd found his Rosey. She had saved him, brought him back from the brink. He probably only had a year left, maybe two at the most, when she had come along.

With those thoughts swirling in his head, Jeremiah realized that Dillon's mate couldn't be among his pack members. It would have been obvious as soon as he walked through the door. He would've gone straight to her and threatened every other male in the room.

"You there, Alpha?" Huck's voice came through the phone, and Jeremiah realized he'd been lost in thought.

"Yeah." He pinched the bridge of his nose, then looked up, letting his eyes roam over his office as he tried to work through the information in his head. "Just trying to process this. Good work, Hucks. You and Orson start heading—" Jeremiah froze as his eyes landed on a picture on one of his bookshelves. "Shit."

"What is it, Boss?"

There was alarm in Huck's voice, but Jeremiah didn't hear it. A light bulb had just flicked on. "Dammit all." He snarled as his teeth started to lengthen.

"What the hell, Alpha?" Huck's voice had become like a buzzing bee in his ear.

"Shut up, Huck. Let me think," Jeremiah commanded. Dillon clearly hadn't found his mate among the females present at the Colorado pack, but there was one female who wasn't at the mansion. There was one female who was still away on a mission. A female who had taken a detour through Texas. A female who, after taking the detour through *Texas*, instead of coming home, had decided to go visit her friend in Missouri.

Jeremiah's knuckles turned white as he gripped the phone in his hand, and he heard a crack as the device gave way under his strength. There was a low growl coming from him that filled the office and no doubt came clearly through the phone. Huck, wisely, stayed quiet.

No damn way. There is no way this lone wolf is my daughter's mate. He wouldn't have just let her traipse off to another pack and not follow her. What kind of male would do that? But then again, maybe the kind of male that would leave his pack when faced with hunters would also leave his mate.

The seconds turned to minutes as Jeremiah considered the implications of what he suspected. But it was more than a suspicion. Deep down, he knew the truth. Tanya had somehow met this wolf, while she and his other wolves had been traveling in Texas. They must have realized they were mates. But, again, why the hell would they have left one another? Why would Tanya have chosen to go to Missouri and Dillon come here? There were simply too many unanswered questions. Jeremiah needed more information. And to keep from killing Tanya's possible mate before he knew if she even wanted him.

"Change of plans, Huck," Jeremiah finally said. "You and Orson get your butts down to Coldspring, Texas as soon as possible, take a flight this time and rent a car. Talk to anyone and everyone who might have known Dillon Jacobs. Friends, family, whatever. If a waitress so much as brought him coffee in a diner six years ago, I want to hear about it. Leave no stone unturned. I want to know everything about what this rogue has been doing down there."

"You got it, Alpha."

"And, Huck, don't breathe a word about this to anyone. If you do, I'll skin you and hang your pelt over the fireplace in the main hall. I'm dead serious." He slammed the phone down, not bothering to wait for a response. He knew he'd be obeyed because Huck knew Jeremiah didn't bluff. Now he just needed to figure out how to deal with Dillon Jacobs until he could get his daughter home and figure out what the hell had happened between them. Because something *had* happened. There was no way Dillon wouldn't have followed Tanya to Missouri, if he'd known that's where his mate was going.

Jeremiah poured himself a glass of whiskey from the decanter on the edge of his desk and then sat down. He sighed and ran a hand through his hair. He sipped the amber liquid and forced himself to calm down. Dillon should be up soon, and Jeremiah would confront him about his lies by omission. He leaned back in his chair and took a deep sip of his drink. "You couldn't have given me a son?" he muttered his words for the Great Luna, though he didn't really mean them. Mostly.

CHAPTER NINE

> "Pain is universal. It's one of those things that anyone can bond over, even enemies, because we all feel it in some form or another. The pain could be caused by completely different things, and yet a bond can form simply because we understand the agony the other person is feeling." ~Dillon

Tanya took a cool rag from Daniel and ran it across Lisa's face. Her friend burned with fever, and despite shivering from the chill, Tanya used a tepid cloth to bring the fever down. They had tried medicine, but Lisa simply threw it up. The night had gone from the old woman lying peacefully to violent bouts of dry heaving, fever, chills, and Lisa calling out in moments when she wasn't lucid, which was more often than not. Tanya thought nothing could be worse than her friend dying, but she had been wrong. Watching her slip away into death peacefully was much preferred to this.

Tyler slipped his arm under Lisa's frail shoulders and helped turn her when she coughed again. "Hold the bucket closer."

Tanya moved Lisa's sick bucket in nearer and forced herself to remain stoic. She couldn't break down, no matter how torn up she was inside. Why couldn't Lisa have been spared this? Tyler had told Tanya about the cancer and explained that Lisa had times when she did well and then times when she would be violently sick. The old woman had requested that he not tell anyone, but any wolf paying attention would have smelled the sickness on her. At this point, it was obvious. Tanya wanted to kick her own ass for not picking up on it. She had been so focused on the crap taking up space in her head that she had completely missed the scent that now filled the room like smoke from a fire.

"What has you so broken, mate?" A voice suddenly filled her mind.

Tanya nearly dropped the bucket. She pulled it away and turned to hand it to Austin, who dutifully took it. She knew he would empty it and then bring it back. Her emotions were frayed like an aged rope, and Tanya realized the guard she had maintained between her and Dillon had crumbled. She hadn't even noticed.

"Talk to me, Tanya." Dillon's deep voice was gentle.

Her heart squeezed tight in her chest as her emotions warred inside of her. The part of her that had been waiting for her mate her whole life, eager to begin a life with him, wanted to lean on the strength Dillon was already offering. His concern came through their bond, and it called to her. But then the stubborn part of her that was scorned by his actions wanted to push him away.

"I understand you're mad at me, and you have every right to be, but let me help you shoulder this burden. Please."

Tanya picked up Lisa's hand again after Tyler got her resettled on the bed. For the moment, after having thrown up once more, the woman was no longer coughing or groaning. Lisa lay still, and if it weren't for her chest rising and falling, Tanya would have thought she was already gone.

"It's my friend, Lisa," Tanya finally said as she ran her thumb across the frail hand in hers. The skin felt paper thin, and the veins were protruding bright blue against the pale flesh. *"She's dying."* Though Tanya hadn't said the words out loud, it felt as if they reverberated against the walls in the room and were now being echoed back at her. Lisa was dying. The woman who had mentored her, been a source of comfort, a safe place for her to take her frustrations and worries, was leaving this earth forever. Tanya would never again be able to pick up the phone and call or visit her. She would be gone.

"I'm so sorry." Tanya heard the sincerity ring strongly in his words. She could feel his emotions, and she could tell he was attempting to mute them. It was as if he understood she was struggling to handle her powerful feelings of loss, and he didn't want to burden her with his own emotions. She could also feel that he understood her pain personally. He'd lost someone he loved dearly, and perhaps if she wasn't in her own hell, she'd ask him who it was. *Maybe one day.*

"I'll tell you anything you want to know." He'd picked up on her thoughts. *"I'll do anything you need."*

Tanya wiped the tears from her eyes with her free hand. Her vision blurred so that she couldn't see Lisa's sweet face. A female from Tyler's pack named Shelly was wiping the old woman's face with a cool cloth. She glanced up at Tanya, tears running down her face, as well. Shelly was a sweet girl, around Tanya's age, and it didn't surprise her she was close to Lisa, too. Lisa was an easy person to be around. She listened well and gave good advice. And if you didn't want advice, but just someone to vent to, she would do that, as well. "Dammit," Tanya muttered, her voice choked with emotions.

Shelly reached across and squeezed her arm but didn't say anything. She didn't need to. The pain in the room was palpable. The rest of those in the room were still on their knees. Other pack members flowed out into the hall and no doubt filled the small house. They had been there all night, heads bowed and fists over their hearts. They would stay that way until the human, whom they claimed as a pack member and honored the same way they would their alpha, left this world.

"She's very loved," Dillon murmured.

Tanya had almost forgotten he was there in her mind. And that she couldn't keep the bond locked down anymore was a testament to just how badly she was hurting. *"She is."*

"Can I come to you?"

"No," Tanya answered quickly. *"I can't, Dillon. I can't deal with you and this. Please. If you care for me at all, then give me this. I just—"* The words died. She felt him pulling her pain into him through the bond, attempting to ease it. But emotional pain wasn't like physical pain. It couldn't be dulled or taken away. It had to run its course.

"Okay," he said softly. *"I'll wait here for you, even if that takes months or longer. I'm not going anywhere."*

She frowned as his words broke through the storm in her mind, like clouds parting for a moment. *"When you say 'here,' what do you mean?"*

She felt his hesitation before he answered. *"I'm in Colorado at the pack mansion."*

Tanya squeezed her eyes shut. *Shit.* "My father—"

"*He doesn't know who I am to you. Your father's reputation is well known.*"

"He's an ass." Tanya remembered all the conversations she and Lisa had over the years about her irrational, controlling father. "*If he finds out about us, well, it will look very bad that we've met and aren't' together. Especially if he learns about...*" She couldn't finish the sentence. Tanya just didn't have the fortitude to deal with that part of her life at the moment. She shook her head and pinched the bridge of her nose. This was the last thing she needed right now.

"*I haven't said anything about you, exactly,*" Dillon assured her. "*He knows I've met my mate because my mate marks are visible. I've requested a probation period to become a member of this pack, and I've asked him to give me time to earn his trust with respect to sharing anything about my mate.*"

Dillon stopped, seeming to wait to see if she would object. At the moment, Tanya couldn't think too clearly because of Lisa and the fact that her father would kill Dillon if he found out about Dillon's past.

He continued, "*Your father knows I was a member of the Montana pack and that I left. That's a whole different story, but not something we need to talk about right now. I just want you to know I'm not a rogue. I never was. I ran from something very painful a long time ago because I didn't know how to deal with it. Just...*"

He paused, and Tanya found herself holding her breath, waiting to hear what he'd tell her next. Maybe she was just trying to distract herself from her current situation, or maybe she was thirstier than she realized for knowledge about her mate. Perhaps a mixture of both.

"*Just know I'm not going anywhere, and if you don't want me to come to you, then I will respect that.*"

She released the breath she'd been holding and nodded, even though he couldn't see her. *"Thank you. And please, be careful. Do as he asks. Be the perfect pack member and give him no reason to doubt your ability to fall in line. Knowing my father, he's already digging for information on you."* She let those words hang without elaborating on what would happen if he dug enough and figured out about Dillon's past. Her father was hotheaded on the best of days. When it came to his mate and Tanya, he was flat out crazy.

"Don't worry about me. I'll be fine. Be with your friend, and please be safe." There was a light caress against her face, and then she felt him pull back enough that his presence wasn't filling her mind. He was still there, but not intrusive. A silent reminder that if she needed him, he would answer in a heartbeat. *"Always,"* he said in response to her thought.

Tanya didn't respond. Instead, she focused her attention back on Lisa. Her friend still breathed, though her breaths were shallow and accompanied by a wheezing sound that seemed loud to Tanya's sensitive wolf hearing. Her beast was in mourning, as she loved Lisa just as much as the human part of her. The wolf wanted to curl up next to their friend and offer her comfort and warmth. But Tanya wouldn't be able to help in her wolf form, so she forced her beast to be still. Inside, it was whining, pacing, and wishing there were an enemy to kill. But this illness was something the beast didn't understand. It couldn't be killed, at least not in the traditional sense of the word. And apparently, even when the humans did everything they could to fight against it, the illness could still win. "It isn't fair," Tanya whispered. "She doesn't deserve this." Lisa was the best of the best. Even in death, Lisa deserved dignity, not to be reduced to this mess.

Tyler spoke up, his voice, strong but gentle, filling the

room. "Many of us don't deserve the hand we are dealt. It's how we handle it that matters. What do we do with the challenges we face? How do we respond? Lisa has taken this disease head-on and hasn't complained once. She never asked, 'Why me?' She handled her illness with dignity, offering comfort to others even while she was in need. Lisa will be remembered for a lifetime of kindness, service, friendship, selflessness, and love."

"Don't forget I fed you, too." Lisa's frail voice seemed to fill the room even more than Tyler's.

The room fell silent as Tanya leaned closer to her friend. "Lisa?" The woman's eyes were closed, but then her cracked lips turned up in a small smile.

"I'm not quite gone yet, little wolf." Lisa slowly turned her head toward Tanya. Her eyes blinked open. They were dull, but there was peace in her gaze. "But it is time."

Tanya shook her head and held Lisa's hand tighter. "No. Not yet."

"We can't live forever, Tanya." Lisa took a shaky breath, her chest rising. Then she coughed and breathed out. "Nothing would be amazing if we lived forever. Sunrises would be mundane. Coffee wouldn't smell nearly as good."

Tanya laughed as moisture filled her eyes. "This isn't supposed to be funny."

"Says who? I'd much rather be laughing as I leave this life than crying." Lisa squeezed Tanya's hand, though her grip was weak. "I love you, Tanya. I love all of you." There were murmurs around the room and sniffles. Tanya doubted there was a dry eye in the house, other than the ones of the old bat who had the nerve to laugh on her deathbed.

"I'd rather you be laughing while not dying." Tanya's heart ached at the thought of losing such a shining light from the world. Lisa was one of those people who did things for others because it was simply the right thing to do. As she stared back at her friend, a thought occurred to her. "What happens after this life for you?" Tanya knew that her own life would end one day, and she would go to be with her Creator, the Great Luna. However, humans weren't created by the Great Luna. Tanya wondered what would happen to Lisa in the afterlife.

Lisa's face softened as she seemed to understand what Tanya was thinking. "I will spend eternity with my Creator. He has prepared a wonderful place for His children, or so I have read in my Bible."

Tanya sniffled. "Is that why you're not afraid or sad?"

"I am both of those things, child. But I have come to terms with His will. I have accomplished what He wanted me to accomplish, and now He calls me home. What a wonderful feeling it is to have the hope that you will stand before your Creator and hear 'Well done, my good and faithful servant.'"

Tanya choked back her emotions. "I can't begrudge you that. I won't. But, damn it, I'm going to miss you, and to know that this is goodbye forever..." Tanya shook her head as she tried to regain her composure. "I would have treasured you more. I would—"

"Shh. You gave me so much in my life, Tanya. Laughter, tears, joy. Remember those times. You will have me until you go home to your Creator, and once you're with Her, you won't need those memories anymore. Promise me."

"I've already promised you," Tanya growled.

"Promise me," Lisa persisted, "that you will live as if any second could be your last breath."

Tears ran down Tanya's cheeks, falling onto their

clasped hands. She nodded, unable to speak for fear that she would lose control of her emotions.

Lisa held Tanya's gaze as a single tear streamed down her wrinkled face. She gasped several times and seemed to fight for her next breath. Tyler laid his large hand on Lisa's forehead, drawing her eyes to him. His face held such adoration that it was palpable. This alpha loved her as if she were one of his own.

"You can let go, little human," he said affectionately. "Tanya will be fine. Go to your eternal rest, my old friend."

As if she had been waiting for permission from her alpha, Lisa closed her eyes, her face relaxing as her lips softened. She took her final rattling breath, and then there was nothing. Just silence.

Tanya's eyes crinkled slowly, and her chin trembled as she pressed her lips together. She leaned down until her forehead rested on Lisa's shoulder. Her body quaked as she lost the battle to keep from sobbing. The walls of her restraint broke, unleashing a torrential storm of emotion from deep within her.

"I'm so sorry, mate." Dillon's voice filled her mind with such tenderness that she only cried harder. To his credit, he said nothing more, but he kept his presence in her mind, offering comfort and letting her silently know he was there if she needed him.

She *did* need him, but that wasn't something she could deal with right now. Breathing in Lisa's familiar scent, she pulled back and lifted Lisa's hand, pressing her lips to it. "Thank you," she whispered and then gently laid it down, resting it on Lisa's unmoving stomach. Tanya pushed up from the bed and looked over at Tyler. "I'd like to help with her send off."

Tyler's eyes shimmered with unshed tears. "Wouldn't expect less."

Dillon's heart pounded in his chest as Tanya's words beat against the inside of his mind. She wasn't just hurting. She was in utter agony. He tried to take some of her pain through the bond, but her despair threatened to suffocate him. He knew where she was now, but she begged him not to come. How was he supposed to stay away when she needed him? She had just lost someone she loved fiercely, and she needed him, but she wasn't ready for him.

Every instinct inside him screamed at him to go to her, care for her, and shelter her through this tragedy. The only reason he wasn't already in his truck was because a rational part of his brain held him in place. If he respected her wishes and showed her he cared enough to do as she asked, maybe it would help prove to her that he was more than just his past. He wanted a chance with Tanya, and he knew he was walking a tightrope. That she had opened up to him, even a little, was huge.

He closed his eyes and felt the bond between them. It wasn't completely open, but she'd left it so he could at least feel her presence, and he took advantage. Dillon stayed close, resting like a shadow in her mind. He'd know if she changed her mind, and he'd be on his way to her in a heartbeat. Dillon's wolf rumbled inside him as he reveled in the connection she allowed. Both man and beast were humbled. *"We have to do as she asked,"* Dillon told his wolf. *"If we want a snowball's chance in hell, we are going to have to be what she needs, no matter what that means for us."*

His wolf agreed, even though he was chomping at the bit to run to Missouri. *"We will prove we are worthy of her,"* his beast said, letting the man take the lead in their mating.

"Hopefully, I won't screw it up," Dillon muttered as he ran a hand down his face. He was pulled from his thoughts by a soft knock on his door. He hadn't slept much the previous night. After the woman, Penelope, had brought him a burger, Dillon spent the remainder of the evening pacing the room. His mind was a torrent of thoughts. Mostly, he wondered about his new mate, what she liked and didn't like, how she smelled in the morning, what kind of things made her laugh.

Occasionally, those thoughts reminded him of Lilly. He already knew all those things about her, and that made him miss her. Then his wolf would come screaming to the forefront, growling and scolding him. The beast reminded him what kind of pain these thoughts would cause his mate. Then a fresh wave of guilt washed over Dillon. He cursed himself and tried to think of ways to make amends to Tanya. This led him to try and push the bond further open, and each time he was met with resistance. Tanya held fast to the sliver she left open between them. There was only one time that he pushed it open a tad farther, and he was shocked when he felt pain rippling through the bond. Now he knew why she had been feeling that pain.

Dillon's musings about his mate and Lilly were occasionally interrupted by thoughts of the Colorado pack. It had been thirteen years since Dillon had lived among a pack. The feeling was alien to him, and he wasn't quite sure he was comfortable. He hated the thought of himself as a lone wolf. When he'd decided to leave Montana, he never imagined himself as becoming a rogue. Though he hadn't interacted with the other pack members before retiring to his room, Dillon continually heard them moving about the mansion. And the vast number of smells in the building threatened to disorient him. That was something he'd have to get used to again.

But it wasn't just the proximity of so many other wolves. There was something amiss with this pack. He saw it on the faces of the pack members as he'd walked through the large home the night before. They lived in... Dillon wouldn't exactly call it fear *per se*. Perhaps unease was the better word, as if they were walking on eggshells, like children afraid to upset an angry alcoholic father. And Dillon thought he had an idea of what kept them on edge —Jeremiah. Dillon remembered hearing about the alpha being a hard man back when he was still a member of the Montana pack, but he'd apparently grown more tyrannical over the years, and his iron-fisted rule was reflected in the downcast eyes of his pack members. And his encounter with the alpha the day before had just proven it to him.

Dillon groggily rubbed his eyes, trying to clear the sleep. With a grunt, he made his way to the door and opened it. It was the woman from the previous evening, Penelope. Apparently, she was Jeremiah's favorite errand girl. She held a tray with breakfast. She greeted him with a tentative smile and offered it to Dillon.

"Thank you." Dillon took the tray and set it aside. "I didn't know that room service was a typical thing in this pack. I figured last night was a one-time occurrence since I arrived so late."

"It's not. At least, I don't think it is. We don't have many visitors." She pursed her lips and her brow furrowed. "Honestly, I was a bit surprised when he asked me to bring your supper. Jeremiah isn't known for his generosity."

"Supper and now breakfast," Dillon smiled and tried to keep the skepticism from his voice. "Maybe your alpha is changing his ways."

Penelope snorted. "I wouldn't count on that." She snapped her mouth closed and glanced back and forth down the hall, like she'd done the night before. She seemed to relax when she noticed there was no one around, her eyes settled back on him. "No, the breakfast wasn't his idea. I just thought you might like something to eat in peace without the pack staring at you or bombarding you with questions."

Dillon's eyebrows rose. "You brought this on your own? Jeremiah didn't order it?"

She nodded and then tentatively asked, "Maybe you could keep that to yourself?"

"That was very thoughtful, Penelope. Thank you." Dillon dipped his chin. "And if anyone asks, as far as I know, the tray was simply sitting outside my door."

"Jeremiah did send me," she admitted. "But not with breakfast. He wants to see you as soon as you're up. Better eat fast."

"Thank you, Nell."

She fidgeted, looking uncomfortable with the gratitude. "Welcome." She started to turn slowly as if to walk away but then looked back at him. "So, are you staying?"

"Why do you sound like you're asking me if I have a contagious disease?"

Her eyes darted to his briefly every few seconds, but she couldn't hold his stare for long. He hadn't noticed her doing that last night or even at the beginning of their conversation, which meant he was leaking some of his dominant power and making her wolf, dormant though it may be, cower in front of him. No doubt this was because of his thoughts about how Jeremiah dominated his pack. Dillon had managed to keep it under control with the alpha, and he would absolutely have to lock that crap down from here on out. Dillon attempted to get his emotions under control in an effort to help Penelope relax.

Her lips turned down as she lifted one shoulder. "I don't mean to sound rude. It's just that Jeremiah doesn't like outsiders. He never has."

"Yeah." Dillon chuckled dryly. "I got that impression already. I've asked for a probation period as a trial member."

Penelope's eyes widened. "Seriously? Why?" she blurted and then once again seemed to sink in on herself.

"Because sometimes we need a new home," he answered honestly. "And this one seemed like a good one." He didn't add "because my mate lives here." No matter how badly he wanted to claim her in front of anyone and everyone.

Dillon didn't waste any time eating his breakfast. He quickly changed and threw his dirty clothes into his duffel bag. Before he left the room, he made sure to pull every ounce of his dominance into himself. *"Keep your crap together,"* he told his wolf. The beast was silent, which he took as a good sign.

As he headed out into the hall and began to follow his nose in the direction he'd come the previous evening, Dillon couldn't help but think how things could have been different if he'd just stayed with his pack. Under other circumstances, Dillon wouldn't have had a problem walking straight up to Jeremiah and declaring Tanya his.

But Dillon had never imagined he'd be meeting his mate after having a years-long affair with a human.

Stupid human, his wolf growled.

Thank you. You've already made your position on the matter quite clear, Dillon replied. *But I've smartened up a bit. I'm not going to do anything that will provoke the alpha ... at least not yet.*

He took several deep breaths and shook out his hands at his sides. As he walked, he passed several pack members. He nodded politely and made brief eye contact but didn't stop. Dillon was going to have to play things Jeremiah's way if he wanted to be able to stay, and by "stay" he meant stay alive. Tanya would come home eventually. When she did, they would hash this out, and he'd make her take him as her mate. Though, he might have to beg, but that was okay. He'd do whatever he had to, dignity be damned. Dillon would latch onto her leg and make her drag him around the pack grounds if that's what it took.

When he reached the door that he recognized from the night before, Dillon pulled his shoulders back and latched onto his inner submissive persona. *"We don't have an inner submissive persona,"* his wolf grumbled, sounding highly offended. *"Use your imagination,"* Dillon growled back.

"Come in," a gravelly voice said after Dillon finally knocked.

He pushed the door open and scanned the room. This time he paid more attention to the details, taking in how spacious it was, with a fireplace on one wall. Exposed wooden beams, polished to a sheen, ran along the ceiling. Dillon had trouble imagining Jeremiah atop a ladder, holding a rag in one hand and a can of polish in another, scrubbing those beams himself. No doubt he had someone do it for him. Two large glass doors led out to a wooden balcony, giving a view of the surrounding woods for miles. The mountains dipped and rose around them in all their glory. Dillon was surprised to see a full bookshelf lining one wall. As much as he couldn't see Jeremiah dusting, he also couldn't see the alpha reading. The office smelled of cedar and pine.

Jeremiah sat behind a large desk made of dark wood, with what Dillon thought was a forced smile upon his face.

"Good morning," Jeremiah motioned to one of the two armchairs across from his desk. "I trust you slept well."

Not at all, considering all I did was worry about your daughter. "I did, Alpha. Let me thank you again for your hospitality. The food and the accommodations are outstanding." Was he laying it on a little thick? Probably. But men like Jeremiah liked their ego stroked.

"No problem at all, Dillon," Jeremiah made a dismissive gesture with his hand. "I can't have it thought amongst the packs that the Colorado alpha treats guests or potential new members with anything less than care and respect."

"They won't hear that from me." Dillon smiled as he rested his left ankle on top of his right knee. "So far, I've got nothing but good things to say."

Jeremiah leaned back in his chair and steepled his hands in front of himself. His eyes narrowed and seemed to hone in on Dillon like a hawk seeking its prey. "I called up the Montana pack and spoke with your former alpha."

Dillon tried to keep any surprise or emotions from his face as he nodded. "I would expect nothing less." Though he'd actually hoped, albeit in vain, that Jeremiah would have waited a bit before he started looking into him. He'd hoped that his honesty would have gone a little further in instilling some faith in him. Apparently, that was a big fat no.

"Let's just cut to the chase, Dillon." Jeremiah sounded annoyed. "You're here for your mate. Where is she? Because, if she *was* here, you'd have certainly claimed her the minute you stepped through my door."

Dillon ran his palms down his thighs and nodded. "No disrespect, Jeremiah, but that is a topic that needs to be handled between me and my mate before I discuss it with anyone else. You, especially as a respected alpha with a beloved mate, must understand this." Dillon waited a moment to see if the alpha would respond. But the man seemed to be waiting to see if Dillon would say more. "When we have figured it all out, then we will need a pack, a home. And I'm hoping that will be here. I still need a fresh start, and I truly hope this can be it."

There was a tense moment while Dillon waited to see if the alpha would lunge across the desk and rip his throat out. When that didn't happen, Dillon tried very hard not to let out a sigh of relief. He really didn't want to have to fight his mate's father. In all honesty, he wanted this to work. Even if he did have to live under Jeremiah's arbitrary rule. He'd do it for Tanya.

"Very well." Jeremiah rubbed his hands together. "I will continue to give you the benefit of the doubt. Though, as I've warned you, my wrath is swift once my judgment is made. I do hope that this will all work out, especially with your mate involved. It's not just you that you have to think of."

"Agreed."

"With that out of the way, beginning today as your probationary period, you'll start on patrol duty." Jeremiah pushed up from his desk. "You see, Colorado is a highly sought-after territory." Jeremiah gestured out the double glass doors to the picturesque Rocky Mountains around the mansion. "Because of that, I'm constantly besieged with challengers. Rogue wolves rise up all the time, trying to make a play for this pack."

Dillon's eyes went wide. "Really?" He tried to keep the skepticism from his voice. What Jeremiah was saying wasn't unheard of, of course, but it was rare. Challenges for an alpha position didn't happen often. And Dillon had never heard of rogues trying to take a pack over completely. Most of the time, challenges came from within, or at least from members of a rival pack.

"Absolutely. But over the years, I've gotten good at sensing when something like that is going to happen."

Dillon's eyes twitched as he used all of his will power not to roll them. *Sensing when rogues were coming? What are you, a sprite?* "And you have a sense that you're about to be attacked by rogue wolves who want to take over your pack?" *Good job not sounding sarcastic.*

"You didn't roll your eyes either," his wolf pointed out. So helpful when he wanted to be.

Jeremiah turned away from the window and looked at Dillon. "I have reports from my sentries that there are rogues getting too close. I need to be diligent and stop any attack before it happens." He stood and walked around the desk.

Dillon immediately got to his feet, as well. His wolf didn't like a less dominant wolf standing over him.

"This will be your first assignment. Any questions?"

Don't say, "Can we invite the rogues for dinner?" Don't say it, Dillon. He mentally growled at himself. "No, Alpha. I'm good at hunting."

"Excellent." Jeremiah clapped him on the back. "You'll report back at the end of the day. Head out to the front door. The others accompanying you are already waiting."

Dillon gave a sharp nod, turned on his heel, and headed toward what was most likely going to be a day of running through forest where no rogues have been near in years. *Just follow orders.* He felt like this hadn't been so hard when he lived in the Montana pack. Either he was out of practice of having an alpha and it wrangled him and his wolf, or it was just the person giving the orders that bothered him.

"It's both," his wolf said coolly. *"We are meant to lead. You know this."*

Dillon didn't acknowledge his wolf's words. He couldn't entertain that kind of thinking—not right now when it was crucial he be the compliant wolf that kept from being gutted.

CHAPTER TEN

"Some people say to never encourage a crazy person's delusions. Well, if the crazy person is your mate's father, you may have to go along with them. Just be careful. This might sound hard to believe, but crazy people do crazy crap. And when a powerful alpha does crazy crap, people get hurt." ~Dillon

Daniel held out the phone to Tanya. "It's your dad."

She was in the kitchen of the main house of the Missouri pack compound, looking in the phone book for local funeral homes where they could get a casket for Lisa's body. Tanya felt uneasy about sending her friend off in the traditional way of her people—by burning her body. Tanya preferred the idea of having a place where she could come and visit Lisa. Tyler had agreed to let Lisa be buried on the pack land with a memorial and a bench where people could sit next to the gravesite. The alpha had said yes with no hesitation, which made Tanya cry, as it was probably the exact opposite way her father would have reacted.

Tanya took a step back when she saw the phone. The last person she wanted to deal with at the moment was her controlling father. She had a feeling this wasn't a phone call to see how she was doing, especially now that she knew Dillon was at her pack.

Daniel shook the phone. "Tanya." She finally sighed and took it. Tyler propped up against the counter with his arms folded in front of his chest. She noticed his eyes glowed slightly with his wolf, but that was the only sign of his agitation.

Tyler and Tanya's father, Jeremiah, tolerated each other and were amiable, but that was as good as it got. Tyler thought Jeremiah was a controlling ass with a god complex, and he wasn't wrong. Jeremiah knew that Tyler was equally dominant and couldn't be intimidated. They never truly felt the need to challenge each other, but Tanya had a feeling that might change one day. If her father ordered her home, she'd have to obey. Knowing Tanya would want to stay for Lisa's funeral, Tyler would not take that well. He might even give Jeremiah his opinion about the matter, and that wouldn't lead anywhere good.

With shaking hands and a pounding heart, Tanya put the phone to her ear. "Hello."

"Tanya, how is your visit with Lisa going?"

Her father's voice was gentle, which made her defensive. She scrunched her brow, trying to figure out her father's intentions. Typically, he had two modes with her: overprotective or annoyed. Essentially, he wanted to control her in both cases. While Tanya believed he loved her, she also thought he saw her as a reflection of himself. Any mistake she made was a mark against him, and any choice she made that he disagreed with was somehow an attempt to spite him. At times it seemed to her that he thought that her desire to visit the Missouri pack to see Lisa was her way of saying she preferred Tyler as an alpha to him. When she was younger, this wouldn't have been true, but she had outgrown the days when she saw her parents through rose-colored glasses.

"Actually," she began slowly, "it's not going too well, and I need to ask your permission"—she swallowed hard—"to stay longer."

"What's happened?" His voice grew stern. She could picture his sharp, hazel eyes narrowing.

"Lisa..." Tanya stopped, took a breath, and cleared her throat. Austin's hand came down on her shoulder, reminding Tanya she had pack with her who would stand by her. "She passed away less than an hour ago."

There was silence for a few heartbeats, and then to her complete shock, Jeremiah said, "I'm sorry to hear that. I know she meant a lot to you."

Tanya found herself irritated that her father sounded so genuine. It had always been a battle to get permission to come visit her friend. But Tanya held her tongue. He hadn't denied her yet, and she didn't want to provoke him to do so.

"She did. We are planning her funeral. I would like to stay for that if you will allow it." She held her breath, waiting for his refusal.

"Of course, you must stay."

Tanya's mouth dropped open as she glanced at Austin, Trevor, and then Daniel, knowing with their wolf senses, they could all hear their alpha. What alternate universe had she just stepped into?

"If Tyler is willing to allow you to stay, I mean," Jeremiah continued, "then you should. It would be irreverent not to pay your respects after she's been such a good friend to you. We never want it said that a Colorado pack member would show such offense. And definitely not my own child."

Tanya nearly growled but managed to hold her wolf's tongue. Of course it was about him and how others would perceive him and his pack. It had nothing to do with the fact that Tanya was hurting beyond words and that Lisa deserved to have a funeral surrounded by people who loved her. "Thank you, Dad. I don't know exactly how long it will be—"

"Don't worry about that," her father interrupted. "Just keep me posted. As long as Daniel, Austin, and Trevor are with you, then I know you're safe."

Tanya lifted her other hand and pinched her arm so hard that she winced. She was sure she must be asleep. She wished it were a nightmare and she would wake up to find Lisa alive and her dad calling to demand she come home. That would be better than this hell.

"Okay," she said, though it sounded like a question. "Give my love to Mom, please."

"I will. And Tanya..." He paused. "I really am sorry."

Tanya closed her eyes. A tear escaped and ran down her cheek, leaving a cool trail. Large arms enveloped her, and she buried her face in the familiar smell of Tyler, the alpha she had wished so many times was her father.

"Tanya," Dillon's voice sounded strained in her mind. She knew her pain was probably radiating through the bond, causing him physical pain, but she couldn't block it. *"You don't have to block it. That's what a true mate is for."* She felt fingers on her face, and they weren't Tyler's. *"I'm here."*

His love surrounded her just as sure as the Missouri alpha's arms did. Tanya tentatively reached through the bond and let him feel her gratitude. It was intimate and terrifying but so comforting that she nearly begged him to come to her.

"Our mate," her wolf said with so much longing in her voice that Tanya felt guilty for asking him to stay away. *"Only he can give us what we need."* Tanya knew her beast was right, but she wasn't ready to face all that would come with Dillon when he finally stood before her.

She hadn't realized her father had ended the call until Tyler took the phone out of her hand. Tanya had just been standing there, holding it with the dial tone ringing in her ear. She patted the alpha, stepping out of his embrace, and then walked over to the kitchen sink. Tanya pulled off a paper towel from the roll, wet it with cold water, then pressed it to her face. The heat that infused her face from her tears and emotions cooled a bit, and she pushed the whole weird conversation with her father into a box and shut it—for now.

When she lowered the paper towel and turned to face the room again, the eyes of her pack mates, Tyler, and several of his pack members were on her.

"Let's go pick out Lisa's casket," she said, feeling a little stronger. "She deserves the best."

Tyler nodded. "And the best she will have."

Dillon's chest ached over his female's anguish. It was eating him alive to have to hold back his instincts. She was shattered, and he just wanted to help hold her together. He picked up on her feelings for the Missouri alpha, and even though she saw him as a father, it grated against Dillon that Tyler possessed his female's affections. *Is it wrong for me to feel that way? Yes. Does that matter to my irrational wolf? Nope.* Dillon kept a presence in her mind but also refocused on the matter at hand.

He and the three other pack members—Kevin, Rusty, and Gabe—had been searching the forest surrounding the Colorado pack mansion all day. So far, they had found nothing—not a single trace of any rogue wolves. As he knew they wouldn't. It just didn't make sense for rogues to be attempting to attack or encroach on a pack this size. It must be some sort of test to see if Dillon would blindly do as he's told, even if he thinks the alpha is full of shit. Dillon was pretty sure Jeremiah saw the skepticism in his eyes when he'd been in his office, though Dillon did his damndest to hide it. To Dillon's delight, the other wolves had been amiable all day, even pleasant. They weren't side-eying him or acting as if paying him any sort of attention might get them smacked across the face like a child who'd asked the same question one too many times to an irrational parent. They seemed like different people away from the mansion. It was as if they could lighten up and be themselves out from under the heavy shadow that Jeremiah subconsciously cast over the entire headquarters.

"You guys ready for some lunch?" Dillon asked the three males.

"Are we going to jog to a fast-food restaurant?" Kevin asked.

"What?" Dillon frowned. "No, I mean, let's hunt up a meal." He found that he was eager to hunt with a pack.

He'd been hunting alone for so long, he hadn't even realized that his wolf was starved for the companionship of other pack mates.

Kevin looked at Rusty and then Gabe.

"What?" Dillon folded his arms across his chest and met Kevin's gaze, who lowered his eyes immediately.

"Jeremiah doesn't like us to hunt," Kevin said. "We can phase and let our wolves run, but he doesn't want us taking down prey."

Dillon's arms dropped as his head tilted. His wolf perked up at this bit of information. "Hold up." He lifted a hand. "You're telling me your alpha doesn't allow you to hunt?"

All three males nodded slowly. None of them looked at him; their eyes stayed on the ground. Dillon realized his irritation was leaking power out of him. He'd been doing so good at keeping it under control, but between hunting and now this bit of information, his wolf was beginning to get agitated. Dillon took a deep breath and pulled back, forcing his wolf to calm down. Kevin's shoulders relaxed first, then Rusty and Gabe followed suit.

"Apologies. I just don't understand. Why wouldn't he want you to hunt?"

Kevin glanced around the woods as if he were afraid Jeremiah might jump out at any moment. When he looked back at Dillon, his eyes glowed with his wolf. "Hunting strengthens our instincts. It draws our wolves to the forefront. It brings out the—"

"Dominance," Dillon cut him off. "It forces everybody into their rightful place in the pack." He shook his head as he realized what their alpha was doing. By preventing his pack from hunting, which would naturally organize them by dominance for the hunt, he prevented the wolves from knowing their place in the pack hierarchy. It basically just kept everyone beneath Jeremiah, and by threat of death, no one engaged in dominance fights.

"Yeah," Rusty said slowly, his eyes darting around.

Dillon wasn't sure how much he could say around these three males. If his instincts were right, they were only loyal to Jeremiah out of fear, not respect. And if that were the case, then Dillon might get them to open up about their alpha. But if he was wrong, they might run to Jeremiah and tell him that Dillon was digging.

"Okay, look." Dillon ran a hand down his face. "I'm not a member of your pack, but I'm hoping to be. At some point I'm sure Jeremiah will let everyone know that I'm in a probationary period. You already know I'm more dominant than any of you," he said honestly. "I have no desire to put you in your place. I just want to hunt." He looked around the forest, which was so different from the flat land of Texas. "It's been a long time since I've been able to hunt with a pack. My wolf and I both just want to do what comes natural."

The three males seemed to weigh his words as they looked at one another and then back at him.

"There's no catch," Dillon assured them. "I will not run to Jeremiah and tattle. And if you don't trust me or are worried you'll get in trouble, then we can just jog somewhere, as you suggested."

He saw the eagerness in their eyes as they looked into the surrounding woods. Dillon could practically see them salivating. Their beasts were starved for the same thing he was, and yet they had been living in a pack while he had been a lone wolf. How much worse it was to have what you needed dangled right in front of your face but be unable to grab it. He really wanted to kick Jeremiah's ass.

"Okay." Kevin breathed out, giving a sharp nod. He seemed to be the leader of their trio, which meant he was most likely dominant to the other two. And it was evident when he made the decision for all three of them that they understood his place over them. In fact, they looked relieved.

Dillon smiled, and his canines lengthened. "How do you guys feel about whitetail bucks?"

They shed their clothes with the excitement of children about to receive a Christmas toy they had been wanting for the whole year. As soon as they phased, Dillon's wolf immediately knew the order of their little pack. He was dominant to all of them and therefore took the lead. They fell in line behind him as he took off into the forest.

After an hour, they returned to their clothes and phased back. Dillon felt rejuvenated, as if he had just been reborn.

"How did you move that fast?" Kevin asked as he pulled his jeans back on.

"Seriously." Rusty nodded, his eyes wide. "I've never even seen Jeremiah move like that."

Dillon put his shirt over his head and then sat on the ground to put on his shoes. "My wolf is fast, but that's not the only reason I took down that buck." He motioned to them. "We worked as a team, as a pack." He paused as he finished tying his shoes. "That's how a hunt should be. We use the strengths given to us and share them with each other to accomplish something together."

When he raised his eyes back up, the three males were staring at him as if he'd grown a third head. "What?"

"We've never hunted like that," Kevin frowned "The alpha will sometimes hunt with his top three, but those are the only wolves permitted. I feel like a part of me has been missing, like a leg was cut off, and I just got it back."

"You're a *Canis lupus*." Dillon pushed up to his feet. "You weren't meant to lead solitary lives, not even within the pack. Your alpha should lead you, not feel threatened by you."

"Careful." Rusty hissed, looking over his shoulder. "You can't let anyone hear you talk like that especially if you want to be a member of this pack."

"*Anyone else,*" Kevin corrected. "*We* won't say a damn thing. But Rusty's right. There are pack members who would tell Jeremiah what you're saying, and he would take it to mean that you want to challenge him."

Dillon's brow rose. "So speaking the truth is considered mutinous?"

"Whose truth?" Kevin's voice was filled with derision.

Dillon nodded, understanding filling his mind. Their alpha had set the standard for truth, but it was *his* truth, which wasn't truth at all. It was a lie constructed to control those who he felt threatened his position in the pack. "I'm sorry." Dillon's wolf growled as he thought about these three good men being oppressed because of their alpha's fear. "Your pack deserves better. A good alpha wants to see his wolves thrive, not cower in fear."

"*Careful,*" his wolf warned. "*We need to be sure we can trust them.*"

Dillon's gut told him he could trust the wolves. He could see it in their eyes—the earnest need to be led by someone who valued them and not just saw them as someone to subjugate.

Gabe made a sound like a whining wolf. Dillon knew that if the younger male had been in his wolf form, he'd have his tail tucked, trying to make himself as small as possible.

Dillon held up his hands. "That's all I'm going to say. I

don't want to get you in trouble. But just know"—he looked each of them in the eye—"you deserve better." He turned and motioned for them to follow. "Let's do one more sweep and see if we come across these so-called rogue wolves."

He heard Kevin chuckle, but then he turned it into a cough. They'd clearly been conditioned not to have an opinion.

"He is no alpha," Dillon's wolf said, referring to Jeremiah.

"No," Dillon agreed. *"He's a dominant male who wants to be more than he is. A wolf who probably was never able to accept his place in his pack, and the only way he can hold his place is by coercion and fear tactics."*

"We will not submit to him once we claim our mate," his beast rumbled.

Dillon had no arguments there, but he'd keep those emotions stuffed way, way down. As they started off again, he checked on Tanya through the bond and found she seemed to be a little less volatile. She was occupied, her thoughts busy, so he let her be. But Dillon made sure to pour his affection through the bond. Even if he couldn't physically be there with her, he *could* still let her know she had his support.

The group had searched the entirety of the forest south of the mansion before lunch, so they decided to spend the afternoon in the woods north of the pack headquarters.

"Why are we out here hunting again?" Rusty murmured. "If there were rogues out here, we'd know about it because any of the other supernaturals that choose to live in this realm around us would have probably informed us."

"Who knows." Gabe huffed. "Our alpha isn't exactly the sanest patient in the mental hospital."

Kevin growled. "Careful." He looked around them. "Things have a way of getting back to him."

Dillon continued to listen to their hushed conversations as the afternoon wore on. It was extremely apparent to him they weren't happy with Jeremiah's leadership. Kevin, obviously very protective of the other two, kept warning them to be careful with their words, but then occasionally he'd throw out a comment that showed his own irritation.

Dillon opened his mouth to ask them about it, but then snapped it closed. He was here to claim his mate, not cause any disruption in the Colorado pack. Still, he couldn't help but feel for the wolves living under Jeremiah's authoritarian rule. His own alpha in Montana had been a servant leader, the concern for his wolves his highest priority, and Dillon had always thought that was how an alpha should lead.

The four men walked along a creek bed, searching the ground for tracks, human or wolf. Dillon suddenly stopped and held up a hand. The other three wolves froze behind him. Dillon listened hard with his wolf's hearing. He heard nothing, and that was what concerned him. The forest was never this silent. There was always birdsong or something scurrying in the undergrowth. Sometimes the sounds were too quiet for human ears to detect, but to a wolf, the forest was anything but calm.

Suddenly, the silence was shattered by the sound of men leaping from the branches above.

"Vamps!" Rusty pointed to the monsters—five in all—dropping all around them.

"Back to back," Dillon yelled. He extended his claws and took in their attackers. Dillon didn't have time to size them up properly before the first one hissed and leaped at him, a dark blade in its hand. Then all hell broke loose.

Growls and screams erupted from both wolves and vampires alike as they engaged one another. Dillon blocked the strike of the vamp in front of him and swiped out with his clawed hand, raking the monster across the face.

"Why do I feel a sudden surge of violence coming through this bond?" Tanya's voice filled his mind, and part of him wanted to throw a fist in the air at the fact that she'd reached out to him. But the part of him that wanted to stay alive kept his focus on his opponent.

"Can't talk at the moment, T." The nickname rolled naturally through the bond as if he'd called her that all of his life. *"Dealing with some vamps."*

He took another swipe across the opposite side of the vampire's face. The monster gave an inhuman scream and fell back. Dillon didn't give it time to recover. Seeing one of the vamp's comrades to his right looking to get a strike in, Dillon moved to his left. In a flash, Dillon grabbed the injured vamp and took its back. With a practiced motion, Dillon snapped the bastard's neck, but he didn't let it fall. Instead, he held the body between him and his next attacker. The vampire hesitated, looking for an opening. He tried to circle, but Dillon kept the dead vamp in between them.

"VAMPIRES!" Tanya's panicked voice reverberated off the inside of his head. *"What the hell do you mean 'dealing with some vamps?' Does my father know? Where are you? Why in the world are you fighting vampires, dammit?"*

Dillon tried to pour reassurance into the bond. He wanted her to know he was fine because he didn't have time to answer her rapid-fire questions, if he wanted to stay fine, that is. The attacker's patience ran out, and he rushed in. Dillon let the body drop, then shoved both hands forward, claws extended. The vamp impaled himself, his eyes bulging as Dillon pierced his internal organs. Dillon ripped his hands outward, bringing as much of the vampire's intestines with him as he could. The attacker took another step forward and fell.

Dillon quickly looked around. *"It seems that you might have an infestation just inside the farthest border of the Colorado pack land,"* he quickly explained. *"I don't think your father knows. Or maybe he does, and he was hoping they'd kill me."*

"Have you lost your freaking mind?"

"It's possible." Dillon noticed that he'd managed to even the odds. *"I haven't been quite right since we parted ways. And now you're dealing with this horrible loss. The least I can do is kill some vampires around your pack."* Despite the damage he'd dealt, the Colorado pack members weren't faring well.

"You better not die, Dillon Jacobs." She growled. *"If anyone is going to take you out it will be me. That's my right as your mate."*

His lips turned up as his wolf practically pranced because she'd basically just claimed them. Did the claim also come with a death threat, probably a legitimate one? Sure, but he'd take what he could get. *"I have no intention of dying. At least not until I've gotten to hold you one time and look into those beautiful eyes again."* He was laying it on thick, though it was the complete truth.

He moved toward the other three males where each fought a vampire, and none of them looked like they had the upper hand. But one wolf in particular looked worse than the others. Rusty was on his knees, a giant gash in his side pouring blood into the forest floor. The vampire in front of him reared back, a blade in his hand, ready to take Rusty's head from his body.

"Dillon, please. I'm being serious," Tanya continued. He could feel genuine fear pulsing into him like electricity, and it only fueled his beast more.

"I've got to save Rusty—"

"Rusty! Why the hell is he fighting vampires? Who else is with you? Blasted all! None of you better die before I have a chance to tear into your hides for scaring the shit out of me when I'm trying to pick out a freaking casket!"

"You've got quite the mouth on you, little mate," he teased, hoping it would calm her down. *"I promise not to die, or let Rusty die, or anyone else who I will not name that is present, and I promise to check in with you as soon as this is done."* He tightened down the bond because he had to focus as he lunged, phasing in midair. His dark grey wolf barreled into the vampire just as the stroke fell. The vampire went sideways, and the blade was knocked wide. Dillon saw out of the corner of his eyes that it buried itself in the dirt a couple of inches away from Rusty's leg. Dillon came down on top of the vamp. Before the monster could react, the wolf's jaws were clamped around the vampire's throat. He jerked back and violently shook his head, saliva and blood flying through the air as Dillon ripped out the vamp's throat. But he didn't stop to savor the kill. He turned and leaped toward the vamp that was fighting Kevin. With a howl of rage, Dillon charged forward again, claws extended and fangs bared. He jumped onto the creature with lightning speed and tore into its flesh with powerful swipes of his claws before finally sinking his teeth deep into its throat and ripping it out in one ferocious bite.

He didn't know if it was because of the emotions from Tanya, the anger at Jeremiah, or the comradery he felt for the three males, but something made him fight extraordinarily viciously. Maybe it was a mixture of all three, but he was not going to let one of them die, not as long as he still drew breath. The final vamp realized it was outnumbered. It shrieked and turned to run, but Dillon wasn't about to let it get away. He snarled and rushed forward, leaping onto the vampire's back. The monster went down face first, and Dillon clamped his jaws around the back of his neck. He wrenched and pulled, snarling and slavering all the while. Finally, with a sickening crunch, the head came free of the body. The wolf tossed his own massive head backward and released, sending the severed vampire head flying into the bushes.

Dillon quickly turned in a circle, taking in his surroundings, looking for any additional threats. After a few moments, his wolf was satisfied there were no more vamps hanging around, waiting to attack. Dillon phased and walked back to the group. Rusty was laying on his back on the ground. Kevin's head was covered with blood dripping down the right side of his face. Gabe's pants were ripped on the thigh, and thick blood oozed out.

Dillon motioned to Kevin's head. "That going to be okay?"

Kevin nodded. "Looks worse than it is." He handed Dillon a pair of pants from a backpack. Dillon took them and put them on with a nod.

"How about him?" Dillon asked as he knelt by Rusty.

Kevin grunted. "I'm no healer, but I think the bleeding is slowing. I believe he'll be okay if we can get some pressure on it to slow the bleeding and then get him home."

Rusty winced. "It's just a scratch."

Dillon took his shredded clothes and wadded them up, placing them into the gash in Rusty's side.

"What the hell was that about?" Gabe stared around with wide eyes. "We haven't had any trouble with vamps in a while."

Kevin shrugged. "Who knows with those bastards? Could be a new coven in the area, or it could just be a group that was out hunting human hikers."

"Regardless, we better get these two back." Dillon motioned to Rusty and Gabe. "They're bleeding like stuck hogs which is going to attract predators." Dillon reached down and made to scoop Rusty up, but Kevin put a hand on his arm.

"I've got it. One of us that isn't injured needs to be on the lookout." He glanced at Gabe. "Gabe can manage with a limp. And we will make fun of him relentlessly for being so slow that a vampire managed to get the upper hand."

"If I'm slow it's because I've been training with you," Gabe muttered. "My great- great grandmother moves faster than you."

Dillon chuckled at Gabe. "Don't worry. It will only stick until another wolf does something to be teased about." Dillon guessed they were about ten miles from the pack mansion, and the sun was sinking low behind the trees. Ten miles wasn't insurmountable for their kind. Uninjured, and not weary from a long day of scouting the woods, they could probably make it back in an hour. But the gash in Gabe's legs said that he wasn't going to be sprinting. Rusty was out of commission and would be carried by Kevin, who may or may not have a concussion, though he didn't seem disoriented, so that was a good sign. All that said, there was no way they would make it back before dark. And where there was *one* vampire, there were usually more. Five vampires in the area could only mean trouble, no matter what the reason. Dillon looked at Kevin and recognized the determination in the man's face. Finally, Dillon nodded.

"I'll go ahead and make sure our way back is clear. If you need me for anything, if so much as a leaf looks out of place, or if you get too tired to carry on, give three howls, and I'll be back in a heartbeat."

Kevin nodded and extended a hand. "Thank you." Dillon shook it and then stepped away. He removed the pants Kevin had given him and passed them back. "See you back at the mansion." He phased and took off down the trail.

"Are you still alive?" Tanya pushed through the bond that he'd closed while he'd been trying to keep his promise of not dying or letting any of her pack members die.

Dillon kept his wolf senses on high alert as he answered, *"I realize you have no reason to trust me."* He paused as his gut twisted at the truth of his own words. *"But I keep my promises. Each of your pack members with me are alive. Not all entirely well, but alive."*

"Injuries?" Her voice was curt, and Dillon could feel the tension coming through their mate bond.

"Kevin took a blow to the head, Rusty has a pretty decent scratch on his side, and Gabe's leg is torn up. I am unhurt. All in all, we are in good shape." Dillon sniffed every rock, leaf, and branch on the trail, and he listened as keenly as he could, straining to hear anything that might warn of another attack *"How are you holding up?"* Dillon didn't allow himself to wander into her thoughts, no matter how badly he wanted to know how she was doing. He wanted her to tell him herself. He wanted her to trust him enough to share with him.

"Are those the only pack members that were with you?" She ignored his question. She seemed worried that there was

someone specific that might have been with him. Was there a male she was close to?

He forced his jealous and possessive nature down his throat because he had no right to feel that way. *"Yes. That is all."* And, because he just had to prove what an ass he had already shown himself to be, he added, *"Was there someone in particular you were concerned about?"*

"I worry about everyone in my pack," she bit out. *"I'm just wondering what you four were doing out there on the edges of the pack land on your own. Did my father send you out to hunt? And if so, what were you hunting?"*

The skepticism in her voice only confirmed what the three males had told him about Jeremiah not letting pack members hunt prey. He continued to run his nose all around the ground, raising his head and lowering it, sniffing out any scents that shouldn't be present. So far, everything was as it should be. *"He told me there'd been signs of rogue wolves near the compound,"* Dillon explained.

Dillon felt confusion slither down the bond. *"Rogue wolves?"* Skepticism filled her voice. *"There's no way there would be rogue wolves anywhere near my father's pack. As you pointed out earlier when we spoke, his reputation of being a ruthless ass is quite well known among wolves and other supernaturals, as well."*

"I figured there weren't any rogues, but I wasn't about to tell my," he emphasized the word, reminding her that he was there on a trial period, *"alpha that I didn't believe him. I'm to do what I'm told, and that's what I did. I don't think he was expecting vampires to be out and about. These were older vampires since they were able to be out in the day."*

"You're right," she said, her voice resigned. *"I told you to be careful, and part of being careful is toeing the line with him.*

But be prepared for anything, Dillon. I promise you he's going to be looking into you."

"He already has." Though he hated to make her worry, Dillon would keep nothing from her. *"He contacted my former alpha."*

"Would he have said anything that would cause my father to think there was more to you than just a wolf who left his pack?"

Like perhaps the fact that you lived a whole life with someone else without considering how it would make me feel. She didn't say those words, but Dillon could practically hear them being shouted at him through the torment that she continued to feel over his past choices.

"I'm sorry." He knew the words were inadequate. There was nothing he could do to take away the sting of what his actions caused. *"I don't deserve a chance with you. But I won't give up trying to get one. You will have to kill me to get rid of me. Don't worry about what your father does or doesn't know or what he will find out. That's for me to worry about."*

"Sure, I'll get right on that." She was silent for a moment, though she didn't close the bond. *"Are you back at the mansion?"*

"No." He let her ignore his comment, for now. *"We've got about seven more miles to go."* He could hear the other males behind him moving at a decent speed, considering they were injured.

"Focus on getting home. You might run into more vampires. Please keep my pack mates alive," she ordered. *"Maybe once you get back and are safe, we can..."* She paused, and he felt the tension in her. *"Maybe we can talk."*

Dillon wanted to howl with happiness that she was willing to entertain the idea of using their bond to communicate. That was more than he had hoped for, and he'd take any breadcrumbs she was willing to give him.

"I'm here if you need me before then." Dillon pulled back enough that he could feel her but so that he wouldn't feel intrusive to her. He wanted her to know she had control. They would move at her speed for as long as they needed to.

His attention returned fully to his trek. Mile after mile passed, and Dillon detected nothing out of place. It appeared that if any other vampires had been in the area, they were gone now. When he reached the pack mansion, he phased. He ran through the front entryway, yelling, "I need the pack medical personnel!" He knew they didn't have a healer. No one had even seen or heard of a gypsy healer in over a century. Packs had to make do with members learning medical skills. Taking one of their own to a hospital was out of the question, considering they healed so much more quickly than humans and their DNA looked different. The good news was *Canis lupus* were tough as nails.

Like most packs, the Colorado pack kept a stockpile of extra clothes on a shelf just inside the front door for just such emergencies. Dillon quickly threw on a shirt and pants. The first person to appear was Penelope, and Dillon was glad he'd gotten his clothes on before she came around the corner.

"What's going on?"

"Where's Jeremiah?" he barked, his voice sounding harsher than he intended. She flinched, so he took a breath and softened his voice. "We were attacked by vampires."

"I'm here." Jeremiah's large form appeared from the common room. "Where are the others?"

"They're right behind me, in human form. Rusty was hurt badly. He couldn't walk."

Jeremiah pushed past Dillon out the door. Dillon followed and saw the alpha scanning the surrounding woods. He could hear the man muttering under his breath. "Cursed vampires." He turned back to Dillon. "How much farther behind were they?"

"They should be here any minute," Dillon scanned the forest. "Kevin and Gabe were both injured, as well."

"Yet you managed to escape unhurt?" Jeremiah's eyes narrowed on him.

Dillon didn't miss the accusatory tone of Jeremiahs' voice. He turned and stared at the alpha. This time, he didn't hesitate to lock eyes with the man. "I came ahead to make sure we wouldn't be ambushed on the way back." Dillon growled. "I did what I thought was best for our pack."

Jeremiah sniffed and turned back to the forest. Just then, the three men emerged from the woods—Kevin and Gabe hobbling along on foot, Rusty in Kevin's arms. Jeremiah watched them come but didn't move from the porch. Dillon fought the urge to run to Kevin and take Rusty himself but knew the pack was expected to take cues from the alpha. If Jeremiah wasn't telling someone to help them then he didn't want someone to help them. *Ass,* Dillon mentally growled. He had a feeling it was going to be a nickname for his soon to be father-in-law.

When they reached the steps, Jeremiah motioned them inside. "Take him to the infirmary." He turned to Penelope, who was standing off to the side, watching them with large eyes. "Nell, see to him. You're the closest thing we have to a healer."

Kevin climbed the steps. As he stepped past Dillon,

Rusty put out a hand and grabbed Dillon's arms. "You saved my life, Dillon. I won't soon forget it."

"Get him inside," Jeremiah barked.

Rusty let go, and Kevin hurried inside, with Gabe and Penelope following.

When they were alone, Jeremiah turned to Dillon. He stared at him, his eyes roaming over Dillon's face as if he could decipher some sort of deception. After the time he'd spent with the three males, hearing how they felt about their alpha, not to mention Tanya's own opinion, Dillon wasn't about to give Jeremiah a reason to kill him. This pack needed someone who could possibly stand up to their current alpha. It might take time, years even, but one day Dillon would be that person. He just had to bide his time.

"I take it you didn't find any rogues?" Jeremiah finally asked after at least a minute of silence.

"Not a one." Dillon crossed his arms in front of his chest. "Which, honestly, alpha, as strong as your pack is and as well-known as you are for your strength, I can't imagine rogues even attempting to get into your land." He quickly held up his hands. "I'm not saying it doesn't happen. I, of course, believe you. But I'm glad it wasn't the case this time. Maybe it means they've learned their lesson."

Jeremiah grunted, but his face seemed less angry and more smug. "How many vampires?"

"Five."

"So you were not evenly matched," The alpha's brow rose. "How is it that you didn't get a single scratch on you, but I have three injured pack mates?" The skepticism in his voice that Dillon could possibly fight off multiple vampires was, frankly, insulting.

Dillon's hackle rose as his arms dropped to his sides, his

hands curling into tight fists. "Surely you don't think that I was working *with* those vampires?" His teeth ground together as he felt his wolf rising to the surface ready to rip out Jeremiah's throat. *It would be one less thing to worry about,* his beast pointed out. Dillon ignored him.

Jeremiah's lips dropped down into frown. "No." He shook his head and actually looked a little upset that he believed his own words.

Ass, Dillon thought again.

The alpha shrugged. "I just find it peculiar that there were five of them and four of you, and you managed to remain unharmed."

"Doesn't always matter the number of foe." Dillon made sure to calm himself down and swallow his pride. "Fighters all have different levels of skill. I am older than each of those men." He motioned to the door they'd disappeared through. "I've been fighting a lot longer."

"Mm-hmm," Jeremiah nodded. "Why is that? Have you had a lot of enemies to fight in your life?"

"I fight when necessary. Not for any other reason," he said matter-of-factly.

The alpha tilted his head as if needing to look at Dillon from a different orientation. "I suppose for now I'll have to take your word on that. Your actions will reinforce if you're telling me the truth."

"A man's word is all he has until he can prove those words to you through actions. You're giving me that chance, and I appreciate it." Even Dillon could hear the sincerity in his voice when he spoke. Because it *was* the truth. Jeremiah could have just killed him for coming onto his pack lands uninvited. Not that it would have gone over well with other pack alphas when they'd heard, but it was still Jeremiah's prerogative, and it would have been the voice of a live alpha against the lack of voice from a dead lone wolf. So, yes, he was grateful.

"I hope that's the case, son." Jeremiah's last word almost sounded like a threat.

Dillon swallowed. Just that one word "*son*" and the way it was said made Dillon think Tanya's worries might already be warranted. Jeremiah was digging further than the Montana pack.

"You can continue to show me you're a man of your word during this probationary time. You can help by training my fighters, your future pack mates." He started toward the door, walking past Dillon, then said over his shoulder, "Don't make me regret this decision."

He sighed and leaned his head back, looking up at the night sky now darted with silver stars. Dealing with the likes of Jeremiah Ellis was exhausting. The air was crisp now that the sun had set, and Dillon enjoyed the slight burn he felt in his lungs when he breathed. When he lowered his head back down, Dillon ran a hand over it and started forward. He needed to check on the three males and then he could use a shower. He hoped that maybe Tanya would still be willing to talk to him. He was worried about her. She sounded exhausted when he'd spoken to her earlier. His arms longed to hold her tightly to him and protect her from the weight of the world. Dillon wanted to give her everything she needed and make her life easier. Unfortunately, he had a feeling that he was going to make it worse before it got better. "Damn," he breathed out as he marched inside. "*One minute at a time*," his wolf told him. *Focus on this minute.* There was no point in worrying about things he couldn't change. It would only cripple him and make him feel hopeless. A male *Canis lupus* looking for his mate, or waiting on her, had no room for hopelessness. He would do as Jeremiah bid and train the alpha's warriors. He would give his mate the gift of the best damn fighters of any pack to help protect her, and he would do it until she came home. Then he could fall at her feet and pledge his faithfulness to her. Hopefully, that would be sooner rather than later.

CHAPTER ELEVEN

"Have you ever wanted to close your eyes and hope they didn't reopen? Not because you wanted to die, but because you just didn't want to deal with the difficult things in your life. You're tired and beat up, and there are no more places for metaphorical bandages on your body. I just want to lay my head down, close my eyes, and just breathe. Breathe and nothing more." ~Tanya

Orson and Huck made their way down the sidewalk of Main Street in Coldspring, Texas. Huck had been pleasantly surprised at how easy it was to find out information about Dillon Jacobs. Everyone in town seemed to want to talk about him. Apparently, his sudden disappearance was the biggest thing that had happened in Coldspring in years. No one could believe it because he'd been such an outstanding member of the community, and everyone had their own theories as to why Dillon had left town. Dillon had only been gone a few days, but the news must have spread throughout the town like wildfire.

The waitress at the diner where they'd had breakfast said one woman would know for sure what had happened to Dillon—his girlfriend, Lilly Pierce. But to the disappointment of every busybody in town, Lilly had refused to tell anyone anything. Huck hoped they could convince the woman to talk. He didn't want to threaten anyone; Huck wasn't that kind of wolf. But he also knew what Jeremiah would do if they didn't get the information he wanted. The waitress told them Lilly worked at Book Lover's Den bookstore, which was where they were now heading.

"Odd that Dillon would leave his girlfriend, don't you think?" Huck asked as they walked.

"No. What's odd is that he had a girlfriend to begin with. If she wasn't his true mate then what the hell was he doing with her?" Orson glanced around at the sleepy town. "But there is something else I find even more strange than that."

Huck glanced sidelong at his pack mate. "What's that?"

"We've yet to run into a single wolf." Orson motioned around them. "And yet, I keep getting a hint of *Canis lupus* on the air. I haven't heard anything about a pack being in Coldspring, Texas. Have you?" People shuffled along the sidewalk, many of them glancing at the two males. It was obvious they weren't from around these parts. Coldspring was small enough that anyone new in town was immediate news.

"Me either," Huck considered. "Which means his girlfriend is most likely human."

Orson pointed at him. "Exactly."

Huck scrunched up his face. "Hmm, it's not completely

unheard of. It would actually be more taboo if he'd been dating a she-wolf."

Orson continued as they made their way in the direction of the bookstore. "And the waitress said this Lilly woman and Dillon had been together for years. Finding his mate after being with someone that long, that's got to be a kick to the gut for everyone involved."

"Sucks, especially for his mate." Huck noticed that they were across the street from where the waitress had pointed. It wasn't a big store, but then in a town this size, nothing was big.

"So we think that he's found his mate and that she must be in our pack since that's where he showed up. Who do you think it is?" Orson asked as they started across the street.

"I don't know, but I think the alpha already has an idea."

"Why?"

"Well, he swore us to secrecy, didn't he?" Huck pointed out. "Jeremiah threatened to skin me if I breathed a word to anyone about this mission. And I believed him, too. Why else would he be so hush-hush about this?"

"Well"—Orson glanced at Huck—"recently there was one female down this way from our pack. Maybe they came through Texas on their way back home."

Huck glanced up at the sky. "Son of a troll." He sighed. "That would not be good."

His pack mate shook his head. "Nope. It would definitely be pretty much the worst possible outcome. Considering it's looking like Dillon had a serious relationship with a woman who wasn't his true mate."

"If we somehow confirm that"—he held up his hands and shook his head—"I'm not telling the alpha. Let Jeremiah and Dillon work that out themselves. Let's talk to this Lilly chick and find out what's going on. Then we'll get our butts back to Colorado. And maybe along the way we'll figure out why we're scenting *Canis lupus*."

They stepped up to the Book Lover's Den bookstore and pushed open the door. A few customers milled about inside, but the wolves couldn't see anyone with a name badge or uniform that indicated they worked there.

Huck tilted his head up and took a deep breath. "Smell that?" He pitched his voice so only Orson's wolf hearing could hear him.

Orson took a sniff and nodded. "*Canis lupus*."

Huck glanced from side to side, searching for the scent. "Keep your eyes open."

Orson shrugged. "What? Am I really going to walk through this store with my damn eyes closed?

"You know what I mean, jackass."

The pair moved farther into the store, all of their senses on high alert. A long counter holding cash registers ran the length of one wall. Behind it, a door led to the back of the store. Orson motioned with his head to the door. "The scent is stronger here. It must be coming from the back."

Then the wolves froze. "You hear that?" Huck asked as the sound of soft crying came from beyond the door. It was so faint that Huck had to strain his ears. Huck glanced around, but none of the customers looked up from the books they were perusing.

The two wolves went around the counter and leaned closer to the door, Huck's ears pricked up. A woman wasn't just crying. She was sobbing. Huck heard muffled speaking. He and Orson looked at one another with narrowed eyes.

"It's tough, Lilly," a feminine voice said. "And I know

you're hurting. But I'm here for you, girl. Lord knows I didn't get out of bed for a week when Mark left me."

"You don't have to worry about that anymore, darlin'," a male voice rumbled. "I told you he's not important."

"Calm down, Gerald," the female chided. "I'm just trying to make Lilly feel better. This is girl stuff."

The sobs, which must have been Lilly's, quieted. "It's not just that Dillon left. That hurts. It really, really hurts. But I don't blame him. He made it clear from the beginning that what we had was temporary. So I knew it was coming."

"Was there someone else?" the male asked.

"Gerald!" the female that wasn't Lilly gasped. "How could you ask that?"

"Forgive me, Jennifer," Gerald said, though he didn't sound very sorry. "I know I'm still new, and it's not really my business. I'm just worried about you both."

Huck rolled his eyes. This guy wasn't worried about anything but his own interests.

Orson nudged his arm. "Wolf?" he mouthed and pointed to the door.

Huck nodded. He'd been thinking the same thing. This Gerald dude was the *Canis lupus* they'd been smelling. But according to his own words, he was new in town.

"How'd you know?" Jennifer asked.

Huck heard Lilly sigh. "I can't really tell you, Jennifer, but I knew. I've known for a long time. But I just didn't realize it would be this soon."

"Lilly, what's going on?"

"I don't know how to say this." Lilly sniffed loudly.-"But I've just got to tell someone, or I'm going to go crazy."

"What is it?" The concern was evident in Jennifer's voice.

"I'm—" Lilly paused.

Huck wanted to growl at her, "Spit it out, dammit."

"I'm—" She paused yet again.

You're what? Huck mentally barked at the woman. *A supernatural race that we actually haven't heard of? You're half troll? No, I got it, you're—*

"I'm pregnant." Lilly's words cut off his mental rant.

"Okay," he whispered. "I did *not* see that coming." Huck's stomach hit the floor as his head turned slowly to look at Orson, whose eyes were as wide as a full moon.

"By the man who left you?" Gerald sounded way too damn interested, even eager.

"Do you have to be here? I mean, no offense, Gerald, but Jennifer's known you all of a few days and this is well, it's private."

Jennifer gasped. "Oh, snap."

Understatement, Huck silently argued with the woman named Jennifer.

"I don't mean to intrude." Gerald's voice took on a gentler tone. "When Jennifer was on the phone with me, she mentioned you were having a rough time. So I brought you lunch. I only wanted to help. I'll be on my way. Jennifer, call me when you get off work."

"I will. Just go out that back door instead of going through the store. I don't need the boss knowing you were back here."

Huck heard the male's footsteps and made a note to go around and follow the scent as soon as they got as much information as they could.

"Do you think Dillon would leave because she told him she's pregnant?" Orson whispered.

Huck shook his head. "No way. Our young are too few and far between. Half-wolf or not."

"Lilly seemed to act like this Gerald guy was new to

town. He had to have shown up in the last couple of days," Orson pointed out. "That's not good."

"Rogue?" Huck offered.

"Probably." Orson nodded. "Which is even worse."

The wolves heard scuffling, and neither of the women said anything for several moments. Huck could only imagine Jennifer was giving Lilly a hug.

"Oh, my gosh. That's why Dillon left isn't it? That son of a bitch!"

Again, if he did, that would be an understatement, Jennifer. Keep up. Huck glared at the door that kept him from seeing the two women. Huck took a moment to turn and see if anyone had noticed them. He casually leaned himself so that it looked like he was just waiting on someone. It didn't seem like anyone had taken an interest in them. In fact, the store was relatively empty. He glanced down and saw that lunch time had passed. Everyone must have headed back to their jobs, having taken their breaks to come do some book shopping.

"No, no, no." Lilly sounded desperate, trying to dissuade her friend's train of thought. "That wasn't it. He doesn't know."

"You're kidding." Jennifer huffed and sounded a bit deflated. "You haven't told him?"

"He left before I got the chance." Lilly's voice sounded wobbly again as if she were once more on the verge of tears.

"Oh, Lilly."

And there it is, Huck thought as Lilly's sobbing returned in force.

Huck shook his head at Orson.

"When are you going to tell him?" Jennifer asked.

"I'm not," came Lilly's shaky reply.

"Lilly, you have to."

"No, I can't. There's a lot about Dillon you don't know, Jennifer." She sniffed. "No one around here knows. And I can't tell anyone, but it's enough for you to know that Dillon cannot be a father, not to my child."

"Wait, are you talking about, like, top-secret government-spy stuff? Is he an escaped convict?"

Huck snorted. If it was only as simple as either of those things.

"The stuff humans come up with," Orson murmured.

Lilly sighed again. "Something like that."

"Not even close, female," Huck interjected, though the females obviously couldn't hear his rebuttal. He looked toward the entrance of the store to see if the Gerald guy had come around. He wouldn't be surprised if the male had scented them. If he was a rogue, he'd wait to ambush them. A respectable pack wolf would walk straight up and introduce himself.

"Well, try not to worry, Lilly."

"Yes, Lilly," Orson whispered. "Don't worry that you're having a half-werewolf baby. No big deal."

Huck mentally cringed. "He seems to have told her about himself at least. But now she's here all alone with no one to help her go through this." He paused. "Except this Gerald character." He shook his head. "That's not a good sign."

"Makes me want to kick his ass," Orson rumbled. "She sounds like a good woman. An understanding female. She wasn't even mad that he left. And you're right. This Gerald dude is bad news."

"I'm here for you," her friend continued. "We all are. The people in this town stick together. You know that. If you need anything at all, you just ask. I think Gerald would hunt him down for you and kick Dillon's ass if you wanted."

Lilly's voice quavered. "Thank you, Jennifer. And no, I don't want that."

"And one thing's for sure, girl. You're going to be one hell of a mom."

Huck jerked his head to the front of the store. Orson nodded, and the pair made their way out. When they got outside, Orson looked at Huck. "I was not expecting that. Not the baby and sure as hell not another wolf mixed up with human females."

"Nope." Huck blew out a deep breath, puffing out his cheeks. "That is crazy. Can you imagine having a baby with a human? The only half-wolf I've ever met is Penelope, and she was raised by our pack. I don't know if she even knows who her parents are, wolf or human."

Orson shook his head. "She's never talked about it."

Huck mentally rolled his eyes. *She's never talked about it because our alpha doesn't like to acknowledge that they have a dormant wolf in their pack. He considers her their dirty little secret. It's only because of the alpha female that Nell was allowed to live with them.*

"Can you imagine being raised by a human?" Orson scrunched up his nose as if the idea was repugnant.

"If it was one that seemed as kind as this Lilly chick"—he motioned over his shoulder toward the bookstore—"then it might not be a bad thing. Considering Tanya's been raised by *Canis lupus,* and she seemed to have drawn the short end of the stick. At least when it comes to her father." Huck glanced at him then up and down the street. "Well, I think we've gathered enough intel to satisfy the alpha. But we need to see if we can figure out who this Gerald is and if he has any more wolves with him. He must be very new to town since no one has mentioned him."

Orson whistled. "Boy, I can't imagine what Jeremiah is going to do when he finds out about this, but I damn sure wouldn't want to be in Dillon's shoes when he does."

"Me either. I'm pissed at Dillon, and I don't even know the guy. He even entered into this relationship knowing that he would most likely have to leave her. The least he could have done was taken steps to prevent pregnancy. But now here's this woman with a half-supernatural child that she will be raising alone. Not to mention that Dillon won't know his child." Huck couldn't even imagine not knowing his child, be it full *Canis lupus* or half-human. "And now there's a wolf in town who knows about this dormant. It's a messed-up situation. Maybe we should wait and tell Jeremiah once we get back. He'll probably want to kill Dillon, and if Tanya's his mate, that would hurt her. I might not like our alpha, but I care for Tanya."

"Yeah, but if we call him and tell him what we know, then *we* might live to comfort Tanya when her mate is killed," Orson pointed out, though Huck could tell he didn't fully mean it. He didn't want Tanya hurt any more than Huck did.

"Might as well get it over with." Huck made the decision for them.

Huck and Orson walked down the street, looking for a place to contact their alpha. "There." A dilapidated gas station stood before them. On the outside wall hung a grimy pay phone.

They approached the phone, and Huck dug in his pockets. "Damn. Got any change?" He held out a hand to Orson.

The other wolf dug in his own pockets. "Nope."

Huck passed him a couple of bucks. "Go inside and grab

us some drinks. Make sure to get a couple of quarters. And pay attention to your surroundings."

"On it." Orson took the money and sauntered inside.

Huck surveyed the small town nestled among acres and acres of cattle land. He thanked the Great Luna that he lived in the mountains of Colorado. There were such plentiful game in the Colorado wilderness to hunt, huge mule deer, and even elk. Not that their alpha ever let them hunt like they should. Huck clenched and unclenched his fists. *Bastard.*

Huck could imagine there was probably game aplenty in this wilderness, as well. He thought he could remember Texas was overrun with wild hogs. Those would probably be a blast to hunt. He thought about suggesting the idea to Orson. What if they were to get in a quick hunt before they went back to Colorado? Who would know? Then again, they did have a hunt to go on, and their prey was named Gerald. *Who are you Gerald, and what's your game?*

He turned and looked into the gas station window. *What the hell is taking Orson so long?* Huck could see his partner trying to decide which stick of beef jerky to buy. *Dammit, Orson. Come on.* With the rogue on Huck's mind, he was antsy to be standing in one place too long.

As he turned back around, Huck caught a glimpse of a man coming around the side of the gas station. Immediately, his wolf perked up. The scent hit him, and he recognized it as the same one he'd smelled at the back of the bookstore. Gerald was followed by another man, then another. Six in all. He was around the side of the building, and there was not another soul in sight. As a gust of wind hit him, the scent of *Canis lupus* filled Huck's nostrils. He realized he hadn't smelled them before because the wind was blowing the wrong direction.

Oh, shit. Huck let his claws extend as his wolf attempted to take over, but he kept his beast under control while he quickly debated what to do. He wasn't a coward, but being outnumbered six to one, running definitely crossed Huck's mind. But that would leave Orson alone with these goons. Huck wouldn't do that.

"You're not from around here," Gerald said as they surrounded Huck in a semicircle. "Though your scent is now familiar. Tell me, how long have you known Lilly? And where is this Dillon character?"

Huck tried to surreptitiously glance back into the gas station to see if Orson had realized what was happening. *Damn wolf is probably buying a slushie.* "Don't know her at all, and don't know about this Dillon character. Just passing through to get what's supposed to be a world-famous slushie. And I like a good book when I travel. That's the only reason I stopped in." Huck glanced again back toward the direction Orson should be coming.

Gerald shook his head. "Don't bother calling out to your friend. My wolves are looking for a fight, and loud noises make them jumpy. You yell for help, and they attack. But I'm a reasonable alpha. I like to ask questions first, then fight second."

Huck's brow rose. "Alpha? I wasn't aware that there was a pack in these parts."

The wolf shrugged and motioned to others. "This looks like a pack to me. And it also looks like you are encroaching on my territory."

Huck glanced around. "If we'd have known there was a pack here, we'd have checked in. As it is, there's not been a pack in Texas in quite some time."

"And I'm not a fool. You've not just been looking for a book. You've been poking around, asking a bunch of questions around town." Gerald ignored Huck's response. "Why?"

Huck shoved his hands into his pockets and rocked back on his heels. "Our alpha sent us here on a mission. That's all I can say." Huck hadn't even considered that if they found Gerald, they might find more wolves. Rogues typically traveled in very small numbers because they couldn't get along. Three or less. And if it was larger than that, they didn't stay together long because their constant fighting simply got them killed. So to see double the normal numbers together was surprising. That meant they most likely were a group of rogues that had managed to build a hierarchy that kept them under control. Which meant Gerald was a damn dominant wolf.

"No." The so-called alpha narrowed his eyes. "I think you can say more. If you don't, I'll have to let my wolves loosen your tongue."

Just then, Huck heard the gas station door open, which he assumed was Orson exiting the building. The wolves in front of Huck turned at the sound. Huck didn't waste time. He leaped at Gerald and slashed out a claw. But the alpha was lightning quick. He recovered just in time to duck the swipe, then he buried his fist in Huck's stomach.

Huck's breath whooshed from his lungs, but he raised up and leapt at the alpha. There were yells and snarls, as the other wolves fell on him. Then all Huck could see was fists, fangs, and claws. He was being pushed around to the back of the building where he knew no one would witness the attack.

"What the hell," Orson yelled as a pair of wolves broke away from Huck. They were going after his comrade.

Huck snarled and cursed his attackers, and he even managed to get a good hit on one before feeling something hard strike him in the back of his head. He went down in a heap. The world went fuzzy, and he heard ringing in his ears. Everything faded to darkness. He couldn't have been out longer than a minute or two because when he came to, Huck felt himself being lifted and dragged across the parking lot. He was hoisted up and tossed effortlessly into the back of a van. Huck heard a grunt and turned his head. His vision returned just enough for him to see Orson land beside him like a sack of dirty laundry. He thought his friend was alive, but he certainly wasn't conscious. Pain radiated in his own head, and he fought to stay awake. The last thing Huck heard was squealing tires before the darkness took him under.

CHAPTER
TWELVE

"Growing up is about learning to make hard decisions and sticking by them. It's about accepting that there are things you cannot change. You can either let them destroy you or make you stronger. It's about taking a stand that might be unpopular. In short, growing up is damn hard, and there's no stopping it." ~Tanya

Tanya was exhausted, both mentally and physically. She had spent the entire day preparing for Lisa's funeral, something she never thought she would have to do. However, she couldn't just leave it to Tyler and his pack. Lisa may have been a human member of the Missouri pack, but she was like family to Tanya. They had shared many years of laughter, tears, and complaints about her father, which had cemented a friendship Tanya would treasure for the rest of her life.

Now, Tanya stood in Lisa's bedroom. She had asked Tyler if she could stay in Lisa's home until the funeral, which was a few days away. Tanya knew it would probably be the last time she would ever be there again, and her father would expect her home as soon as it was over.

Tanya took a deep breath and let her old friend's scent saturate her lungs. She looked around the room, reminiscing about the times she had laid on Lisa's bed, listening to her talk about the drama within the Missouri pack, her life, and her unfulfilled dreams. Tanya could still see Lisa's smile and the way her eyes crinkled at the corners when she laughed. She had a full body laugh that Tanya couldn't resist joining in with.

As Tanya sat down on the bed, she noticed various medicine bottles lined up neatly on the bedside table. A worn Bible sat by them, and next to that, rested another book with an aged cover. She lifted it and saw the word 'journal' written on the front. Tanya scooted over on the bed, pulling her legs up and leaning her back against the headboard. As she crossed her ankles and ran her hand across the cracked cover of the journal, she pursed her lips.

Tanya asked the empty room, "How mad will you be at me if I read your thoughts, old lady?" She imagined Lisa's spirit sitting there beside her. "It's not like you can scold me, but I wouldn't put it past you to haunt me and do scary crap like make doors close on their own and rocking chairs rock with no one sitting in them." Tanya glanced around the room as if Lisa would suddenly appear and tell her to quit touching her things. Because that's exactly what Lisa would do and then probably smack Tanya's hand. Tanya smiled slightly. "Damn, I miss you already."

Tears welled up in her eyes, but she took a deep breath and blinked them away. Tanya didn't want to cry anymore, even though she knew there would be many more tears to come. For the moment, she just wanted to stop feeling anything. If she didn't know that Lisa didn't drink, she'd go in search of some alcohol. But it took a lot of liquor for one of her kind to get drunk. *Not that getting drunk would help anything*, Lisa's voice filled her mind. Not her actual voice, of course, but the memory of something Lisa would have said. "I don't need your lecture," Tanya said to the imaginary Lisa. "If I want to get drunk, I damn well will."

"Could you refrain until I'm there to watch your back?" Dillon's voice filled her mind.

Dammit. She needed to pay closer attention to the walls. They had come crumbling down earlier that day, and she'd been unable to re-erect them.

"I need some space tonight, Dillon," she said as gently as she could. He'd been through a lot facing off with vampires and keeping his promise to ensure pack mates stayed alive. Tanya didn't want to be a bitch even if she was still struggling with their whole situation. She thought maybe she'd be able to talk to him, to ask some questions, but she just didn't have the energy.

"I hope you're able to get some rest tonight, mate. If you need me, I'm here."

He pulled back, and she felt him in the recesses of her mind, far enough away that he was offering her privacy, for which she was very grateful. Not all males would be so accommodating, especially with their unclaimed mate. The males of her kind were possessive, and that was putting it lightly. Dillon was proving that he had some serious self-control and compassion. "Shit." And she was crying again.

She flipped the journal open, needing her mind to focus on something else, and privately promised Lisa that whatever she read in the pages of the book in her hand, she'd never share with another soul. The pages were aged, showing that this book had been in Lisa's possession for a very long time.

Dear Journal, the first entry began. There was no date, which Tanya found odd. Didn't people date their diary entries? Then again, what did she know about journaling? The closest she'd ever come to keeping any sort of journal would be the list of people she wanted to kick in the shins for being jerks. That was a form of a journal, right? She snorted. Lisa would have said absolutely.

I'm not even sure if that's how I should start each entry. I mean, who is a journal? I suppose I could be talking to God instead of an inanimate object called a journal. Okay, let's go with that.

Dear God,

This has been a hard day. A hard week. Hell, it's been a hard month. I feel like I should be pulling myself together, and yet I just find that the best I can do each day is breathe. That's an accomplishment, isn't it? If it's not, then it should be considered one. It needs to be added to the list of things you can get an acknowledgment for. Where? I've no clue. Maybe just a shout out from someone on the street who sees that you're upright, walking, and therefore breathing. Is applause too much to ask for after your husband has died and you've somehow managed not to join him six feet under?

Tanya's mouth dropped open as she reread the paragraph. Lisa had been a widow? How had Tanya not known? Why hadn't Lisa told her? "I told you everything, you old bitty," Tanya growled. "And you leave out this very important part of your past? If you were alive right now, I'd throw something at you. And it wouldn't be something soft." She blew out a breath and refocused on the page.

How is it possible to be only twenty-five and a widow? Only four years married and now he's gone. It's not fair. And I know that life isn't fair. Really, I do, but it's so much easier to say that to some other poor chump.

Tanya snorted at her friend's words. Lisa had always been a sassy pants, even years ago.

But it's a completely different pill to swallow myself. In fact, I'd rather just vomit that sucker up and have my husband back. Thanks. Today's one of those days where I can be a smart-ass about it. Tomorrow I'll most likely be a sobbing mess. Just the other day, I broke down in the grocery line. I dropped my bread and eggs on the ground and ran out like I was being chased by something scary. Which, to be clear, I was. I'm constantly chased by the thoughts of all the things I will never share with the man I expected to spend my life with. What will I do now? I suppose I can become the creepy cat lady. Not crazy because crazy has been overdone. Creepy, however, hasn't been touched. So I'll be the creepy cat lady. That's all I can do tonight. I'm running out of smart-ass things to say, and I'm slipping into my pity party segment of the evening. Goodnight, God. I'll be talking to you tomorrow. Most likely, it will be every bit as fun as this conversation has been.

Tanya's heart felt like a hand had wrapped around it and was squeezing as hard as possible. Her lungs were closing off, and she sucked in short breaths in an attempt to breathe. She could feel the emotion bleeding from the pen onto the pages like blood from her own veins. Even if she hadn't known Lisa, the words would have been etched on Tanya's soul, as if they were somehow her own emotions reflected on the page.

The pen had been pressed so hard into the pages that Tanya could feel the indentations as she ran her finger across the paper. Had there been anyone there for Lisa to talk to besides the journal she'd written to God? Had there been a person for Lisa like she was for Tanya? She could picture a younger version of Lisa sitting in her room all alone, surrounded by the emptiness that had once been filled with the sound of her husband's voice. Tanya could imagine how suffocating that might be. She pressed her hand to her chest as the ache dug deeper, all the way to her back, knocking the wind out of her. She was scared to turn the page. If that was Lisa being a smart-ass about her grief, then Tanya didn't want to read a page where she'd been a sobbing mess, as her friend had written.

"Mother of pixies, Lisa," Tanya snapped. "This is what you show me on today of all days? You couldn't have shared this a few years ago, like 'Hey, Tanya, look at this old as dirt book and all the things I've endured, and look how awesome I am despite what I've been through?' Is that too much to ask?" Okay, so considering it was Tanya's snooping that had brought the journal to light, it wasn't really Lisa's fault, but Tanya needed to be pissed because otherwise she'd just curl up in a ball on the floor.

Instead of turning the page, Tanya flipped through several more, jumping ahead in the journal. She stopped at random and read.

Dear God, It's been a while. Life got busy. I found it easier to deal with my grief if I didn't have to think. Honestly, writing to you sometimes just made it worse. Not because of you. I mean, I don't believe that you did this. It's just a part of life. Death is the beginning because the second we breathe, we begin to die. Some lives last longer than others, but each one has a purpose. I know that now. I've gone and become a nurse. That was challenging, but a good distraction. Sometimes I still cry occasionally, though it's been three years since Toby passed. I used to think about him every day. But now, I have days that go by when I'm able to live life without his memory constantly haunting me. And the memories I do have are good ones that make me smile.

I'm coming to you for a different reason today. And I'm sorry that I've let it go this long. I'm not just stopping in to ask for something. Mostly, I just want to pour out the confusion I'm feeling. You see, I've become close to someone. I wasn't looking for him. In fact, I didn't think it was possible to love someone the way I loved Toby. I thought he was it for me, and my future was destined for either half-relationships where I settled for second best or that I would just be alone. Being alone appealed to me more than the former. But then, I was walking through the grocery store and bumped into this man. He was so apologetic and worried that he'd hurt me. He's a lot bigger than I am, so it wasn't a stretch that he could have hurt me. Long story short, that wasn't the first time we ran into one another. Turned out that he works at the same hospital I do. He was new and worked on the south wing while I worked on the north.

It's been a year since we started dating. I fell hard and fast, and I felt guilty, like there was this cancer inside of me—"

"Foreshadowing much, Lisa?" Tanya growled while her eyes stayed glued to the page, unbelieving of what she was reading. "I feel like I'm going to vomit."

Was she talking to a dead woman? Yes? Did she care? Nope. Maybe she was going crazy. Tanya could handle crazy. What she wasn't sure she could handle was just how much Lisa's words were affecting her. She sighed and then continued reading.

His name is Charles, and I told him about Toby, of course. I wasn't going to treat my first husband like a dirty secret. Charles was extremely understanding. I couldn't comprehend how he wasn't jealous or worried that I wouldn't be able to love him the way I loved Toby. And believe it or not, me and my big mouth asked him all of this one night. It was like I was trying to get him to kick me to the curb. But you know what he said? I mean, you do, because you're God. But I'm going to tell you, anyway.

He told me that one of the greatest gifts you gave humans was the ability to choose to love. It's not forced on us. You don't force us to love you, and yet you still love us. You've given us the capacity to have room in our hearts for more than one person. We don't only love one of our children; we love all of them. Just because we care for one friend doesn't mean we can't care equally for another. Charles said it was the same for loving a partner. But that no matter how attracted or infatuated I might be with him, ultimately it would be my choice to love him. He asked me if Toby would want me to spend the rest of my life alone, in a constant state of grief over my loss of him. And I know the answer to that question is "No." Toby would never be so selfish as to want that for me. So ultimately it came down to me. My choice to either decide that loving Charles would somehow be betraying Toby or accepting that I could love another and it didn't take away from my time with my first husband.

I asked Charles how it made him feel to know that I loved someone before him, that I had memories and firsts that I wouldn't be able to have with him. He said he wouldn't have wished for me to be alone all the time before I was able to meet him. He said he was happy that I had someone to care for me and love me. How in the world did I find this man? Was it you? Did you send him to me?

I've decided that I can't let my past determine my future. It will always impact the direction of my life, of course. But how I let it impact my life is up to me. I will take the lessons I learned in my first marriage and carry them over to this one. I will find joy in the fact that someone will choose to love me even though he wasn't my first love. To be fair, I wasn't his first love either. He dated a woman for a long time who said no to his proposal. Her loss. And no, I don't hold that relationship or those feelings against him. It would be cruel to do so. Every experience in life shapes us into the person we are becoming. I want to be better than I was yesterday. I want my grief to become joy and my sorrow to be something I can use to help others who might find themselves in the same position. Such a time as this, right?

I'm grateful you gave me Toby. And I wouldn't change those four years even though I lost him. I am also grateful for Charles and the future I have with him. Hopefully, I won't go so long without sharing my life with you. One thing I have learned over the past year is that the best way to learn about love is from the one who created it to begin with. Though I have not written much to you, I have read my Bible. And if you can love me, despite all of my shortcomings, then I have the capacity to do the same, because you put that love in me. Help me know who it is that will need that love, who it is that I will one day share this story with. And thank you, God. Thank you for Toby and Charles and all the people who have loved me and showed me that I have room in my heart to love more than once with just as much fervor.

There were many more pages filled with writing. Tanya noticed that over the years the handwriting became less smooth, and toward the end it was nothing but chicken scratch. She envisioned Lisa, with her feeble hands, shaking as she wielded the pen, still wanting to share her thoughts with the God she obviously loved. Maybe later, a long time from now, Tanya would read more of those pages, but for now, she felt as if she'd been run through the ringer, beat with a stick, hung out in a storm, and pelted with sleet only to then be subjected to the blistering sun and burned to a crisp. In short, she felt like shit. "Thank you, Lisa. I totally needed that right now."

What irked Tanya even more was that Lisa's words were the truth. They were words Tanya needed to hear, or in this case, read. But that didn't mean she wanted them. It was easier to consider Dillon the enemy. It was easier to think that he purposefully hurt her because then she didn't have to face her own shortcomings. Was she so selfish that she would begrudge him love just because their kind were destined to have a soul mate? She'd like to say no. But the anger inside of her proved her to be a liar. It might never stop being taboo or unacceptable for any of their kind, male or female, to have a relationship with someone who wasn't their true mate. But Tanya had to admit that it was harder on the males to refrain from taking a human partner. The darkness that lived inside of them would eventually turn their beasts into feral wolves. That must be a very difficult thing to face alone. They weren't robots. The male *Canis lupus* couldn't just turn their feelings off. And she didn't believe that their own Creator would only give them the capacity to love one person. Maybe that love was very different from the love they would give their true mate, but did it honestly make them betrayers? What if she had fallen in love with a human male? Would she want her true mate to try to understand and forgive her, despite the inevitable feelings of betrayal?

She snorted and shook her head. Of course she would. It would destroy her to be rejected by the male created for her. No matter their past choices, their souls were meant for one another. And unlike humans, they would never be complete without each other.

Tanya set the journal beside her on the bed and ran a hand down her face as her head dropped so that her chin almost touched her chest. Her body was exhausted. Her mind, even more so. And her wolf longed for their mate to wrap her in his arms and tell her he was there. She wouldn't go through tomorrow alone as she stood beside Lisa's grave site and watched the casket being lowered into her eternal resting place.

As she lifted her head, her eyes widened, and she pushed herself up even straighter. Standing at the end of the bed was the Great Luna in all her glory. Tanya immediately slid from the bed and kneeled on the floor, bowing her head in reverence. "Creator," she whispered as tears filled her eyes. The only thing better than her mate's arms was her Creator's.

"My child," the Great Luna said, her voice full of compassion and love. "I feel your pain, and I ache with you. I created you to be with your one soul mate because strong bonds create strong families, which create a strong, healthy pack. I created your relationships to be committed through the Blood Rites which tie you together for life. Yes, you have the capacity to love others. But my best for you comes in the form of the one I've set apart for you. Does that mean you don't forgive? Absolutely not."

Warmth enveloped Tanya and her chest, which had been twisted tightly inside of her, loosened so she could breathe easier.

"Forgiveness is the greatest kind of love you can give another. But you see what has happened between you and my son, Dillon. Pain comes from stepping off my path for you. There are consequences of going your own way. But I can take those consequences and use them for good. There is nothing that I am surprised by. Dillon is no less yours now than he was before his decision. But it must be your choice to love him regardless of his past. Just as it must be his choice to be understanding of the pain his choices have caused you. Do you want bitterness to eat you out from the inside, touching all of those who come in contact with you? Or do you want grace and forgiveness to be your legacy for generations to come?"

Tanya lifted her head as she felt the Great Luna's hand

on her chin. Tears streamed down her eyes as the goddess lowered herself and pressed a kiss to Tanya's head.

"Don't turn away that gift I have given you because of pride. Build the life I have intended for you and see the great things that I will do with you and Dillon. I saw you before you were a thought in your parents' minds. I planned your future, and it is for good and hope. Do not give that up so easily."

The light filling the room faded, and Tanya covered her face as she wept. She wanted what her Creator had for her. She wanted to leave a legacy for generations that would be a blessing. Tanya would not let anger and bitterness be what ruled her.

"Dillon?" she called out through the bond. The weariness she'd felt earlier eased a bit after the Great Luna's touch.

"I'm here."

She took a deep breath. *"Will you tell me about yourself?"*

Tanya felt his relief but also his hesitation. He didn't want to hurt her. She could feel his desperate need to protect her from anything, even himself.

"Please. I want to know the man I will spend my life with. The good, the bad, and the ugly. I assure you, I am not perfect. No matter how much I'd like to think I am."

He huffed out a laugh and then seemed to make a decision. *"I was born into the Montana pack by parents who couldn't have been better examples of what it meant to love without conditions,"* he began.

Tanya stood back up and settled on Lisa's bed, getting comfortable as she listened to the rumble of his voice.

"I had an ideal childhood within a small but strong pack. We lived in peace and abundance. And I thought life would always be that easy. I longed for the day when I would meet my

true mate, and I could share with her the kind of faithfulness that my father showed my mother." He paused, and Tanya found herself reaching through the bond, picturing his hand and wrapping hers around his. He, in turn, held on tightly as he continued. *"I never imagined tragedy would touch my perfect world. But that was before hunters discovered wolves—large wolves living in the Montana mountains. Wolves the size of which they'd never seen. And killing one became an obsession for many of them. We were the ultimate prize in their need to have the largest predator stuffed in their homes to show off like a shiny trophy."*

Bile rose in Tanya's throat as she listened. She wanted to tell him to stop, but she also felt like he needed to tell her. Dillon needed to share this story with someone that would completely understand. Even if he once shared it with the human woman, that female would never fully understand what it was to be *Canis lupus*, to be hunted like an animal and treated as if your existence were simply for sport.

"One day, while my parents were out hunting on their own, without the pack, they were ambushed. Both were killed. Something inside of me died that day."

He seemed to be ashamed of that admission, though Tanya wasn't sure why. He wasn't responsible for the death of his parents, and no one could fault him for feeling destroyed.

"Yes, I had the right to grieve." He answered her confused thoughts. *"But instead of being there with my pack, grieving with them because I wasn't the only one hurting, I ran. I only thought about how their deaths affected me. I wanted to get as far from their deaths as I could, though obviously that wasn't possible."* He sighed, and Tanya felt the heavy burden on his shoulders. *"Their deaths followed me, as did the anger that*

grew inside of me. I lived for a decade as a lone wolf in the small town of Coldspring. And that was where I met Lilly."

She winced at the woman's name, but then took a deep breath and drew strength from not only Lisa's words but her Creator's, as well.

"I could lie and say she was just a distraction from the pain that still lingered. But I won't disrespect you that way. She became a friend, then someone I loved. I gave her something I never should have, but I won't lie and say that I never cared for her. I regret my choices, leaving when I should have stayed with my pack. Remaining faithful to the woman I would one day meet and share my soul with. But I can't change them."

Tanya swallowed as she prepared herself for the answer to the question she was about to ask. *"Did you tell her what you are? Did she know that you would never really be hers?"* Tanya wasn't trying to be mean. She didn't know Lilly. She didn't know what kind of woman she was. But she couldn't help but feel curious about the type of female that would have drawn Dillon to her.

"After a time, yes. I told her. I didn't think it was fair to her that she did not know what she was getting involved with and what would one day happen. I gave her the choice to walk away because I would never truly be hers."

Tanya was surprised to realize that she felt sorry for Lilly. To love a man that couldn't love her to the same extent in return. *"And she chose you, anyway."*

"She did."

"I want her to be a villain. I don't want to admire her, and yet it would take a very loving woman to make such a choice. Did she ever show bitterness at her circumstances?"

Dillon seemed hesitant to answer. But then she felt his resolve. *"No. She was gracious. She said that the true mate I would one day meet would be the luckiest woman on earth. I pointed out that my future mate might not feel that way when she learned of my relationship with a human."*

He didn't say it, but Tanya saw the memory in his mind. *"If she's a woman worth having, she will forgive you,"* Lilly had said.

"I believe you're a woman worth having, whether or not you forgive me, Tanya. I was yours, and yet I shared that with another. It would have never happened if I had stayed where I belonged—with my pack, being what they needed me to be."

Tanya considered his words and then sighed. *"We are the sum of our wise decisions and our poor ones. When I show that I am perfect without fault, then I can judge you. I won't deny that I'm hurt. And it might take time for that to heal. But I won't give up what was created just for us. My soul, my wolf, and even me, want a chance with you."* Saying the words, admitting them not only to him but to herself, as well, lifted an enormous weight that had settled on her shoulders and threatened to crush her to the ground. New breath rushed into her lungs, and new tears filled her eyes—only these tears were full of hope. Their trials could make them stronger or tear them apart and leave a legacy of brokenness for their pack. She refused to be that.

"Thank you." Dillon's voice was full of anguish, hope, and love.

That love flooded the bond like a dam being broken and rushing into an empty gorge. The places inside of her that her own despair had shadowed lit up with the possibility of love and a new life.

"I know you still want me to stay here," he told her, obviously having seen the thoughts in her mind. *"But know that there is no place I want to be other than by your side."*

Tanya could feel the truth and sincerity in those words, and she soaked them up like a dry desert getting rain for the first time in a century. *"I was dreading coming home. But now it doesn't seem like such a tragedy waiting to happen. I can't promise that I won't have moments where I find myself struggling to understand, but I promise to talk to you about it. I promise to give our relationship everything that I can."*

"All that I am is yours, Tanya. Faults and all, I am yours and will be til death and after."

CHAPTER
THIRTEEN

"Tragically, we are unable to choose the life that we are born into. We can only do our best with the hand we have been dealt, then strive to overcome any difficulties that come with that hand. We can count ourselves successful if the way we play our hand results in a better hand being dealt to our children than the one we received." ~Penelope

"Sometimes I feel like my life will never have meaning." Penelope stared out the window at Dillon, who was sparring with the warriors of the Colorado pack.

Rose sat skillfully braiding Penelope's hair. She clucked her tongue at the girl. "Of course your life has meaning. How could you say something like that?"

Penelope wanted to roll her eyes, but such disrespectful actions had been conditioned out of her. Jeremiah didn't like it when she rolled her eyes or did anything else he found offensive, like breathe, for instance. "Because I'm basically a servant in a pack where I don't really fit in." Penelope forced her voice to remain steady, despite the emotion caught in her throat. "I don't fit anywhere. Human, but not human. *Canis lupus,* but not *Canis lupus.* I'll never be more than this."

Rose's hands rested on Penelope's shoulders, and Penelope imagined the disappointed look in the alpha female's eyes staring back at her. Rose was one of the few in the pack who treated Penelope with kindness.

"The Great Luna has a purpose for you, Penelope. It's more than this. I wish I knew how to give it to you or help you achieve it."

Penelope turned to face Rose and saw the pain that often filled the alpha's eyes when she looked at her. "You've done enough." She hoped the alpha heard the sincerity in her words. "Your compassion is something I treasure. I know I was dropped on the doorstep of this mansion, but you took me in and have always treated me as if I'm valuable."

Rose bowed her head, shaking it slowly. "There's no doubt you're valuable, Penelope." When Rose raised her head, tears streamed down her face, and her bottom lip trembled slightly. "I'm sorry that you don't feel that way. I'm sorry I haven't made you feel that way."

Penelope grabbed Rose's hands. "No, no, don't say that." She swallowed hard and pressed her lips together to keep her own tears from falling. If Jeremiah walked in, he would scold her for crying. The stoic alpha hated tears. "You, of all people, have made me feel loved and welcome."

"You shouldn't have to feel welcome in your own family," Rose huffed. "It should be a given that you belong. You're not a guest, dammit. You're pack."

Penelope didn't want to tell Rose that she'd never felt like anything more than a guest, and often more like a burden. She frequently saw guilt in the alpha female's eyes when Penelope was treated with scorn by Jeremiah or the other pack members. That's not to say some weren't kind, but mostly, especially with the males, their attitude followed Jeremiah's.

"What's going on in here?"

Jeremiah's booming voice filled the room, and Penelope immediately stepped back from Rose. One thing that seemed to annoy him the most was his mate showing Penelope any affection.

Rose discreetly wiped her eyes before turning to face her mate. "I asked Penelope for help with some cleaning. We were just finishing up, and I was letting her know what needs to be done next."

Jeremiah's eyes darted between her and his mate, as if trying to determine if Rose was telling the truth. Considering he could simply look into her mind through their mate bond, Penelope wondered why he wasn't already accusing Rose of lying. Finally, he focused on Rose. "You don't ask her to help, mate," he grumbled. "You tell her what you want done and then leave her to do it."

Penelope lowered her gaze, hiding the resentment she knew must show in her eyes. She bit her lip to keep from telling him off and simply waited to see what else he would say. He had undoubtedly sought one of them for a reason.

"Penelope, take water and refreshments to the training area for the warriors working there. Don't bother them. Simply set everything out and refill as necessary. Understood?"

Though she wanted to respond sarcastically, she said, "Of course, Alpha." The title tasted like ash in her mouth.

She despised addressing him with any form of respect because he deserved none. A true alpha would be worthy of the title.

She hurried from the room, but before Penelope was out of earshot, she heard Jeremiah say, "I don't understand why you insist on keeping her around. She's a dormant. That whelp will never have a mate. She's just deadweight."

Penelope's feet stopped moving as his words pierced her heart, a heart she thought she had protected with stronger walls.

"That's cruel, Jeremiah. She's a living person with the same rights as you and me," Rose replied. She was the only pack member who could get away with talking to Jeremiah like that.

"We live in a world of survival of the fittest. A pack is only as strong as its weakest member," Jeremiah snarled. "She makes us weak."

Penelope had heard enough. She'd heard it all before. Jeremiah loved to point out what a burden she was. She often asked herself why she didn't just leave. The answers remained the same: she worried about Rose, she loved Tanya, who had always treated her with the same kindness as her mother, and being a lone female wolf, dormant or not, was dangerous. Maybe if Jeremiah allowed her to learn to fight alongside the pack's warriors she could venture out on her own. But he treated her like a servant, and servants didn't learn to defend themselves.

She sighed as she entered the kitchen and began gathering items for the warriors. Perhaps Dillon would be willing to work with her in secret? He seemed like a much kinder wolf than their alpha and appeared to have more respect for a dormant like herself. It was something she would have to consider. But Penelope knew if she approached him, she'd need to be very careful. If Jeremiah found out, he might just go ahead and finally put her out of her misery like he'd always threatened to.

"MY GRANDMOTHER CAN HIT HARDER THAN YOU DO." KEVIN heckled Dillon from where he, Rusty, and Gabe sat just on the edge of the sparring circle.

Dillon ignored him as he focused on the two wolves that had challenged him. Apparently it had gotten around, no doubt courtesy of the three troublemakers on the sideline, that he'd taken out five vampires nearly by himself. So now, every wolf in the pack was eager to take him on. He hadn't had to do any sort of recruiting for some training lessons. They'd simply lined up, especially once they heard Jeremiah had ordered it.

One male was in his wolf form, while the other was still in his human skin. They seemed to use a tag team method, which was not doing them any good. If they'd both attack him at once, they'd have a much better chance at taking him down. As Dillon moved around the sparring ring, he waited for the perfect moment to strike. The wolf circled him, snarling and snapping, but Dillon was too quick for it. With a swift movement, he darted behind the wolf and landed a well-placed punch to its side. The wolf yelped, but it didn't go down. Instead, it turned around and lunged at Dillon again.

The one in human form, sensing an opportunity, charged at Dillon from the side. Dillon saw him coming and quickly ducked and rolled, putting some distance between himself and his attackers.

Dillon knew they would think he was stepping back for a breather. So, instead of hesitating, Dillon rushed forward toward the human. Before the man could react, Dillon punched him square in the face, sending him flying back into the circle. The wolf's eyes widened in surprise before his body hit the ground with a loud thud. He groaned but didn't try to rise.

Meanwhile, the lupine wolf was still circling Dillon, looking for any opportunity to attack. Dillon remained vigilant, keeping the beast off balance. Finally, the wolf gave a frustrated snarl and charged wildly. Dillon sidestepped with practiced agility and swung his arm around the beast's furry neck, pulling back with all his strength. With a yelp of surprise, the wolf stumbled back and fell to its side with Dillon on top. It thrashed and rolled, but Dillon pushed all of his weight down on the wolf and wouldn't let go. No matter how hard it tried, the beast couldn't shake Dillon free. Eventually, the wolf quit fighting. After a few seconds, it gave a small whine of submission. Dillon released him and rose to his feet.

Dillon could hear cheers and catcalls coming from the pack members that had surrounded the sparring circle, things like "Two on one, and they still couldn't beat him," and "I've never seen a man move that fast." Dillon found it hard not to preen like a peacock. Apparently, hunting the feral hogs and coyotes in Coldspring for so long had kept his skills sharp. But he wasn't terribly proud of besting these two warriors. They fought hard, but they clearly hadn't been trained properly. Anyone from his old pack back in Montana could have bested them.

The defeated wolf phased back into a human. Dillon

extended the man a hand. At first, Dillon thought he might not accept, but he finally reached out and took it, allowing Dillon to help him up. Dillon tried to read the expression in the man's eyes. He saw a defeated look he didn't like. Being bested in the sparring ring shouldn't be shameful. It should be an opportunity to learn, to improve your fighting skills, so that you can defend the weaker members of your pack.

Gabe jogged over and tossed the man a pair of sweatpants.

"You did well." Dillon helped the wolf up. "And you, too." He nodded at the other one.

Pointing to the first wolf, Kevin walked over and said, "The one you knocked out is Wade. And the other one with the puppy dog eyes is Dean."

"Shut up," Dean retorted as he put on the sweatpants.

Dillon motioned for everyone to follow him to a group of logs arranged as a seating area. About fifteen wolves, including Kevin, Gabe, Rusty, Wade, and Dean, sat down. Dillon noticed five more wolves standing at the back of the group, arms folded and suspicion in their eyes. *The loyal disciples.* He met their gazes. One by one, they looked away. Dillon had yet to find a male in Jeremiah's pack who was more dominant than he.

"The reason Jeremiah asked me to work with all of you is to find your weak points," Dillon began. "I didn't fight you to make you feel inferior," he added, looking at Dean. "Do you understand?"

Dean nodded, and Dillon realized he had hit the nail on the head. These wolves had been humiliated when they had failed or were defeated, instead of being taught where they went wrong and then given another chance. If rogues attacked Jeremiah's pack, they would likely not stand a chance because these wolves did not fight like a pack. It was every man for himself.

"You're only as strong as your weakest fighter," Dillon continued. As soon as the words were out of his mouth, growls erupted around him. But they were quickly silenced as the wolves at the back of the group took aggressive steps forward. "What?"

"Jeremiah has expressed that same sentiment," Kevin said softly. "The weak ones must be cut loose."

Dillon recoiled as if someone had slapped him. "What? No." He leaned forward and rested his arms on his knees. "You must find their strengths and use them accordingly. Every pack member is essential, and every pack member has a purpose. Not everyone is meant to be a warrior." Dillon watched in shock as the eyes of the wolves staring back at him widened. It seemed as though light bulbs flickered on over their heads. It was as if Dillon had just informed them that they were *Canis lupus*, and despite all the evidence already present, they were only now coming to understand it.

"So if someone isn't a warrior," Dean spoke up, "then what good are they?"

The fear of rejection was evident in the young male's eyes. This was a wolf that Jeremiah had undoubtedly shamed many times before. "He or she could do lots of things. They could be good at gathering intelligence, being a liaison with other supernaturals, or someone who helps take care of the pack compound. It's not like werewolves go easy on things," Dillon explained. Chuckles filled the group. "Just like humans have their strengths, so do we. Some of you are probably good teachers. Some of you are good with numbers and can handle pack finances. There are roles for everyone. And when you do have to work in an area that isn't your strong suit, you just try harder, and those around you will offer more patience and grace."

Dillon's stomach turned at the idea that Jeremiah had shredded the confidence of his pack and made them feel shame for not being the best or even good at something. But then, that was how tyrants operated. They kept the people under their control oppressed, so that they felt too weak to rise against them. Only insecure men led in such a way. An alpha who knew his worth as a male and leader didn't need his pack to fear him. He earned their respect and, therefore, their willingness to follow him. They trusted him because he showed he cared for them as individuals and that the pack valued them.

"Why aren't you with your own pack?" Wade asked.

Dillon glanced down at his clasped hands and then made a decision. If Tanya would accept him as her mate, and Jeremiah didn't try to kill him, he'd hopefully become a member of this pack. And these males deserved the truth. "My parents were killed by hunters over a decade ago. And I couldn't deal with losing them." As he shared his story, the males who had been standing at the back of the group slowly dispersed until all that remained were the fifteen and a few females who had joined them. "I'm here because I need a new home, a pack. I have no ill will toward my former pack, and they hold me no ill will. Sometimes we just need a place to start over." When the time came for him to face off with Jeremiah, and Dillon was now convinced it *would* come, he wanted them to trust him.

"What about those marks?" Kevin asked. Dillon had seen the questions in the three males' eyes since they'd gone hunting together and they'd seen him shirtless. Anyone else who'd seen them hadn't been brave enough to ask, or they thought Jeremiah would punish them for doing so because it would essentially look like they were questioning his judgment to let Dillon stay.

"I've met my mate. But it's going to take some time and trust building before I'll say more about it."

Heads nodded around the group as they all seemed to understand, like any *Canis lupus* would, that true mates were a private matter until they decided to make it public.

"Even though we might not all be great at fighting," Dillon said, focusing back on the matter at hand, as the afternoon wound down, "it's still important that we all learn to fight." He looked at the group of females. "Even the females, maybe especially the females. If ever a coven of vampires or pack of rogue wolves descended on this place, you'd have a better chance of surviving if everyone had training."

"The females aren't allowed to fight," Rusty whispered and leaned forward from where he sat on a log.

Dillon bit back his snarl. Of course they weren't.

"Well, except for T," Kevin added. "That's Tanya. Jeremiah and Rose's daughter. He allows her to learn to fight."

"Only because she'd do it behind his back, anyway." Gabe laughed.

There was a murmur of agreement, and Dillon smiled. He liked that his mate hadn't lost her fighting spirit under the stern thumb her father most likely kept on her.

"Same time tomorrow?" Dillon asked the group. They all nodded and dispersed. As Dillon stood up, Dean jogged over to him.

"I know I'm not great—" he started, but Dillon held up a hand.

"You haven't been given the opportunity to see what you're capable of, Dean. Most of us are natural fighters. We're wolves. Predators. It's what we do," Dillon explained.

He wrapped a hand around Dean's neck and pulled him closer, his hold firm but not cruel. "You've been held back. Don't count yourself out just yet, okay?" He was careful not to say that it was Jeremiah who'd been holding him back. That was understood by the look in Dean's eyes.

Dean's eyes widened, and he appeared almost teary as he met Dillon's gaze. "Thanks. I'll remember that."

After Dean left, Kevin stepped up beside Dillon and nudged him with his shoulder. He leaned in close and spoke in a low voice. "Dean's parents died a few years back. The alpha claimed it was rogues. He's had a rough time ever since."

Dillon glanced at him. "You don't believe your alpha?"

"Do you? He sent us out hunting for them, remember? Did we find any?" He shook his head.. "We haven't had rogues around this pack for a decade, Dillon," Kevin replied. "I'm one of our six patrollers. I'd know if there were rogues. That's why I *was* surprised when he sent us out yesterday. But I've learned to keep my mouth shut and my head down."

Dillon was incredulous. "Why do you all put up with it? Why not challenge him?"

"He doesn't fight fair." Gabe came up on Dillon's other side. "He was challenged back when he first took over the pack. When the challenger submitted, Jeremiah killed him anyway. The male had a mate and a child."

Dillon swore under his breath. "So he murdered the female as a result of the mate bond and left a child without their parents." He shook his head. "Where is the child now?"

"The child," Gabe replied, "was an eighteen-year-old pup and probably would have been more dominant than Jeremiah—"

"Would have been?" Dillon interrupted.

Gabe nodded. "As soon as his mother dropped dead, he went after Jeremiah. And instead of treating the young male like a kid who'd just lost both his parents, Jeremiah acted like Reese was actually challenging him and killed him, as well."

Kevin shook his head. "Given a few years of experience, Reese could have challenged him and taken him on, but at eighteen, nah. He was just angry and hurt, and he went for the man who'd caused that pain. Reese didn't want to be the alpha of the Colorado pack."

Dillon ran a hand through his wavy hair. It was a mess from all the sparring. *He* was a mess, and now his thoughts felt just as nasty as his sweaty body did. Hearing about all the death and corruption in Jeremiah's leadership made Dillon feel like it was catching, and it might somehow infect him, as well. "You guys need to get your rest," he told the three males who'd fought against the vampires with him. "Tomorrow, I'll expect you to be training. Each of you should be leaders in this pack."

"Don't let the alpha hear you say something like that." Gabe began to walk away, still a limp in his step. "Them's fighting words."

Dillon's lip curled up as his wolf pushed forward. "Believe me, I'm counting on it." The more Dillon learned, the more he was convinced that, even if he did become a member of this pack, he could not follow Jeremiah. The man wasn't worthy of his respect or loyalty.

THREE DAYS PASSED IN THE BLINK OF AN EYE, THOUGH THEY WERE eyes that were continually red and swollen. Like Tanya's eyes, the sky was crying as Tanya watched Lisa's casket being lowered into the deep hole that members of the Missouri pack had dug the night before. She didn't consider that it was rain because there was no way that even the elements wouldn't be affected by such a sweet person being taken from the world. Tanya knew Lisa wasn't perfect, but she was as close as they came.

They'd placed her beneath a large tree which shaded the bench that had been placed a few feet from Lisa's final resting place. All different types of flowers had been planted around the grave and brought life to a place that was meant to hold death. At some point Tanya was sure she would appreciate the gesture, but at the moment she wanted to rave. As thunder rolled overhead she found herself wanting to shout right along with it. Why couldn't Lisa have been one of their kind so that she could have lived longer? Why did Tanya have to love her so much that the pain of losing her stole her breath?

She felt an arm come around her, and she leaned into the familiar scent of Daniel. Her wolf internally growled because there was only one male that she wanted touching her. Tanya didn't disagree, but she didn't want to stand on her own two feet at the moment. She wanted to lean on someone else, and she'd yet to come to a place where she could let herself reach for Dillon in any way more than just for conversation. She enjoyed talking to him and found him to be kind and genuine. Lisa would have liked him. She would have called him a "catch."

Tanya wiped the tears from her face and sniffed. She hated crying because it always made her nose run, which was freaking annoying. Tanya found herself rolling her eyes at herself as she thought about something so trivial. She was watching her friend being buried and yet she was worried about a snotty nose. *"Being vain isn't an attractive trait."* Tanya heard Lisa's voice in her mind. It wasn't actually Lisa of course. It was simply Tanya's imagination in a desperate attempt to hold onto the old woman who always kept her on her toes.

"You okay?" Daniel gave her a little squeeze.

"You do realize that's a dumb ass question, right?" Tanya wanted to take the words back the minute she spoke them, but once they were out there, there was no taking them back. "I'm sorry —"

"Don't," Daniel cut her off. "It was a dumb question. I just don't know what I can do to help. I feel helpless. It's a really crappy feeling."

She started to speak, but he held up his hand. "Don't try to comfort me because I can't comfort you. I'll most likely bite you."

Tanya's lips turned up slightly. "Like I would comfort you? I'm not trying to waste the air in my lungs."

Daniel snorted, gave her a final squeeze, and then dropped his arm. Her body relaxed, and she felt guilty that she wasn't comfortable with his touch any more despite the fact that he was practically a brother to her. Her mom had told her that once she found her mate, the touch of other males wouldn't be welcome, especially by her wolf. She'd thought her mom was exaggerating. But she hadn't been.

"Dillon?" Her mind reached out to him without really deciding to do so. Tanya suddenly just wanted to hear his voice. She didn't want to be that needy chick, but her friend had died a few days ago and was being buried today, her father was acting extremely suspicious and would most likely lose his cool when he found out who Dillon was, and

she was falling for her true mate. Which should make her happy, but she also wanted to stay mad at him because something inside of her wanted to punish him. Which, yes, she knew, wasn't very mature of her at all, and Lisa would totally have called her out on that.

"I'm here," he said immediately. *"I didn't want to bother you this morning. I figured you'd have a lot going on."*

Of course, he was being considerate. Ugh, why couldn't he be a jackass? He sort of seemed like a jackass at the gas station. But then, neither one of them had been expecting to meet each other, and he'd built a whole life without her. *Don't go there, Tanya.* She would not let their past dictate their future. Wasn't that what she'd decided last night? Yes, it was. But this morning was not last night. No, she just felt like a freaking mess all over again.

"It's okay to be a mess, Tanya," he said gently. A strike of pain hit her side and she gasped. She heard Daniel say something, but Tanya didn't understand him because she was too focused on the fact that it wasn't her own body that had actually been hit.

"What is going on?" She closed her eyes and tried to force him to let her see through his eyes.

"Your father is having me train his warriors, been doing it for the past few days" he said, a slight groan in his voice. *"I've managed to keep you from feeling the pain, but right now I'm a little distracted."*

"What's wrong, Tanya?" Daniel's voice broke through when she felt his hand on her side where she'd instinctively grabbed.

"Nothing." She shook her head and patted his hand. "Just a cramp."

"Are you training them, or are they kicking your ass?"

"I've got to focus, beautiful. Kevin is determined to see me get put on the ground."

She felt another jab, and then the pain was suddenly cut off. Dillon slipped from her mind at the same time she felt the featherlight touch of a hand on her face.

"Why are men such apes?" she muttered before stepping back from the grave they were now beginning to cover. Tanya had no idea how long she'd been standing out there. Everyone had said all the words they wanted to about Lisa and dispersed. Tyler had asked Tanya if she wanted to say something, but she'd declined. Anything she was going to say would be done in private, where she could gripe at the old lady for leaving her. Not that she actually believed it was Lisa's fault. But for the moment, Tanya was angry. Life was not happening the way she'd imagined it would play out.

"We can sit out here as long as you'd like," Daniel told her as she turned and saw that almost everyone else had cleared out. There were only a few people left. Tyler stood off to the side, leaning against a tree, watching as some of his wolves filled in the grave. Austin and Trevor were farther away, sending glances her way, looking as if they feared she might have a mental breakdown at any moment. It was a legitimate worry. She mentally shrugged.

She looked over at the bench, then at Daniel. "Do you mind if I have some time alone?"

Daniel's face looked pained. It was so natural for wolves to want to care for their pack when one was hurting. Touch was essential, and she could tell he just wanted to hold her, not for any reason other than she was a pack mate, and he cared about her. After several heartbeats, he finally nodded and then turned, heading for the other two males from their pack. Tanya looked at Tyler, and he simply bowed his head and then walked away.

Tanya sat on the bench and simply stared at the quickly filling hole. It seemed like such a barbaric thing to do. Burying a person in a box in the ground. Sending them off in a pyre of burning glory was much less nefarious. But then, human ways were often strange to her, and Lisa always found that amusing. The first time Tanya slept over at Lisa's house, Lisa had been shocked when Tanya had jumped up onto her bed in her wolf form and wrapped herself around Lisa's prone body. Such behavior wasn't the slightest bit odd to Tanya. The memory filled her mind, and her lips turned up in a small smile.

"Tanya, why are you furry and in my bed?"

Considering Tanya couldn't speak to Lisa in her wolf form, she'd phased to her human form, which then left her butt-ass naked—also not a huge deal to her—which caused Lisa to slap her hand over her eyes.

"Wolves sleep in piles sometimes," Tanya explained. She tried to pry Lisa's hand away from her face. "It's a way to stay warm."

"You have fur, you ridiculous wolf. Why would you need to sleep in a pile to stay warm?"

Tanya stopped trying to pry Lisa's hand and thought about it before shrugging. "Because touch is essential to wolves. We like to sleep in piles. Why? Don't humans do that?"

"If they're into orgies." Lisa slapped Tanya's hand, keeping her eyes clamped shut. "Put on some clothes or fur. Now. There will be no naked sleepovers, and you're lucky I'll let you put your furry self in my bed. I don't enjoy shedding."

"We don't shed, dork," Tanya huffed. She jumped up

and grabbed a pair of shorts and a shirt from one of Lisa's drawers. Pack shared possessions, often without asking. Lisa also found that to be odd. "I'm decent." She sighed and then plopped back down on her friend's bed.

Lisa opened one eye, as if she didn't trust Tanya to be clothed. Then she opened the other. "We've talked about you walking around naked, Tanya. And wearing my clothes."

"You're pack. Therefore your clothes are fair game." She tilted her head to the side and pursed her lips. "What's an orgy?"

Lisa threw her hands up in the air. "What does a human have to do to get some sleep around here?"

"Explain what an orgy is, and then I'll totally let you sleep. With me. In my fur, which will keep you warm and is very soft. You're welcome."

Lisa's lips pressed tightly together as if she was trying hard not to laugh.

Tanya wiped the tears from her eyes as the memory faded. Her eyes regained focus, and she realized the wolves were done filling in the grave. Now she sat alone next to a pile of dirt with flowers all around it.

"Is that what you wanted?" she asked, as if Lisa sat right beside her. "To be a garden? Because that's what you are, Lisa. You're a freaking garden. I'm tempted to let my wolf pee on you." She waved her hand. "I'm kidding. That would be gross. But not totally undeserving since you left me in my time of need." She sighed and leaned forward, resting her elbows on her knees and her chin in her hands. "I just wasn't ready. I don't know if you can ever be ready to lose someone you love. But I wasn't. I'm going to miss the hell out of you, old woman."

There was nothing more to say. She'd cried herself dry,

and Tanya knew no amount of griping at Lisa's grave would bring her friend back. It was time for her to head home and face her future. Lisa would kick her butt if she didn't grow a pair, as she often told her to do, and accept what the Great Luna had given her. Dillon wasn't perfect, but their Creator had never promised a perfect soul mate. She'd simply promised the completion of their soul. The rest would be up to them.

She pushed up from the bench and pulled her shoulders back and her chin up as she walked from Lisa's grave. "Don't worry," she called back over her shoulder. "I'll be back to visit from time to time. And I'll tell Tyler to make sure nothing digs you up and chews on your bones." It was a morbid thing to say, but Lisa would have found it hilarious.

Tanya let out a deep breath and gave a last nod to herself. Yes, it was time to go home.

CHAPTER
FOURTEEN

"Sometimes bad things happen because there are bad people in the world. No one is out to get you. The world isn't somehow keeping score of your rights and wrongs and giving you cosmic karma. There is evil in the world, and therefore, evil things happen to undeserving people." ~Huck

Huck's muscles ached with every strained breath, the metallic tang of blood thick in the air. He knew they didn't have much time; the wolves that captured them would surely be back soon. Huck rolled onto his side and glanced around the room. He knew they were in the basement of a suburban house because he'd momentarily regained consciousness when the rogues had dragged him and Orson inside. The basement had bare concrete floors, old pipes and insulation, and an ancient, rusted freezer. The room was wide and open, with piles of trash in the center. The walls were lined with old boxes and crates with layers of dust. It smelled of decay and mold.

Huck and Orson had been hauled down a flight of stairs, then thrown into a makeshift cell. Huck stared at the iron bars of the cell that he could tell had been hastily bolted to the concrete floor and the wooden joists of the ceiling. He knew he could break out if he had enough time and was operating at full strength. He heard a door open and groaned. *Too late.*

Footsteps thundered down the stairs and then ice-cold water hit his face. Huck's eyes snapped open as he sputtered. "I wasn't unconscious, asshole," he snarled at the same time he heard another splash and then Orson cursed.

"Don't care." A younger looking wolf stood just on the other side of the cell doors, holding the now empty bucket while staring down at him with a maniacal glee. Huck thought the dude was a hinge shy of a functioning door. "I was told to hit you with some ice water, and what the alpha says, goes."

"You realize he's not actually an alpha because your little merry band of psychos aren't actually a pack, don't you?" Orson said. Huck shifted so that he could see his friend wiping water out of his eyes.

The other male who'd thrown water on Orson backed up, and both wolves leaned against the wall on the opposite side of the cell. Huck's eyes bounced back and forth between them. They were young, probably not even thirty in wolf years. He opened his mouth to speak but snapped it close when another set of footsteps sounded on the stairs. A moment later the "alpha," Gerald, stepped into the room and glared down at them through the bars with glowing, gold eyes.

"Now, we'll start again. What the hell are you two mongrels doing in my territory?"

He snarled, spittle flying from his mouth as his teeth elongated. Huck could tell the man was not in control of his beast—not a good sign.

Huck pushed to his feet. He was weak, but he wasn't about to let this mad man stand over him as if he was Huck's alpha. "As I told you before, there isn't a known pack in Texas. So the more important questions are: Who the hell are you? And why is there an unregistered pack here? That would make you rogues. The real alphas in the United States territories won't stand for rogue wolf packs." Out of the corner of his eye, he saw Orson climb to his feet, as well. His friend bit back a groan, and Huck could sympathize. He felt as if their captors had beaten him while he'd been out of it.

"I'm not concerned what the so-called 'real' alphas will stand for," Gerald bit out. "What I am concerned about is why you were hanging around my girl's bookstore and why you were traipsing all over town asking questions about Lilly Pierce."

Huck squeezed his eyes shut as he tried to clear his pounding head. "Jennifer? She's your girl?" He remembered the woman that had been talking to Lilly in the bookstore. "She hasn't been your girl long, according to Lilly if I remember the conversation correctly. In fact, it didn't seem like Lilly wanted you anywhere near that conversation."

Gerald's eyes began to glow brightly. "Neither of those females is your concern. What *is* your concern is answering my questions. You can do it and die quickly. Or not answer them and die slowly." He shrugged as if their decision was of little consequence to him.

"You haven't been here long, have you?" Huck continued, ignoring Gerald's threats. Why would he bother cooperating if this man was going to kill them no matter what he said? But maybe if he pissed him off enough the alpha would make a mistake in anger. "Did you only come into town once Dillon was gone? Was he more dominant than you and you had to stay hidden with your tails tucked between your legs until the big bad wolf was gone?"

"What the hell are you doing?" Orson whispered. "Do you want to die by entrail strangulation?"

"You have it wrong, pup," Gerald snarled. "*I* ran Dillon out of town. As soon as I claimed this territory, he ran away like weak prey. He wasn't even worth chasing."

He noticed several of Gerald's wolves give him a skeptical look but then schooled their features quickly. "Sure." Huck snorted. "I'll believe that when I believe that Jennifer, the human, actually wants to be with an animal. Oh, wait." He tilted his head to the side. "She doesn't know you're an animal, does she? Would she still want you if she did?"

Orson sighed. "Could you please leave me out of your 'let's die more painfully' plan?"

"Why are you here?" Gerald roared.

Huck nearly smiled. He was getting under the alpha's skin. Pissed off wolves made mistakes. Instead of answering him, Huck just stared back, meeting his eyes. Even if his wolf wanted to drop his gaze, Huck refused to submit to a rogue.

"If you're not going to talk, then I'll have to convince you."

The alpha ignored Huck's words. *Yep.* They were dealing with an older, most likely unmated, male who'd gone far too long without finding his true mate. Huck was sure the wolf was on the verge of going feral. It would explain why he was messing around with a human. Though Huck also guessed it had something to do with Lilly. Gerald had been way too interested in the human female's pregnancy.

Gerald snapped his fingers, and three more wolves joined the twitchy looking first two who'd dropped their buckets and now had their claws out, literally. The alpha opened the door, and before Huck could lunge forward, the five males shoved into the cell and tore into Huck. His own snarls mixed with Orson's as claws shredded him, teeth punctured his flesh, and the tang of iron from blood filled the room. At some point, he lost consciousness and could no longer feel the pain from the torture. He had no idea how many times this little scenario repeated but it felt unending.

"Splash them again." Huck heard the alpha's voice, and then freezing water hit him again. *What the hell? Did they just have buckets of ice water sitting around?* He sputtered and pushed up again.

As he moved, Huck could only guess at his injuries. Certainly, he had some broken ribs because it hurt when he breathed. Phasing would also be a risk since it could cause more damage depending on how bad the breaks were. But his arms and legs, though bruised and battered, seemed unbroken. He wasn't so sure about Orson. He'd heard his friend groan at times and snarl at others. Huck didn't know if his partner would be able to run if they ever did get an opportunity to escape. If this crazy son of bitch would leave long enough for them to attempt it. Huck tried to move, but nausea rolled through him. His injuries must be a little worse than he thought because before he could try and move again darkness swallowed him.

When he opened his eyes he had no idea how long he'd

been unconscious. Could have been hours. He tentatively moved his head, and the nausea was no longer present. That was good and bad. Good because he hated puking, but bad because if he'd been out long enough for a concussion to heal itself then it could have been over a day. He raised his head and saw that there was no one standing over them or around the cage.

A man sat guarding the door to the stairs up to the main house. He was humming to himself as he read a magazine. Huck recognized him as one of the wolves that had held him down while the others took turns raking their claws across his face.

Huck's mind was fuzzy, but there wasn't time for him to sit around wondering how much time had passed or when the crazy wolf would return with his hyenas. He forced his mind to focus, and finally, a plan formed in Huck's mind. He had no idea how much time they had before the other wolves returned, so there was no time to lose.

"Orson, you alive, bud?" he whispered, careful to speak as softly as he could so the guard didn't hear.

For a few moments, the wolf said nothing. Finally, Orson croaked out, "I'm fit as a fiddle," though he didn't raise his head off the concrete. Huck breathed a sigh of relief. He hadn't been sure that his friend would respond.

"Do you have to pee?"

"What?"

Huck heard the surprise in his partner's voice. "Shh. Listen to me. I've got an idea." Huck quickly explained what he had in mind.

"Really? That's the best you've got?" Orson whispered frantically. "We've been unconscious for who knows how long and 'Do you have to pee?' is what you've come up with."

Huck rolled his eyes, and even that small motion seemed to hurt, so he decided he wouldn't engage in any movements that were not strictly necessary until he had to. "If you've got a better idea, I'm all ears."

Orson groaned and rolled his eyes. "Fine, let's do this."

Huck watched as Orson, with much straining and groaning, rose to his feet. He staggered over to a rusty pail sitting in the corner that by the smell of it had blood and urine in it. He glanced toward the door and saw the guard had lowered his magazine to take note of what Orson was doing.

Huck heard Orson's pants unzip. The man stood swaying for several seconds before the flow finally began. Orson released a long, low sound somewhere between a groan and a wail.

"Shut up." The guard growled at him. Huck dragged himself up to a sitting position. The sound of urine hitting the bucket stopped, then Orson gave one final moan before collapsing in a heap next to the pail.

"Orson!" Huck rose shakily to his feet and made his way to his friend. He took a moment to appraise him. Orson's face was ashen, and he was trembling. Huck turned to the guard. "He needs a doctor."

The guard scoffed. "Fat chance."

Huck growled. "Bring him some damn water then. He's lost a lot of blood."

"I'm not bringing him a damn thing. You think this is a hotel or something? I was told to guard you two whelps, not provide room service."

"And I'm sure your alpha's going to be really happy when he comes back and finds one of us dead. We haven't told him anything yet, and we're not going to be able to if we're dead. I don't know what that bastard has planned for us, but I bet he wants us alive for it. If this man doesn't get some liquids soon, he's done for. I mean how long have we been out? Hours? Days? We could both be on death's door." He was laying it on a bit thick, but then he honestly didn't know if they'd gone days without water. They were werewolves and stronger than humans, but that didn't mean they couldn't die from dehydration and starvation, same as humans.

The guard hesitated for a second, then rose. "No bullshit," he warned, pointing a finger at Huck. "Back up."

Huck raised his hands and moved back to the other side of the cell. The guard opened a cupboard and grabbed a mason jar full of rusty bolts. He tipped the jar, dumping the bolts onto the concrete floor with a clatter. Then he went to a corroded sink and turned on the tap. When the glass was half-full, he walked closer to the prisoners. Huck saw the man staring him down as he approached the cell. He stopped just out of arm's length of the bars. "I mean it. No bullshit. If you try anything, I'll kill you myself and take my chances with the alpha."

"I'm cool." Huck shrugged.

The guard took another step forward and put a key into the cell's lock. Just as it clicked, Huck heard Orson make a strangled noise. He looked to see his friend leap to his feet, a rusty bucket in his hand. By the look on Orson's face, the movement had cost him every last ounce of energy.

"Hey!" The guard was halfway through screaming when a half-gallon of blood and piss splashed across his face. "You son of a bitch!" he sputtered, flinging the door open. With a snarl, he leapt upon Orson, turning his back on Huck.

Huck took his chance, praying to the Great Luna that his cracked ribs wouldn't get worse, lunging and phasing as he did so. As the guard's first blow rained down upon Orson, a two-hundred-pound wolf landed on his back. Huck felt a surge of energy from the beast coursing through his body, even as he felt another snap. *There went another rib.* The wolf had been longing to get his teeth on one of their attackers, and now it had the chance. He clamped down on the back of the guard's throat. Though it took almost all his strength, he shook his head and tore open the man's neck. It was far from a clean kill, but it worked. He felt the guard go limp beneath him, both of them collapsing on Orson. Huck phased back and rolled the guard off his friend.

Orson was covered in the man's blood. Again, he was barely conscious, but he managed a weak grin. "Piss bucket to the face. Works every time."

"Don't forget it was *my* plan."

"Even a blind hog will find an acorn every once in a while," Orson groused as he pushed up on an elbow. "Now, how about you help me up and let's get the hell out of here?"

"Good idea." Huck lifted his friend to his feet, which elicited a moan. "I've got you." He put one of Orson's arms around his neck and started walking him to the cell door.

"Huck," Orson breathed out as wet, wheezy sounds emerged. "I like you and all, brother, but do you mind putting some pants on before you get this close to me?"

Huck chuckled as he glanced down at himself. He let go of Orson, who held onto the cell bars to keep himself from falling. Huck looked at the guard. The man appeared to be roughly his size. "These should work." He quickly relieved the body of its dungarees and put them on. They were a little tight, but they would do for now. Huck went back to Orson and helped him out of the cell.

"Much better." Orson grunted.

They made it to the stairs before Orson stopped, his breath coming in great gasps. "This ain't going to be easy."

"I got you." Without giving him any warning, Huck lifted his friend in a fireman's carry, which drew a yelp from Orson.

"Shit!"

"You going to kiss your future mate with that mouth?" Huck's voice was strained as he carried Orson up the stairs. "Maybe try to be quiet until we get out of here. I don't think there are any other wolves in the house, but it's better to be safe than sorry." When they reached the top of the stairs, Huck found himself in a dirty kitchen. He glanced around, his senses on high alert. The place seemed empty. With a grunt, he lowered Orson to his feet. The other wolf swayed but leaned against an old, green refrigerator and managed to stay upright.

"I think we're alone, O-man." Huck peeked around a wall between the kitchen and looked into a small living room.

"And I think we're gonna make it."

"Don't count your chickens before they're hatched. We don't have a clue where we are, where those bastards have gone, or when they'll be back. Not to mention how the heck we are going to get out of here when you can barely walk."

"You're wrong on that last one, bud." Orson pointed out the kitchen window. A green sedan rested in the driveway.

"That'd be great if we had a k—"

Huck stopped speaking when Orson pulled a key ring from magnetic hook stuck to the fridge and tossed it to him. "I think you better drive."

"What do you mean they got away?" Gerald slammed the door to the small house they'd used to keep their two captives.

"Frank is laying in the basement with his throat torn out." Oliver stood in the open basement door. "They killed him and got away. Must have taken his car because it's gone."

Gerald ran his hand over his face and growled. If he wanted anything done he had to do it himself. "Just make sure they're nowhere in town and that Lilly Pierce is where she's supposed to be. Check on Jennifer, as well."

Oliver held Gerald's gaze. He was the only wolf who could. They'd been friends a long time, and in a fight, neither of them knew who would win. But they both understood they'd made an unspoken decision to never challenge one another, and Oliver let Gerald lead. That didn't mean his longtime friend didn't give him hell from time to time. "Are you sure this woman is truly worth our attention?"

Gerald growled. "It's like the Great Luna dropped her in our lap, Oliver. We come passing through town, and the first diner we stop at happens to have a woman sitting two tables away that smells like a *Canis lupus* male, yet after scouring the town we find none. Then, the woman I manage to scratch an itch with happens to be this girl's best friend and spills her guts to me about the whole situation, which then leads me to getting to meet this Lilly Pierce, who is pregnant with a *Canis lupus* baby." His words got louder and louder as he spoke as the conviction in him grew. "Yes, she's damn well worth our attention. If Lilly has a female, then she will belong to my son. I'm not going to force Lucas to go through what I've gone through. Living alone all these years."

"Gerald," Oliver said, his voice low. "Lucas isn't your son."

"He's as good as," Gerald snapped back. Gerald didn't talk about the brother and sister-in-law he'd lost, and he wasn't about to start now. Lucas and his sister had been left in the world without parents and Gerald did what any good brother would and claimed Lucas and his sister, Cynthia, as his own. He would do everything he could to give Lucas a fighting chance in this life. For all they knew this child growing inside of Lilly Pierce actually was his nephew's true mate. Maybe that's why Dillon Jacobs wound up in Coldspring to begin with. It had to be fate, Gerald decided. And he would make sure that Lucas got his mate no matter how many wolves he had to take out in the process.

◊

HUCK PULLED OVER AT A GAS STATION TWO MILES AFTER THE GAS gauge touched the E mark. He'd been pushing it hard to get as far from Coldspring as he could without getting pulled over by the human police. They'd managed to nearly make it to Dallas but had finally been forced to stop. He was still trying to decide if they should call Jeremiah and let him know about Lilly or wait until they arrived back at the pack mansion. As Huck pulled into the parking lot, he noticed a door on the side of the building marked Bathroom. They'd need to clean up as much as possible before getting gas. He checked his back pocket, and by the grace of the Great Luna, his wallet was still there. That was seriously the goddesses' work. There was no other explanation for it. "Thank you," Huck whispered as he closed his eyes and let out a shaky breath. They had money, which would get them home. He'd never wanted to be back in pack territory as much as he did in that moment. With their pack, they were safe. Even under Jeremiah's rule, at least they were safe from rogues like Gerald.

"You look like you're in pain," Orson said from his slumped position in the passenger seat. "You shouldn't think. It's going to give you brain damage."

Huck huffed. "I think *you* got brain damage from being hit one too many times by those wolves." He sighed and rested his forehead on the steering wheel. "I think we should wait and tell Jeremiah when we get back. We don't know the whole story. We know that Dillon was with a human, and she got pregnant, but he doesn't know he's got a kid baking." His hand tapped against the side of the steering wheel as he spoke. "And he's most likely Tanya's mate. I have no idea what the alpha will do when all this shit hits the fan, but more than likely he's going to try and kill Dillon." Huck raised up and looked at Orson. "Even though I don't agree with what the man has done, if he's Tanya's mate, it's her decision if he dies, and she should be the one to pass judgment on her mate."

Orson nodded. "Sounds good to me, bud."

Decision made, they cleaned up, got gas, and hit the road again. It was a fourteen-hour drive from Coldspring, Texas to their pack home. They made it in twelve. Huck was still in pain, and though his werewolf blood was doing its best to heal his injuries quickly, the long drive had not done him any good. Unfortunately, Orson had been in no condition to drive, so he couldn't give Huck a break while on the road. And because they both felt like the rogues that had captured them might appear in the rearview mirror at any second, they only stopped for bathroom breaks, did their business as quickly as possible, and got back on the road. He and Orson had learned their lesson about wasting time choosing gas station snacks. Huck would've loved to stop and stretch his legs, maybe take some time at a rest stop diner and have a nice meal, but he kept up an unrelenting pace all the way back to the Colorado mountains.

Thankfully, Orson had slept most of the way, so his friend seemed a bit better when the pack mansion finally came into view. Huck brought the car to a screeching halt in the headquarters' concrete driveway. He wanted nothing more than to take a shower, gobble a handful of painkillers, and sleep for three days. But he knew such luxuries would have to wait. Jeremiah was already going to be upset that he and Orson hadn't reported in, but Huck hadn't dared take the time to stop at a payphone, not that he planned on telling his alpha anything over the phone to begin with. That would have to wait until they were face to face and they could gauge his reaction.

The pair unfolded themselves from the sedan with a chorus of grunts and groans. With a quick stretch, they made their way up the mansion steps. The door opened and Nell appeared.

She gasped at their appearance. "What happened?"

"No time to talk, Nell. We've got to see the alpha, ASAP." They both pushed past her and made their way painfully up the stairs to Jeremiah's office.

"Come in," came his gravelly voice when Huck knocked.

Huck pushed the door open, and they both shuffled inside.

"What the hell?" Jeremiah said before either Huck or Orson could speak. "I haven't heard from you two for over two days. You look like you've been tied up and dragged behind a horse."

"I wish," Orson grumbled.

"Half of that is true, Alpha." Huck explained everything that had happened in Coldspring, starting with the revelation that Dillon had had a human lover who was pregnant with his child and ending with their escape from the rogue pack.

JEREMIAH LISTENED INTENTLY AS HUCK SPOKE, NOT BELIEVING what he was hearing. He wasn't sure what was more surprising: that Dillon had a secret human lover or that a rogue pack was operating in Texas. Well, only one of those things really concerned him. When Huck finished speaking, Jeremiah looked down at his desk. He turned the information over and over in his mind. *That son of a bitch Dillon Jacobs.* How could this degenerate be his daughter's mate? Not only was he a bastard liar, but he had a freaking kid with a human? There was no way Jeremiah could let his daughter be with someone like that. He didn't care if he was her mate or not. This man would cause her nothing but pain. Not to mention the embarrassment of having a half-human stepchild. She was better off without a mate than with this guy.

Jeremiah growled low in his throat. This revelation was problematic, to say the least. He couldn't let his daughter find out about Dillon's past. But how could he keep it quiet?

There was no way to keep something like that from getting out to the pack. Unless...

Finally, Jeremiah looked up. "Did anyone see you two come in?"

Orson shrugged. "Just Nell."

"Hmm." The alpha scrunched up his face and looked at the ceiling. *That damn dormant. She is a constant thorn in my side.* He looked back at Huck and Orson. "I need you both to come with me."

H∪CK WATCHED JEREMIAH GET UP FROM HIS CHAIR AND WALK OVER to the far wall. He reached out and pressed a hidden switch. There was a click, and the bookcase on the wall swung open, revealing a secret door in the wall. Jeremiah went through without a backward glance.

Huck and Orson looked at one another with wide eyes and shrugged. They rose and followed him with tentative steps. Stepping through the doorway, the pair found themselves in a cramped passageway. Ahead, a flight of steps led downward. The passage was lit by dim lamps on the walls, casting the entire area in a soft orange glow. Jeremiah disappeared down the stairs, and they followed. Descending the steps was pure torture. Every time his foot landed on one of the wooden steps, a lightning bolt of pain shot through Huck's injured ribs.

When they mercifully reached the bottom, Huck guessed they'd descended roughly four flights, which would put them somewhere below the basement. A heavy locked door stood before them. Jeremiah turned the lock and pushed it open, passing through into a stone hallway. Orson and Huck continued forward.

"What the hell is going on, Huck?" Orson whispered.

"No idea."

Both knew better than to disobey their alpha's orders, so they dutifully followed. Huck hadn't known the alpha's office contained a secret passage, but he wasn't surprised. It was exactly the thing the man would need. There was no telling what he used it for, but Huck knew it wasn't for anything good.

The tunnel seemed to go on forever, and after fifteen or so minutes, Huck was growing tired of walking. He noticed he and Orson were falling behind. Huck thought he might just lie down and go to sleep right there on the concrete floor. It required an almost herculean effort of will just to put one foot in front of the other.

The alpha slowed, allowing them to catch up. "C'mon." As soon as they reached him, Jeremiah started walking again. Huck stifled a groan.

Huck couldn't guess as to where they might be, as he had no idea which direction the tunnel went after leaving Jeremiah's office. But he thought they must be miles away from the pack mansion by now. Huck knew any chance of sleep and a shower was long gone. Finally, after about a half hour of walking, the tunnel ended at another door, this one equally as heavy and imposing as the first. Again, Jeremiah unlocked it and passed through. Huck and Orson followed. The door opened into a small cave with stone walls pressed closely together. It was dark, but Huck could see a sliver of light coming from up ahead, revealing a small gap in the stone walls. He watched Jeremiah squeeze through the gap and disappear. Huck's curiosity was running wild. *A secret cave that led into the pack mansion?* What other secrets was Jeremiah hiding?

Huck felt an arm grab him in the darkness.

"I don't like this, Huck," Orson whispered, his voice holding a note of panic.

"Me either."

"What should we do?"

"Let's just keep our wits about us, Orson. We fought off those rogues. We can fight Jeremiah if we have to." Huck wasn't sure he believed his own words or the fact that he'd even considered having to fight their alpha. But something didn't feel right. "C'mon."

Huck followed Jeremiah through the crack and saw the light of the forest through the opening of the cave mouth. He heard running water and recognized the place. It was a quiet clearing a few miles from the pack headquarters. A river, deep and swift, ran nearby. Huck hesitated at the mouth of the cave. He glanced around but didn't see Jeremiah anywhere.

Thump! Huck turned when he heard scuffling above him. He looked up to see Jeremiah crouched on a boulder, glaring down at him. Before he could react, Jeremiah leaped from the boulder and landed on top of him, shoving him to the ground. Huck tried to push the alpha off, but he didn't have anything close to the strength required. Jeremiah rose up and swiped at Huck with his long claws, catching him by the throat. His own blood flew out in a bright spray. Huck clutched at his throat, trying in vain to stem the tide of blood. Jeremiah stood and moved back to the mouth of the cave.

Huck watched in horror as Orson emerged from the cave. Jeremiah stepped forward and grabbed Orson by the throat, lifting him off the ground with one hand. His friend tried to cry out, but his voice was cut off by Jeremiah's hand around his neck. With frightening strength, Jeremiah threw Orson against the nearby rocks. *Crunch.* Orson fell limp.

Huck writhed and squirmed on the ground. He knew these were his final moments.

Jeremiah paused and looked at him. "Sorry about this, boys. but I just can't run the risk of you telling anyone about Dillon. If Tanya found out, it would kill her and be an embarrassment to me and my pack. I can't have that. My daughter won't be the laughingstock of the *Canis lupus* world because her mate couldn't keep it in his pants."

As Huck's vision began to blur, he watched Jeremiah walk to a pile of large stones. He moved one and revealed a small cache of equipment. Huck blinked and then saw the alpha had retrieved a length of rope, which he tied to a small boulder. He tied the other end around Orson's waist. Then Jeremiah hoisted the rock with one hand and Orson with the other. He walked to the riverbank and then unceremoniously tossed them both in. Huck heard a large splash when the boulder and his friend simultaneously hit the water.

Jeremiah then turned to Huck. Huck didn't even have the strength to raise a hand in defense. His life was over, and there wasn't a damn thing he could do about it. His best friend had just died at the hands of their alpha, the leader of their pack and a male they should have been able to trust implicitly. They'd been fools. And no one in the pack would know the truth of what had happened here. The rest of them would continue to be fools led by this mad man.

"You don't..." Huck coughed as he tried to speak.

Jeremiah frowned. "I suppose you should get some last words since Orson didn't. Go on then." He motioned. "What are you saying?"

Huck pulled on every ounce of strength he had left. "You don't deserve what the Great Luna has given you. You never have." He coughed again. "And I hope she snuffs your life out with the same amount of care you've given me and Orson."

Jeremiah sighed. "The Great Luna hasn't *given* me anything. I've taken it. I've created my own opportunities. I will not let Dillon, you, Orson, or some brat growing in a human whore's womb ruin all I've worked for."

The last thing Huck saw was his alpha raise a giant stone over his head and bring it crashing down.

CHAPTER
FIFTEEN

"It's strange how once you've made a choice in life to do something that you previously thought impossible, the desire to keep pushing forward becomes unstoppable. You become fixated on achieving that goal. The thought of it not coming to fruition makes you think everything is crumbling around you." ~Tanya

Tanya stared at the book in her hands, listening to the sound of the road beneath the tires of the van. They'd been on the road for hours. Slowly, the encroaching dusk swallowed the day, leaving the moon, stars, and the van's headlights to illuminate their way back to the Colorado pack mansion. After she had said her goodbyes to Lisa, Tyler, and the other members of the pack she'd grown close to, Tanya was anxious to be home.

She wanted to see her mom. She needed to check on her father and see just how much crazier he'd become in her absence. Tanya knew something was up because his response to her request to stay for Lisa's funeral had been absolutely out of character for him. Most of all, she wanted to see Dillon. She had no idea how she would respond once she did, though. Her wolf wanted to barrel into him and rub her scent all over him, hussy that she was. *"As if you haven't thought about it,"* her beast chided. The wolf was like a child, giddy with excitement now that they were headed toward their mate. Tanya wouldn't deny that she was excited, as well. Nervous as hell, but excited.

"I can feel you getting closer." Dillon's deep, rich voice filled her mind.

Warmth infused every cold place inside of her as unseen arms wrapped around her. She should tell him not to take such liberties, even if it was simply a psychic touch and not a real one. It was intimate as hell.

"My wolf and I are hungry to lay eyes on you."

"Not holding back, are you?" She sounded breathless. *Have a little dignity, T,* she told herself.

"Are you going to reject me, Tanya?" he asked boldly. *"Am I going to have to grovel at your feet in front of the entire pack? Because I will. I'll do it for as long as it takes."*

She swallowed and gripped Lisa's journal tighter in her hands. *"Why would you do that? We're still in the beginning stages of this whole thing."* Not that she had changed her mind. She'd meant what she told him. She wasn't going to walk away without trying.

He chuckled, but it didn't sound like he was amused. *"I know you've survived living with a tyrannical dick and somehow managed to remain a tender, caring person. I know you're gracious and kind because you're talking to me right now instead of asking one of your pack mates or your father to kill me. I know you care deeply for those you've claimed as yours. I've felt the love you have for Lisa, and I will be a greedy bastard and tell you now that I want all your love focused on me. I want to be on the receiving end of that love. I know enough, Tanya, to know that the Great Luna gave me something precious when she gave me you. I will protect it and you with all that I am."*

"Damn." Tanya breathed out.

"You okay, T?" Daniel asked from the driver's seat.

She coughed and nearly dropped the journal, caught off guard by his voice. Then she cleared her throat. "Yep." She nodded. "I'm good. Totally good. Nothing but good going on."

"Okay, now you're just being weird," Trevor said.

She felt his gaze on her, but she didn't acknowledge them. Instead, Tanya turned to look out the window, her eyes staring up at the sky, wondering if Dillon was looking at the same sky.

"Yes," he said softly. *"I'm laying outside. My wolf is restless now that he knows you're on your way to us."*

"I'm on my way home," she corrected, even though her stupid heart did a little flip at his possessive words. Female *Canis lupus* got stupidly hot by the possessiveness of their true mates. She'd seen it happen to the best of them. Tanya didn't think she'd be one of *those* females. She inwardly rolled her eyes and sighed. "Idiot," she muttered.

"Exactly," Dillon continued. *"You're on your way to me. My home is you and vice versa. Always."*

Okay. She pressed a hand to her chest over her pounding heart. She could practically hear Lisa tell her to jump on that bronco and ride it into the sunset. She quickly shoved that thought aside, hoping Dillon hadn't picked up on it. If he did, he didn't let on—a fact for which she was grateful.

"Can I ask you a question?" she ventured, not really sure if she wanted to open this door now, but she felt like she

needed to get this out before they met again, face to face. She didn't want to start their mating with secrets, no matter how painful. It might be tough, but Tanya would have to keep reading Lisa's journal over and over and remember the Great Luna's words.

"Anything," he said without hesitation. She felt his worry, but also his resolve.

"Are you worried I won't compare to her?" As soon as she thought the words, Tanya wanted to take them back. How could she ask something to which she didn't really want to know the answer? She closed her eyes as she felt fingertips run across her face.

"There is nothing to compare, Tanya," he said firmly. *"No matter what Lilly was, she's not my true mate. She was not created for me and me alone. She will never complete me. She will never tame my wolf. She will not stop the darkness from spreading, and she will never have my devotion the way you do."* Tanya heard what sounded like air being blown out, and she could practically see him letting out a burst of air. *"That probably sounds cruel regarding her, but I don't mean it that way. I don't know that words will ever be adequate, love. I will show you with my actions what you are to me and what you mean to me. That is all I can do. I pray it will be enough so that you never feel you're lacking in any way."*

Tanya wiped away a tear as she felt the sincerity in his voice. The mate bond was a tremendous thing because it was nearly impossible to lie to one another. Lies had smells, tastes, and even felt wrong on the inside. Their wolves could pick up on deceit in one another. And Tanya's beast would put their mate in his place if he did lie to them. Her heart did actually go out to Lilly. It couldn't have been easy to be with a man that had made it clear that she would never have him, not fully. Why she would allow herself to endure that, Tanya couldn't understand.

"Thank you," she finally responded. *"I'll probably make you repeat all of that on a regular basis. You might want to memorize it."* She wasn't joking. *"How is everything with my father and the pack?"*

"Odd." She could feel frustration suddenly radiating in him. *"Why does your father weaken his pack by not allowing them to be what they are? He won't let them hunt properly. He's not honest with them. He belittles them. And he treats Penelope like she's a stain on the pack simply because she's a dormant. I don't understand him, Tanya. What kind of alpha acts that way?"*

Tanya's heart hurt at the description he painted. Not that it was incorrect. It was completely accurate, but she found that she was embarrassed for her mate to see what kind of pack she'd grown up in. And what kind of man her father was.

"You don't have to be embarrassed," he assured her. *"I don't hold your father's deeds against you. Tanya, you're not responsible for him. He's a grown-ass man who knows better. How does your mother deal with him?"*

Tanya's lips turned up at the thought of her mother. *"My mother is the complete opposite of my father. She has a ridiculous amount of grace and love for people, regardless of all their stupidity and poor choices."*

Dillon's humor came through the bond. *"So that's where you get it from?"*

"I don't know about that." Tanya shook her head. *"I have a bit of my father's temper."* That was one thing Tanya liked least about herself. At times, she let her emotions get the better of her. *"But the older I've gotten, and the more I've*

learned about my father and the type of man he is, the less I want to be like him in every way."

"I've asked some of the males why they don't challenge him."

Tanya sat up so abruptly that she nearly dropped the journal. She was suddenly very alert. *"You have to be careful, Dillon,"* she warned. *"If it gets back to my father that you've said something so mutinous, he won't hesitate to kill you. Even if you are my mate. He will see you as a threat."*

"He's power hungry. It's made him very dangerous and has made the Colorado pack unsafe. His warriors don't know how to fight."

"What?" She frowned. Tanya had sparred with some of the males, including the ones in the van with her currently. *"They are good fighters."*

"No offense, love, but I could take multiples on at once and not break a sweat." He didn't sound like he was bragging, merely stating a fact. *"He's so afraid of one of his own being able to take him out that he purposefully keeps them weak. If this pack were attacked by vampires today, it would be destroyed."*

Tanya's mind immediately jumped to the fight that Dillon had been in the other day. He and three others of her pack had been attacked by vampires on pack land. *"Do you think that will happen?"* She looked up at the back of Daniel's head and spoke out loud. "Drive faster, Daniel."

There was a chorus of questions as the three males in the van looked at her. Daniel's eyes kept darting from the road to the rearview mirror, where he could see her.

"I've been patrolling when I have some downtime," Dillon said quickly. *"I haven't picked up any more scents of vampires. Tell Daniel to slow the hell down."* Dillon's voice had turned into a deep growl. *"I'll be pissed if he gets into a wreck and you get so much as a scratch on you."*

Tanya ran a hand down her face and clutched Lisa's

diary to her chest. "Sorry, Daniel. False alarm."

"Are you talking to your mate?" Trevor asked.

"Is he at the pack mansion?" Austin piped in, his eyes a little too eager. Dude really wanted to pick a fight with Dillon.

"Is something wrong?" Daniel finished for the three worried males.

She pointed to Trevor, "Yes." Then she pointed to Austin, "I'm talking with him. And yes"—she looked at Daniel in the mirror. "He's at the pack mansion. And I don't know if something is wrong. He led a hunting party the other day with some of our wolves, per my father's instructions, to look for rogues."

"What?" the three males said at the same time, their voices in various pitches.

"We haven't had rogues around our lands in a long time," Daniel said.

"I know," Tanya replied. "And Dillon didn't come across any during any of his patrols."

"Tanya, quit getting them worked up," Dillon interrupted her conversation. *"I don't want him driving like a madman to get back here when there's nothing happening. I want you here quickly, but in one piece."*

"Don't be bossy, Dillon. You'll find that I don't like to be told what to do." She focused her attention back on her pack mates. "But they were attacked by vampires."

"Are you freaking kidding me?" Austin asked.

"Shit." Trevor spat.

But Daniel's brow simply dipped into a deep V. Tanya imagined he was wondering why her father hadn't kept his beta in the loop about something so serious as the presence of vampires. It wasn't the first time that Jeremiah kept things from Daniel. An alpha treating his beta as if his input weren't important was a complete slap in the face. But her friend had always just brushed it aside, even though it spoke volumes to the pack about how Jeremiah felt about Daniel. Just like everyone else, Jeremiah didn't trust him.

Tanya wanted to reach forward and pat Daniel's shoulder, but she couldn't bring herself to touch him. She felt Dillon's jealousy rise before he could block her from it. She knew it would be something he would deal with. Considering their circumstances, she imagined that Dillon would never feel like he had the right to voice his feeling's in that regard, whereas other males of their kind would be quick to remind their mate of who she belonged to and who she should and shouldn't be touching.

Insecurity, the hunger for power, pride, fear, and greed had crippled her pack. Tanya hated that they'd all been stunted by her father, prevented from being the healthiest pack of *Canis lupus* possible. She didn't want her mate to feel equally stifled, as if he couldn't snarl when he felt possessive. It sounded so stupid in her mind and would sound even more stupid out loud, but it wasn't the way of their kind. They were hotheaded when it came to their true mates. She wanted her male to be just as aggressive as any true mate would be.

"Okay, fine," Dillon snapped, obviously listening to her thoughts. *"I'll rip a hole in his shoulder if you touch him. Is that better?"*

She pressed her lips together to keep from laughing even though her shoulders shook with the chuckle bubbling up inside of her. And she had told Lisa that humans were weird. If that was the case, then *Canis lupus* were just psycho.

"True mate males definitely are," Dillon agreed. *"I don't think that's ever been in dispute."*

"You're not wrong." She snorted.

"Would you please tell Daniel to slow down now?"

"Daniel, my mate asked that you please drive as if you have a glass of water filled to the brim on top of the van, and if you spill any of it, he will rip out your throat."

"Cutthroat." Austin grinned. "I think I might like this guy after all. Once I've kicked his ass, of course."

"That's not exactly what I said." Humor filled Dillon's voice. *"But I'm impressed by your creativity."*

"You're easily impressed then. You need to up your standards." She settled back into the seat, still clutching the diary. Tanya's eyes grew heavy as she finally relaxed and let herself trust Dillon. If he said everything was fine, then she would believe him. And even if things weren't fine, there wasn't anything she could do about it until they arrived home anyway.

"Get some sleep, love. I'm not going anywhere, and we have a lifetime to work through everything while I prove myself to you."

His words, and the sincerity in them, settled her heart even more. Tanya finally let sleep pull her down.

JEREMIAH STALKED THROUGH THE CORRIDORS OF THE PACK mansion, his hands fisting and unfisting at his sides while he tried to cool his boiling blood to a simmer. He'd killed two of his own pack members, and it was Dillon Jacobs's fault. If that fool hadn't gone and taken a human as a lover and then sired an offspring with her, none of this would have happened.

He picked up his phone and dialed the pager to his beta. He should have done this days ago, but he'd been too busy trying to work out the puzzle that was Dillon Jacobs. And then, when Jeremiah heard of Lisa's passing, he hadn't wanted to upset Tanya any more than she already was. He was an ass, but he *did* love his daughter. But now—now he had to make damn sure that his suspicion was right. He had to know if Dillon Jacobs was, in fact, his daughter's true mate.

The door to his office opened, and the scent of his mate hit him like a gentle breeze. Even in haste, she moved with grace and calmness. He could feel her worry through their bond. She knew something was very wrong, but he'd been keeping his mind blocked from her. She rarely questioned him, but killing two of your pack mates caused intense emotions that were hard to hide. He turned and slowly let his eyes meet hers. Jeremiah hated that he saw disappointment there. It was worse than seeing anger.

"What have you done, Jeremiah?" She held her hands clasped in front of her, and he heard the worry in her voice. Rose held her chin high and her shoulders back, looking every bit like the confident alpha female that she was. Some might mistake her meekness and gentle spirit for weakness, but they would be fools. His mate was as fierce as any dominant wolf. The difference between her and him was that she didn't feel the *need* to exert her dominance over anyone. It was something he both admired and resented.

"What I had to do in order to protect Tanya," he answered coolly. "She deserves better." Jeremiah kept the secret of the child tucked away in his mind, but he allowed her to see the knowledge that he believed Dillon to be Tanya's mate.

"This is a cause for celebration." She stepped farther

into the room. "And it isn't for us to judge who the Great Luna has for our daughter. You know this, Jeremiah." Her voice was sharp as a whip and stung just as badly. Her dismay bled into him like poison, burning to his marrow and bone.

"He doesn't deserve her, dammit," he snapped. "Don't you see that?" Jeremiah rested his hands on his hips and leaned his head back, closing his eyes as he pictured his daughter as a young child. He remembered when she was born, how hard the labor had been for Rose. They had no gypsy healer, and the risk of birth complications was high. When he'd laid eyes on Tanya, his heart had never been fuller. He and the woman he adored had made this precious being. The Great Luna had blessed them, and he knew there would come a day when he'd have to give her away to her true mate, but he'd imagined a man of integrity, a man whose actions dictated him to be worthy of Tanya. Not a man ... a man like ... *him*. Jeremiah felt bile rise up in his throat as his own past came back to bite him in the ass. It was a memory he faced every single day. And not because he wanted to but because his sweet, forgiving, gracious mate had a heart of gold, and he didn't deserve her for even a second. But he'd never give her up.

"Can you really judge him?" Rose knew exactly where his mind was. "I love you, Jeremiah Ellis, and I forgave you a long time ago for your past. I have embraced the result of that past. It wasn't her fault. She didn't ask to be the result of a union that should have never happened. She didn't ask to be rejected by her mother, and I wasn't about to turn away your own flesh and blood."

"Don't," he growled as his hands dropped and his wolf pushed forward. His eyes would no doubt be glowing as he glared at his mate, both bitterness and awe inside him for her. "You didn't have to let her stay here. We could have turned her over to the human adoption agency, and she could have found a family that would have been better for her than here."

Rose growled as she stomped over to him and shoved him hard. "She is *your* daughter, just as much as Tanya, dammit." She pressed her finger into his chest and punctuated her words with pointed jabs. "No matter how she came to be, she is ours. Penelope deserves love just as much as a child brought into this world between two people who deeply love one another. It was *your* foolishness that led to the circumstances, but that does not mean she is a damn mistake. And I will never treat her as one."

"And that is why you're my mate," Jeremiah whispered. "Because your goodness balances out my wickedness."

Rose lifted her hand, the very one that has been so violent moments ago, and cupped his face gently. "You let your wickedness rule where it doesn't have to. That has always been a choice, my love. I have tolerated many things from you. But you will not rob our daughter of her true mate."

Jeremiah could rarely tell his mate no. It was the reason his illegitimate, dormant offspring lived in their home. Because the human he'd lain with had dropped her off at his door and hightailed it out of there before he could shove the kid back in the car. He'd been ready to hand her over to the humans, just drop her off at a police station or some other place of human authority, but Rose wouldn't have it. She'd known that he'd been with a human before meeting her, though it was nothing as deep as what Dillon had with Lilly Pierce. Jeremiah had a one-night stand. He'd given in to a moment of weakness, not years of himself to another woman. And as a result of that hour, Jeremiah saw a lifetime of regret every day in the halls of his own home.

The phone on his desk rang, and he met his mate's eyes. "I love you, Rose. But you will not interfere in this. And if you do, I will send Penelope away." Her face blanched. Despite how Penelope had come into this world, Rose claimed her as her own, though they'd never told Tanya the truth of the dormant female. It had been his stipulation for letting her stay. Jeremiah was a coward, but he didn't want to see judgment in his daughter's eyes. As a child, she'd always looked at him as if he'd hung the moon. He never wanted her to see him as anything less. Though in recent years he was pretty sure his tight hold on her was beginning to make her resent him.

He picked up the phone and blocked his thoughts from his mate. "Hello?"

"Alpha." Daniel's voice came through. Jeremiah didn't miss the hesitancy in his tone.

"Is Dillon Jacobs Tanya's mate?" He didn't bother beating around the bush. There was no point. "Don't make me give you an alpha order."

"Yes," Daniel said quickly. He never liked to be forced. It was what made him a good beta, though Jeremiah still didn't trust him with everything. He couldn't. The secrets Jeremiah kept were too dangerous to his reputation. His pack might have forgiven him decades ago, but keeping Penelope a secret all these years would be seen as a betrayal of their trust. It could never be allowed to get out.

"I've learned much about him," Jeremiah told his beta. "He's not who he appears to be. And he certainly isn't good enough for my daughter."

"Alpha, with all due—"

Jeremiah cut him off. "He had a years-long relationship

with a human, Daniel," Jeremiah barked. "He cared so little for the feelings of his future mate that he dared to share himself with another woman, *loved* another woman for years." There was silence on the other end of the phone. Jeremiah imagined Daniel must be in a phone booth, considering he didn't hear the sounds of people at a gas station or wherever else he might have stopped to return his alpha's page. "I will not allow him to sully her with his disloyal hands."

Daniel let out a sigh. "She's an adult, Alpha. Isn't that her choice to make?"

Jeremiah's wolf growled. "I am her father *and* her alpha. As long as she is a member of this pack, she will follow my rules. Dillon will not claim her. When will you be back?"

He felt his beta's hesitation.

"I order you to tell me the truth," Jeremiah snarled. Daniel could not lie.

"A little over an hour," he finally answered.

"Bring her straight to my office." He slammed the phone down and looked back up at Rose, who still stood in the same place.

"Don't do this, Jeremiah," she begged. "She will never forgive you."

Jeremiah thought of the child Dillon had made with another woman. He remembered the crushing pain Rose had felt when she'd learned of Penelope, and he vowed that his daughter would not endure that. "She will one day."

He walked past his mate and mentally prepared himself to do what he knew he had to. It was the only option to ensure that his daughter would not endure the embarrassment and pain of knowing her mate had betrayed her. Dillon Jacobs had to die before he could be allowed to complete the Blood Rites with Tanya.

CHAPTER
SIXTEEN

"There are some things worth fighting for. There are some things worth dying for. Sometimes, the hard part is figuring out which is which." ~Dillon

"DILLON!" Kevin's voice boomed. "Let me in, now!"

Pounding on Dillon's door woke him from a deep sleep. He leaped from the bed and landed in front of the door in one bound. He ripped it open and found not only Kevin but Rusty, and Gabe, as well, standing there looking like they'd just seen their own ghosts. "What the hell? Vampires?"

Kevin shook his head, his face pale, and Dillon could smell perspiration on the wolf. "Worse. Jeremiah."

Dillon frowned. "What?"

"He's calling you out," Gabe answered.

Rusty nodded. "He's challenging you for the right to mate his daughter."

"Dammit." Dillon turned and grabbed the jeans he'd thrown on the floor and pulled them on. He didn't bother with a shirt or shoes. The chances he would get through this without phasing were low, so there was no point ruining any more pieces of clothing than necessary. *What the hell am I going to do?* Dillon didn't want to fight his mate's father. He and Tanya were on the precarious tip of moving in the right direction. The last thing he needed was for her to resent him for hurting her father. "Dammit." He followed the other three males out of his room.

"What are you going to do?"

Dillon shot Kevin a look. "I was just asking myself the same thing. But Tanya is my true mate. I'm not giving her up."

"You're going to kill him?" Gabe sounded a little too happy about the prospect.

"No." Dillon spat. "I'm going to try to reason with the ass."

The three males all snorted.

"Good luck. You can't reason with a madman."

Dillon worried that his newly made comrade Kevin was right. Jeremiah was unstable at best and a downright lunatic at worst. "I don't want you three getting involved. I don't expect you to show me any loyalty or preferential treatment."

Gabe scoffed. "Are you kidding me? You're more dominant than any wolf in this pack by a long shot. You're going to wipe the floor with him. I don't cheer for the losing side."

"Especially when the losing side is led by such a worthless bastard," Rusty added.

Dillon's wolf approved of their loyalty, but the man worried for their safety. Unstable supernaturals could be dangerous, especially if they felt backed against a wall. If

Jeremiah knew of Dillon's past, he would see what he'd done as a complete and utter betrayal of his daughter. Not that Dillon could blame him. The alpha would want blood shed as reparations for the disrespect Dillon had shown Tanya. And maybe Dillon needed to pay for what he'd done, but he didn't want any of Jeremiah's pack being punished for showing loyalty to Dillon.

They rounded a corner and headed down the hall that would lead out the side door and to the sparring grounds. Dillon heard a commotion of growls, voices, and unrest. The pack no doubt felt their alpha's agitation and rage. Dillon could practically sense an electric charge in the air, and he wasn't a member of the pack.

"Dillon?" Tanya's sleepy voice filled his mind.

Dammit. He did not want her dealing with this. *"Morning, T."* He attempted to sound as lighthearted as possible.

"Don't do that," she warned with a snarl in her voice. *"What's going on? No lies, Dillon. That's the only way this will work."*

Okay then. *"Your father has apparently found out that I am your mate, and it seems like he's also found out about my past. I don't think he's too happy to have me as his future son-in-law."*

Alarm filled the bond. *"You have to leave. Get far away."*

"I can't do that, love. I won't leave you. But don't worry, I won't hurt your father. I'll try to reason with him—"

"That's the problem, Dillon," she practically shrieked. *"He's not reasonable. He won't listen to anything you have to say."*

"I have to try. I promise I won't hurt him." As soon as he stepped outside, Dillon saw that the entire pack had gathered and made a circle around the sparring grounds—the area where he'd sparred with pack members only yesterday.

The group parted, revealing Jeremiah standing in the center, also wearing nothing but jeans.

Dillon took a deep breath and walked forward. "Move away from me," he told the three wolves that flanked him.

"Not a chance." Dillon could hear the smile in Gabe's voice.

"We've got your back," Kevin added.

"Don't die," Rusty finished.

Dillon bit his lip and shook his head. "Thanks for the vote of confidence, Rust."

"It's my gift. I totally build people up and make them feel more badass than they are."

As soon as Dillon reached the circle, Jeremiah pulled power from his pack. Dillon could feel the weight of it attempting to push him down. "Kneel," the Colorado alpha commanded.

Dillon held his ground, planting his feet and drawing on the power inside of him. "No. I kneel to no one other than my Creator."

Jeremiah's face turned an alarming shade of red. Had he been a human, Dillon would have been worried he might have a stroke.

"You are in my pack territory." Jeremiah snarled. "You came under false pretense. You lied to me and my pack. Now you have the audacity to challenge me?"

"I am not challenging you, Alpha, and I did not lie," Dillon tried to sound respectful. "But I will not bow, and neither will I fight you. Tanya is my true mate. Whatever is between us is just that—between *me* and *Tanya*. It has nothing to do with you."

Jeremiah laughed. "It has everything to do with me and this pack. You come here thinking you have the right to claim her when you have disrespected her." Jeremiah looked around at the pack and pointed a clawed finger at him. "This man, the so-called true mate to my daughter, the future alpha female of this pack, had an affair with a human woman for years."

Gasps and chatter moved through the pack. Dillon knew he might be losing any allies he might have made. "I made a mistake," Dillon admitted. "I can't take it back. But I can try to make it right."

"You're telling me you expect my daughter to take you as her mate, knowing what she will see in your mind? You expect to build a life with her knowing you first built one with someone else?"

Damn. Put like that, it sounds completely unfair to expect of Tanya. "I don't expect anything. I *hope* she is willing to try."

"Not if I have anything to say about it," Jeremiah spat out. "The only way you will claim my daughter is by getting through me."

With no warning, Jeremiah lunged at Dillon, his muscles coiling like a spring as he extended his razor-sharp claws. His eyes burned with a fiery intensity, as though his wolf were possessed. If Dillon didn't know the man was mated, he would have thought Jeremiah was feral.

Dillon quickly dodged Jeremiah's attack, narrowly avoiding the deadly claws. He raised his fists in a defensive posture and said calmly, "I don't want to fight you, Jeremiah. I could never be responsible for killing my mate's father. I will if you insist, but only to submission, not to death."

Jeremiah let out a guttural laugh, his eyes still fixed on Dillon. "Submission? Hell no." He snarled. "I want to see you bleed. You will die under my fangs and claws this day." His eyes were filled with madness and the determination of a man who truly felt he was justified in his actions. Jeremiah charged at Dillon again, his claws glinting in the light. Dillon ducked under the attack and landed a swift kick to Jeremiah's stomach, causing him to stumble backward.

The alpha regained his footing quickly, and the two men circled each other warily. Dillon knew he couldn't let Jeremiah get too close, so he feinted left and then delivered a powerful right hook, catching Jeremiah on the side of the head. The man staggered backward before raising a hand to his head and touching a trickle of blood that was forming from a newly appeared cut caused by Dillon's fist. He looked at the blood and chuckled.

"You'll pay for that, whelp." Then Jeremiah barreled toward Dillon once more, his claws slashing through the air like deadly knives.

Dillon dodged left and right, ducking and weaving as he sought an opening without dealing a killing blow. Suddenly, he saw his chance. As Jeremiah lunged at him, Dillon dropped to the ground and moved his leg in a swift, sweeping motion.

Jeremiah crashed to the ground, his claws digging deep into the dirt. Instead of jumping on him, Dillon took a step back and stared down at him. Jeremiah sprang back to his feet with a string of curses.

"I won't do this," Dillon said through clenched teeth.

"You don't have a choice," Jeremiah replied. This time, Jeremiah didn't blindly charge. He advanced upon Dillon slowly, warily. Dillon could see him calculating, trying to determine how best to attack.

Dillon held his arms out wide. "We always have a choice. You have a choice right now. You could abandon this folly and become the alpha you were meant to be. You could be the father your daughter needs you to be. The mate your bonded needs you to be."

"What my mate needs is none of your concern." Jeremiah's voice was laced with dangerous intent. "What my daughter needs is none of your concern. The only thing that should matter to you is whether you will live through this. And I vow you will not." He pushed off toward Dillon with a powerful jump. Dillon dove forward, rolling on the ground to avoid the massive hand coming at his face.

"No!" Tanya's voice pierced the air.

Dillon's head whipped around to see her running toward them. The three males from the gas station were just behind her. "Stop her!" Dillon roared at them. He turned back to Jeremiah and realized his mistake. He'd given the alpha the moment Jeremiah needed to get the upper hand. The alpha moved with incredible speed and was on top of Dillon in a second. Dillon couldn't get his hands up quickly enough. Jeremiah's claws headed straight for Dillon's chest. They would slice through his flesh with a force strong enough to break through his muscles, tendons, and bone, all the way to his heart. Just before the deathly blow landed, a smaller form appeared directly in front of him.

"Mom!" Tanya's voice bellowed, a sound so painful that it broke Dillon's heart.

Out of nowhere, the Colorado alpha female was there. Dillon's eyes looked past Rose and landed on Jeremiah's face. It turned ashen-white, stricken with horror. Instead of the alpha's claws piercing Dillon's chest, they were buried in his mate's torso.

Tears streamed down Rose's face. "I love you," she told Jeremiah, her voice shaky. "Too much to let you do this. She's our daughter, beloved. Your rage is misplaced."

"Rose. Rose. Rose." Jeremiah's voice was so broken it was painful to hear. "No, no, you stupid, beautiful woman.

No." He fell to his knees, pulling her to him. Dillon could see death slowly taking them both. As a bonded pair, her death would mean Jeremiah's, as well.

"Oh, my Creator." Dillon breathed out. A wave of realization washed over him, and a heaviness like a giant boulder landed in the pit of his stomach. Tanya's mom had sacrificed herself, knowing her death would also be her mate's. She kept Dillon from having to kill Jeremiah or vice versa.

Dillon looked up at Tanya, who was being held back by Daniel and Trevor. "Mom!"

He nodded at Daniel, and the males released her. Tanya ran straight for her parents and heedlessly hit the ground next to them. "Mom, no." Tanya cried as she held her shaking hands over her mother, seemingly unsure where or if to touch her. Tanya's anguish and hopelessness ripped through the bond. It traveled into him and shredded his soul.

"Why? Why, dammit?"

"I'm sorry," Jeremiah choked out, tears pouring down his face. "He doesn't deserve you. Tanya he—"

"I know what he did, dammit," she snapped at him. "You had no right! None!"

Jeremiah slumped to his side, his hand still buried in his mate's chest as if he didn't have the strength to pull it back. "You're my little girl." Utter despair and sadness filled his eyes.

"I'm a grown woman, Dad. My choices are my own. And your selfish pride did this." She motioned to her mother. "*You* did this. Not Dillon."

"Tanya." Rose's voice was weak. "Look at me, daughter mine."

Tanya turned back to her mom and pressed a hand to her cheek. "Mother." Her voice cracked.

"Forgive him," Rose implored. "He is not a god, only a man. And he will make more mistakes in this life. As will you. You will live too long to be angry and bitter. Love him and help him be a better man, and he will help you be a better woman. That is the gift you can give one another."

"I can't lose you, Mom," Tanya cried. "Not you, too."

"Nobody lives forever, sweet girl."

Tanya growled. "I'm sick of hearing that."

"Dillon," Rose called out. Though the sound was barely more than a whisper, Dillon appeared, hurrying around so the alpha female could see him. "Promise me you will love her even when she doesn't return that love. The feelings of love will wane, but the actual act of love is a choice. Promise me you will always choose love."

"Done." Dillon didn't hesitate. "I promise, Rose, with everything I have within me."

Rose's brow furrowed, and a tear leaked out of her eye. "Oh, Tanya. You will face more trials, and they will cut you to the bone. Trust the Great Luna to be your strength and guide. Don't let bitterness kill what she has blessed you with."

"I won't, Mom. I promise. I've already forgiven him," Tanya said softly. "You've been the best example of what a true mate should be."

Rose's hand lifted, and she beckoned Tanya forward. She whispered something in Tanya's ear that Dillon couldn't hear. Tanya's shoulders shook even harder. She lifted her head and looked around until her eyes landed on something. Dillon followed her gaze and saw Penelope standing in the crowd. Her hands covered her mouth and tears flowed down her cheeks. Tanya lifted an arm and motioned for the girl to come. Penelope ran to her and fell into Tanya's arms so hard that she nearly knocked Tanya over. The girls wrapped their arms around one another, and their weeping ripped through the pack like a tidal wave.

A few seconds later, a burst of power rippled through the pack, and Dillon knew the alpha pair was gone. He looked up to see every member of the pack hit their knees and bow their heads.

Tanya rocked Penelope back and forth, running a hand down her hair. "It's going to be all right, Nell. I promise. I love you. It's going to be alright."

Dillon heard in his mate's mind what Rose had told her, and his heart threatened to beat out of his chest. Penelope was Tanya's half-sister. "By the Great Luna," he whispered. He understood Jeremiah's loathing for him now. Part of the hate he had for Dillon was his own guilt at the choices he'd obviously made in his life. And his mate had to see the result of that choice every day. And yet, Rose had been loving and kind to Penelope, treating her like a daughter, and, no doubt, loving her like one, as well.

Suddenly, the howl of wolves drowned out the sounds of his mate and her sister's cries. No matter how they'd felt about Jeremiah, he was still their alpha, and losing him and Rose would rip a hole in their hearts. That was the bond of the pack to the alpha.

Dillon kneeled as a sign of respect. Though he didn't agree with any of Jeremiah's choices, he could understand to a degree why he made them. The alpha had let guilt and regret rule his life, even though his mate had obviously chosen him over her own anger or grief. She'd wanted to be his. She'd wanted them to build a life together. To some degree, they had. But it was apparent by the ending today that Jeremiah had never given them a fighting chance. Dillon would not make that same mistake.

◊

Rain seems to be a common theme on days that I say goodbye to people I love. Tanya watched Daniel light the pyres where her parents' bodies lay. Penelope stood on her left, gripping her hand. Dillon stood on her right, his strength rushing through their bond. It was the only thing keeping her on her feet.

Tanya had lost three people who meant the world to her in less than a week. She'd gained a mate, a sister, and hope for a future. Her mother had showed her that a person's choices were the things that determined a person's misery or joy. Nobody else could determine the happiness, contentment, or success of her future except herself. Just as nobody could determine that for Dillon. They could strive for it together, but each of them would have to make those choices on their own. It would take Tanya time to forgive her father, but she hoped one day she would. His choices had been horrible, but he'd made them because he couldn't forgive himself, even though his mate had. She didn't want that for Dillon, herself, or their pack.

Today, they would set the tone for their future. Dillon would take the place of the Colorado pack alpha, as was his right because Jeremiah had fallen during their challenge and because he'd taken Tanya as his true mate. Though their bond wasn't complete, in her mind, it was a done deal. Dillon and all his mistakes, flaws, and grievances were hers.

And she was his, for better or for worse, as the humans put it.

"I love you, Mother and Father," Tanya whispered. She bowed her head to her former alphas. She asked the Great Luna to guide them to their eternal resting place and for grace for her father's transgressions. After a time, she looked at Penelope, the sister she'd always had. Tanya gave her a small smile. "No matter how we came to be sisters, I'm so glad you're mine."

Penelope smiled back and wiped her tears away. "Me, too."

How the female wasn't bitter and angry for all the years Jeremiah had mistreated her, Tanya could only guess, but it had to do with Rose—their mom. And that was exactly who Rose was, even if she wasn't Penelope's birth mom. Rose had adopted her and loved her just as she loved Tanya. She could only hope to be half the woman her mother had been.

"She was amazing," Dillon agreed through their bond. *"But then, so are you. I'm sorry it ended this way, love. I would change it for you in a heartbeat."*

Tanya had no doubt he would. His heart was laid bare before her, the bond always open between them. It was obvious that Dillon was determined to be the best mate he could be. And she could see that the pack respected him. He'd proven himself to them in how he'd handled her father's challenge. He'd not gloated or even reveled in her father's demise, despite how he'd treated Dillon. There were some who would struggle to accept a new alpha, and she knew Dillon would have to do what any *good* alpha would do and create order and structure so the wolves knew their place. This would mean security for their pack. There would no longer be wolves on constant edge with the need to fight because they were unsure who was dominant to whom. And knowing their alpha was strong enough to take any of them on meant he could also take on any enemy who would try to harm them. Even on this bleak, sorrowful day, hope rose on the horizon. And for the first time since she could remember, Tanya looked forward to what the future held for them and their pack.

CHAPTER
SEVENTEEN

"Creator, true mate, pack, then allies. That was the order of things. That was how our loyalty worked. Were there still bumps in the road to be expected in our new situation? Absolutely. But now another pack needed our help. And as a step in the right direction for changes in the Colorado pack, we would come to their aid. Because that's what pack does." ~Dillon

"Dillon," Mathew, alpha of the Montana pack, held out his hand. "It's good to see you."

"You, too." Dillon shook his hand, holding Tanya's with the other. "I'm sorry I left as I did." His words needed to be said in person, and so he'd waited until they'd arrived to tell his former alpha.

"We never know how we're going to react to painful things in our life until we're in the midst of them. No one has the right to judge you. Especially if they haven't been in your shoes. I hold you no ill-will."

Dillon nodded and swallowed down the emotion. His former alpha had always been a fair man. He'd led his pack with integrity. Dillon hoped to do the same with his own. "So, what do you know about the human hunters that have been taking out pack members?"

Mathew folded his arms in front of him and rocked back on his heels. "There's four of them, and they've got it in their head that they've found the legendary dire wolves. Because we tend to be larger than our natural brethren." The alpha growled. "So they are hunting for sport, trying to kill the largest wolf they can find. They've killed many natural wolves along with the four total from our pack."

"Are they staying in the forest?" Dillon looked thoughtful. "Camping? Or do they have a hunting cabin?"

"They camp and move frequently. We've been trying to lead them away from our territory but—"

"Bullets are faster than even us," Dillon offered, detecting the hesitancy in Mathew's voice.

"I haven't wanted to put more pack members in danger." The stress of keeping the Montana pack safe was obvious in the lines on Mathew's face and his clenched jaw. This was a man at the end of his rope.

"Let me help you," Dillon offered. "Let's hunt them down and give them the justice they deserve. They answer to our law, not humans."

There were growls of approval from the pack members Dillon had brought with him, along with the Montana pack members present.

Mathew nodded. "Let me get out the map and show you where we saw them last."

. . .

They decided on a hunting party of ten wolves—five in their human form and five in their wolf fur. It would give them the advantage of numbers but still allow them to move quietly as they hunted their prey.

Tanya moved silently beside Dillon in her wolf form while he stayed in his human skin. Daniel, Trevor, and Austin all ran in their wolf forms as they moved in on the male voices they could hear less than a mile ahead. They'd waited until nightfall and traveled under the cover of darkness. As they began to close in, Dillon suddenly froze as a male stepped out of the shadows. The rest of their hunting party, including Mathew and his wolves, felt the shift in the air and froze where they stood. The man didn't seem to see any of them, as the moon was not bright tonight and clouds obscured any light further. The wolves and their dark fur blended in well, and the humans had managed to place themselves on the sides of trees that the man couldn't see around.

What Dillon wanted to know was why they'd not scented the male before being right up on him. Even with the wind not blowing in their direction, they should have, at the very least, heard his breathing or movement.

"Earl," the man suddenly called out. "I think there's something out here. You three get your asses and guns over here, and let's see if one of those dire wolves is lurking. I can practically feel it breathing down my neck."

Dillon bit back a grin. The fool wouldn't be so smug if he knew ten wolves, not one, were breathing down his neck. "Back away slowly," Dillon told his pack members using a subvocal range that only their wolf hearing would catch. "And then circle around from behind the other males as they move this way."

Within less than a minute, Dillon heard the lumbering

humans moving through the brush. Sticks snapped and leaves crunched. How they managed to hunt anything was beyond him.

He glanced down to check on Tanya and bit back a growl when he realized she no longer stood next to him. He sought her out through their bond and saw that she'd circled back around him and was sneaking up on the male who'd surprised them. She took a step and froze just as a twig broke beneath her weight. Everything seemed to move in slow motion.

Dillon saw the glint of something metal as the man lifted his arm—the gun that had been hidden by his side. The man couldn't see Tanya's exact location, or he'd have already shot, but his arm was pointed in her general direction.

The new alpha started moving forward as he saw the man's finger on the trigger begin to squeeze. Dillon wasn't going to make it. He was fast, but not faster than a bullet. The gun fired. Tanya dropped to the ground as a body slammed into hers. Snarls and growls erupted as screams filled the night. It was the last shot any of those hunters would ever fire. The wolves of the Montana and Colorado pack dispensed justice on the four humans who'd decided hunting wolves for sport was a good idea.

Dillon's eyes were only for Tanya as he bounded to her side. She pushed up and shook off her fur. There was a red splatter of blood, but it wasn't hers. Dillon turned to the right, and his hands shook as he saw Mathew's body lying still. He was the one who'd knocked Tanya out of the way. He'd taken the bullet meant for Dillon's mate, directly in his temple. The alpha was dead. No wonder the humans hadn't stood a chance. As soon as Mathew's pack felt his death, they brought down the immediate pain of their loss.

Dillon laid his hands over his former alpha's eyes and closed them. "Go rest, old friend," he said softly. "Your work here is done. You died well." There was no greater gift than to lay down your life for another, and Mathew had saved Tanya's life. Dillon would never forget the sacrifice the Montana pack alpha made.

Two days later, they sent Mathew off in the manner befitting an alpha. As they watched the pyre go up in flames, Dillon felt the warmth, that only came from their Creator, wrap around the small clearing where they stood. He immediately dropped to his knees, and the rest of the pack members did the same.

"I have come to welcome my servant, Mathew, home," the goddess gestured to the pyre. "He served a noble life and represented my love to others. He was an upright and fair alpha, and he shall be remembered as such."

No one made a sound as they continued to listen to their Creator speak. Dillon found it hard not to fall prostrate on the ground in need to thank her that Tanya's life was spared.

"The Montana pack has been vulnerable, its numbers low," the Great Luna continued. "My wolves were meant for community and family. They weren't meant to live isolated lives. Dillon, alpha of the Colorado pack, mate to Tanya and humbled wolf, you will take in the Montana pack. They will be yours just as your current pack mates are now. Family. You cannot defeat your enemies if you're fighting amongst yourselves. Remember that as you move forward in this next stage of your pack's story. Trials are to come. You must be ready. New challenges will threaten your loyalty. Remember why I created you. Remember that you are loved, and that love should shine through your thoughts, words, and deeds."

As the warmth faded, Dillon pushed to his feet and looked around the clearing. No other wolf stood. Instead, each Montana and Colorado pack member bore their neck to him in submission. They were one pack now. And they would learn from their respective pasts and strive for a better future. Emotion filled him as he considered what the Great Luna had in store for them. He prayed he would be the kind of leader that would sacrifice for those who could not fight for themselves and that he would lay down his life to protect his mate and pack. He prayed he would be an example to the child or children he might one day have so that they would know what integrity and goodness looked like.

Dillon looked over at Tanya, the only other wolf standing, and took her hand. "Are you ready for this?"

She smiled up at him. "I was born ready."

He chuckled. "Of that, I have no doubt."

EPILOGUE

"There is nothing more intimate than baring your soul. Not even naked skin compares to revealing your deepest fears and insecurities to another person. It makes you vulnerable in a way that is terrifying. It can create a strong bond or an unequal power dynamic. Choose wisely who you share yourself with, physically or otherwise. Remember that every person you give a piece of yourself to will come with you into future relationships. They will be a memory that your mate will feel. Your mate might think that they must compete with this memory. And once you've both made the choice to move forward, then you must fully let go of the past. You must not allow yourself to continually pick at old wounds. They cannot be a source of contention between you and your mate. In order for your relationship to thrive, then you must *choose* love. Because love is something that we *do*." ~Tanya

Dillon rinsed Tanya's feet as he kneeled on the floor in front of her. They'd completed the bonding ceremony before their pack, but now they needed to do the Blood Rites. He didn't deserve her, and yet he knew he'd never walk away. Not even if she begged him to. As he looked up at her, their eyes locked, and electricity danced in the air. It had grown between them since the day they met. His blood heated in his veins as he ran his hands up her bare calves to the soft skin behind her knees.

"You're more lovely than I could have ever imagined." His voice was a soft rumble in their room. "Not just on the outside, Tanya Jacobs. The light inside of you shines brightly in your love for others, and I will forever be grateful to be counted among those you love."

"I had good examples." She never took her eyes from his. "I'm not saying I won't ever have doubts, but I know you never did anything with malicious intent to hurt me, Dillon. And I would have to be perfect to throw stones at you." Her lips twitched slightly as she continued to look at him. "Though I come close, I'm not quite there."

He chuckled and admired her glowing skin as shadows from the candlelight danced on the walls and music played softly in the background. She took his breath away. Dillon was trying like hell to make this special. He wanted Tanya to forever remember this day as one of the best in her life. It certainly was the best day of his own life. He pushed up from the floor and held out his hand to her. "Will you join me?" The question held depth. He was asking her to join him for much more than their Blood Rites. Through their bond, he showed her the life he hoped to give her. Dillon was asking her to join him on that journey.

Tanya placed her hand in his without hesitation and let

him pull her to her feet. Her body trembled, and he pulled her into the shelter of his larger frame, wrapping an arm around her shoulders. Dillon guided her over to their bed and took a seat. He turned her and pulled her onto his lap so that she straddled him, her nightgown bunching up above her knees to mid-thigh, revealing more tantalizing flesh.

"I didn't think I could want this with you."

The words stung, but he didn't blame her. He never would.

She ran a finger across his forehead, no doubt smoothing out the wrinkles that had formed there. "But I cannot imagine a future without you. Whatever your past, Dillon, you're a man of integrity. And I love you."

Dillon sucked in a deep breath. He didn't know if he'd ever get used to hearing her tell him that, but he knew he'd never grow tired of it. As he pressed his lips to hers and then guided her face to his neck, he tilted his head back so she had better access to his flesh. The divide that had ripped inside of Dillon at his parents' death began to stitch itself back together. As his mate's teeth sank into his neck and she pulled his life force into her, the bond grew stronger between them, and Dillon's soul reached out to its other half.

She kissed his neck then pulled her hair away from her own skin. Dillon cupped the back of her head and leaned forward. He ran his nose along her soft, supple skin, breathing her in deep. He'd forever know her scent and find comfort in it. Dillon bit into her, and her body tensed before relaxing against his. As he sucked on her flesh, her hands moved quickly across his body. Dillon caught her thoughts and grinned. In a flurry of movements and eager fumbling, they managed to undress each other. His teeth left her neck briefly as he removed her gown, only to return once more. His desire grew stronger as he traced the markings on her shoulders that matched his own. She was his, and he was hers. As they joined their bodies, Dillon's wolf howled inside of him as their souls completely united. They would never be parted, in this life or the next.

He made mistakes in his life and knew that he'd make more, but Tanya chose to love him, anyway. She chose to grab on to the gift of their bond and trust that he would always honor it.

"You will always come first," he said through the bond as he kissed her deeply. *"Your needs, your wants, your comfort, your safety, above my own. This I vow to you."*

Tanya's eyes opened and glowed brightly with her wolf, mischief dancing in them. *"And I vow to hold you to that."*

"So, this Jeremiah guy is totally making me look like a saint." Myanin snuggled down on the couch.

Tanya sighed and rolled her eyes as she leaned against Dillon's shoulder.

"*That* is what you got from that story?" Jewel raised her eyebrows.

"What?" Myanin's eyes were wide. "I've heard about your killing sprees. Doesn't it feel good to know you're not the only bloodthirsty bitch making mistakes?"

"The whole point of that story was to answer one question," Tanya said. "Alice will not be able to say no to her true mate, not even if she loves a vampire king."

Myanin looked puzzled. "And *that* is what *you* got from that story?"

Tanya laughed. "No, what I got from that story is that our choices don't simply affect us. The consequences of them, good or bad, are far reaching and long lasting." Her eyes ran over Dillon's face as he stared back at her, the bright green orbs glowing slightly with his wolf. "Our story is one of pain, but also triumph. I also hope that it can be a lesson for others to make different mistakes than the ones we made."

"Can I ask what ever happened to Nell?" Kara asked from where she sat sideways in Nick's lap. His arms were wrapped around her with one hand resting on her stomach.

Tanya bit the inside of her lips and swallowed hard. She'd known this question would come, but she still hadn't really been prepared to answer it. The pain went away. Like Lisa's death, and her moms, Nell's was a wound that simply wouldn't heal. "She died in childbirth." Tanya's words caught on a shuddered breath. "She met her mate a year after our parents died. And a year after that, she went into labor. She and the baby didn't make it."

"And that is the blessing of the mate bond." Dillon pressed a kiss to her hand. "He got to go with his mate and child instead of being left here without them."

"I'm so sorry, Tanya," Jewel told her. "The amount of loss you've suffered, and yet you still seem so..."

"Not a jaded jackass?" Myanin offered.

Tanya chuckled. Myanin might be a little rough around the edges, but she was great for comic relief. "We live way too long to become jaded. What a sad, miserable existence that would be."

Jewel nodded. "Sometimes I still think in terms of a

human life span. Being jaded for sixty years seems much more doable than for a couple hundred or more."

Dillon looked her way. "The point is, we make bad choices, we own them, we deal with them, and then we grow and become better people. Hopefully, the kind of people who can help people like Alice, Lizzy, and Finn. Our pasts don't define us. They refine us and help us become the kind of people the Great Luna wants us to be." He looked at Tanya and then back at the small group. "What Tanya and I have been through will look like a walk in the park compared to what could happen if Alice falls in love with the vampire king and then meets her true mate. A human male isn't as possessive as a *Canis lupus* male, nor does he stand a chance in a fight. But a vampire, not to mention the king of vampires? If he feels toward Alice anything as possessive as he feels about his meals, then a fight between him and her true mate could be a bloodbath, and they wouldn't be the only ones hurt. There would be lots of collateral damage."

"So what I hear you saying is that we need to kill Cain." Myanin sat up and pulled a knife from the side of her boot and began cleaning under her nails. "If Cain is dead, then Alice doesn't have to choose because the choice is made for her. *Boom*! No bloodbath ... except the one I get to cause when I kill the vampire king." She slipped her knife back in her boot and pushed up to her feet. "Okay, story told, lessons learned, plan made. I think we can all get some sleep and then head out to kill the king tomorrow."

Tanya patted Dillon's arm as he muttered under his breath.

"It's not quite that easy, Myanin," Tanya reminded the djinn. "We've got Lizzy and Finn to worry about, as well as all of those dormants."

Myanin waved Tanya's words away as if they were gnats. "I hear ya, Alpha chick. I'm not going to go on a killing spree tonight. But I at least got to give myself something positive to think about after that train wreck of a bedtime story you just told. I mean, it's like reading a book that ends so badly you feel like you've just wasted seven hours of your life that you can never get back, leaving you so depressed you'll most likely need therapy. So not only did the book cost you money to buy, but now it's costing you the expense of therapy." She shook out her hands at her side. "Just point me in the direction of a bed so I can attempt to dream of beheading things and wipe away all the junk you two just planted in my head."

Gerrick stood and followed his mate who had simply begun to wander toward a hallway.

"Go right," Dillon called out. "Then first hall on your left, second door. You can use that bedroom."

"It better not be the dead sister's room," Myanin called back. "I don't want sad, dead-sister mojo messing up my sleep."

"Do you think Gerrick would be mad if Peri put a binding spell on her?"

Tanya shrugged. "She's a little uncouth, Kara, but she's good to have in a fight."

"A little?" Dillon's brow wrinkled.

"Don't be judgy." She pointed a finger at him. "We're all animals here." Tanya glanced at the two healers. "Well, most of us. We all have our uncouth moments."

"She's downright feral," Jewel jerked a thumb at Myanin.

"And Jewel knows," Nick added. "She's a genius."

Kara laughed. "That has nothing to do with knowing if

Myanin is feral. Any idiot can see that just by looking in her crazy-ass, wild eyes."

"Well..." Tanya took a deep breath. "I'll take the crazy-ass, wild-eye chick on my side of a fight any day. Speaking of which, we should all take a note from her crazy book and get some sleep."

The group said their good nights, and Tanya held Dillon's hand as he led her to their room. After he closed the door behind him, he pulled her into his arms and kissed her deeply. His hands cupped her face, and she felt his deep love pouring through their bond. When he pulled back, he rested his forehead against hers.

"You will always come first. Your needs, your wants, your comfort, your safety, above my own. I vowed this to you when we bonded."

"You did," Tanya agreed, her lips swollen from his kiss. "And you have kept your word."

"Even as I told them all about our life? Even as I opened back up wounds that had healed?"

Tanya held his face. "My love, talking about past wounds doesn't reopen them. It reminds us that those wounds didn't kill us. We are still here. We are still fighting for this life we've built, this love that we choose every single day. And we will fight for others to have the same chances we've had. I love the life that we have, in all of its messy glory. And I wouldn't change it. Not a single second." Her words were the complete truth because Tanya knew that everything they'd been through had made them who they were today. Their struggles, their passions, their triumphs and failures had all been used by the Great Luna to help others, to love others. And wasn't that what their Creator had been trying to teach them from their very creation? To love unconditionally, selflessly, and without asking anything in return.

Tanya had realized over the years that it didn't take a second person to make you feel divided over who you loved. You could have created the discord yourself. For love to truly flourish, there could be no divide between created and Creator. For it was the Great Luna who gave them the capacity to love as she did, and it was the Great Luna who would give them the courage and strength to continue to do so.

"I love you, Dillon Jacobs," she said as she thanked the goddess for the man before her. "Until my last breath."

"And even after?" He smiled.

She nodded her head against his. "And even after."

Thank you so much for reading Wolf Divided! I truly hope you enjoyed it. Please consider leaving a review where you purchased this ebook. They are greatly appreciated!

Acknowledgments

So much goes into writing a book and it's not just the author who should get the credit. Thank you to my amazing husband who continues to work with me despite the fact that I'm not always the easiest person to work with. He does it with grace, love, and patience. Thank you to my boys for understanding that sometimes I have to work a lot which means they see me less. Thank you to Jessica for being a sounding board, and for telling me to stop freaking out when I'm freaking out. Thank you to Lindsey for keeping my boys when I need a break and feeding me when I'm too lazy to feed myself. Thank you to Amy for all the research you do on this series and the hard work you put in. Thank you to my readers who have stuck with me for so long on the journey. I am so very honored and humbled. Thank you to Drina, Michelle, Bryanna, LaVerna, Joyce, Renee, and Evie, the "party planning committee," you gals are simply amazing. Most of all, thank you to my God and Savior whom without this wouldn't be possible.

ABOUT THE AUTHOR

Quinn Loftis is a multi-award-winning author of over Forty novels, including the USA Today Bestseller, Fate and Fury. When she isn't creating exciting worlds filled with romantic werewolves, she exercises, reads, and crafts like there's no tomorrow. She is blessed to be married to her best friend for over twenty years and they have three sons, a crazy French bulldog, and a cat that wants to take over the world.

- facebook.com/QuinnLoftisBooks
- twitter.com/AuthQuinnLoftis
- instagram.com/quinnloftisbooks
- bookbub.com/profile/quinn-loftis
- pinterest.com/quinnloftisbooks

QUINN'S BOOKSHELF

The Grey Wolves Series

The Gypsy Healer Series

The Elfin Series

The Dream Maker Series

The Clan Hakon Series

Nature Hunters Academy

Sign up for Quinn's newsletter here:

https://www.quinnloftisbooks.com/newslettersignup

You can also find Quinn writing contemporary romances as her alter ego, Alyson Drake.

https://www.quinnloftisbooks.com/alysondrake